PRAISE FOR NATALIE

"A taut, compelling mystery and a comp[ellin]g [......] [........] novel all in one."

—*Kirkus Reviews* on *What You Hide*

"A chilling, small-town mystery... This page-turning story of teens helping each other through dilemmas will attract and inspire readers."

—*Booklist* on *What You Hide*

"A haunted love story about a couple who bring out the best— and worst—in each other."

—Mindy McGinnis, author of *The Female of the Species* on *We All Fall Down*

"Full of drama and suspicion."

—*Kirkus Reviews* on *One Was Lost*

"An intriguing story line... Readers will be drawn in to the mystery of what happened to Chloe and will never guess the ending."

—*VOYA* on *Six Months Later*

"This romantic thriller will leave readers on the edge of their seats until the very last page."

—*School Library Journal* on *Six Months Later*

"An intense psychological mystery. [This] novel has the feel of a high-stakes poker game in which every player has something to hide, and the cards are held until the very end."

—*Publishers Weekly* on *Six Months Later*

"A smart, edgy thriller."

—*Kirkus Reviews* on *Gone Too Far*

"A gripping whodunit with a challenging ethical dilemma at its center. Richards maintains a quick pace and creates enough red herrings to keep readers guessing."

—*Publishers Weekly* on *Gone Too Far*

"Brimming with suspense and intrigue, *My Secret to Tell* hooked me from the very first page and refused to let go. A thrilling, romantic, all-around captivating read!"

—Megan Miranda, author of *Fracture* and *Soulprint* on *My Secret to Tell*

"*My Secret to Tell* is as addictive as it is unpredictable. Natalie will keep you second-guessing until the nail-biting end."

—Natasha Preston, author of *The Cellar* and *Awake* on *My Secret to Tell*

FIVE TOTAL STRANGERS

ALSO BY NATALIE D. RICHARDS

FIVE TOTAL
STRANGERS

NATALIE D. RICHARDS

sourcebooks
fire

Published by Sourcebooks Fire, an imprint of Sourcebooks
P.O. Box 4410, Naperville, Illinois 60567-4410
(630) 961-3900
sourcebooks.com

Library of Congress Cataloging-in-Publication data is on file with the publisher.

Printed and bound in the United States of America.
VP 14 13 12 11 10

To my fellow travelers,
explorers of water and deserts
and everything in between.

ONE

THE CABIN LIGHTS FLICKER ON AND I BLINK AWAKE, NECK stiff and mouth tacky. An overhead bin rattles. Turbulence. I yawn and one of my earbuds slips out just as we drop through an air pocket, the airplane settling with a jolt. Scattered gasps and snatches of panicked conversation rise in the cabin.

The intercom crackles. "Folks, we're about twenty miles outside of Newark. As you might have noticed, the weather has intensified, so it's going to be a bumpy descent."

My seatmate, Harper, shifts impatiently. "Cue the hysteria."

I laugh because it's true. Infrequent flyers always get twitchy when pilots start tossing around words like *turbulence, bumpy,* or *weather.* Across from us, a woman with dark eyes and thin lips tightens her seat belt to the point of obvious discomfort. I imagine painting this scene. I'd focus on her face, blurring out the rest. The mix of fear and energy in her eyes tells the story.

The woman catches me staring and gives a pointed glance at the loose seat belt across my hips. I ignore her and lean closer to the window to see better. Unlike Seat Belt Sally, I'm not worried about a little choppy air. Unless the plane is plummeting to earth on fire, there's no point in getting worked up.

We can bounce all the way down as far as I'm concerned. I just need to get home to my mom.

Without meaning to, I picture my aunt's hand in mine, thin and waxy and bruised with old IV sites. This is not the memory I'd choose. Aunt Phoebe and I had *great* memories. Making homemade fudge. Trying on scarves. Playing together with her paints and color wheels. All these beautiful pieces of my aunt are smudged and watery, but those days from a year ago, the last ones we spent together—they come at me in high definition.

The smell of disinfectant and medicine. The squeak of my shoes on the hospital floor. My mother's soft, hiccupping sobs. If I let myself think about it too much, it's like I'm still there.

But it's worse for Mom. Phoebe was my aunt, but she was my mother's twin. *It's like losing one of my lungs*, she once told me. *I don't think I'll ever breathe right again.*

A clatter brings me back to the present. In the front of the plane cabin, the flight attendants make their way down the aisle, collecting trash and securing seat-back tables. A passenger is arguing with them. I can't hear what he's asking, but the flight attendant is firm. *No, you can't access the overheads. Sir, I can't allow that, it's unsafe.*

I zip my own bag shut as the attendants move on, pleasant and professional even as the cabin bumps and creaks. Beside me, Harper applies lipstick. With the way this plane is jiggling, I don't know how she's not shoving it up her nose, but she coats it on with utter precision. It's like a magic trick.

I shift in my ratty jeans, feeling sloppy beside her crisp white shirt and wool pencil skirt. Harper's been talking about her college, so she can't be much older than me, but she's sophisticated in a way I doubt I'll ever be.

The plane drops again, enough to make my stomach flip. The wings catch air with a thunk. My teeth clack together, and a flight attendant stumbles in the aisle. Someone begins to cry. I take a deep breath and close my eyes. I guess they weren't kidding about it being bumpy.

The intercom warbles again. *"Flight attendants, please take your seats."*

Harper tucks her long dark hair behind her ear. "Great, now I'm stuck holding my cup."

The plane thumps and shimmies its way down through the clouds. It's a hard go. My teeth clack together. Bags bounce up against the undersides of seats. I spend enough time in the air to know it's probably fine, but I still check the window. *Just get down out of the clouds already.*

In front of me, that woman is still crying, but I don't blame her now. Almost everyone looks nervous. Well, everyone except Harper.

"How long is your layover?" she asks, tucking her lipstick into its cap without spilling a drop of whatever's left of her Diet Coke.

"Forty-five minutes," I say as the plane dips right and then rises. "Tight."

"It won't matter in this mess. We'll all be delayed." Then she grins. "So, did you think any more about our conversation?"

Normally, I avoid chitchat on airplanes at all costs, but before we even took off, Harper pointed out my silver cuff bracelet, a gift from my dad two Christmases ago. She recognized the jewelry maker by sight, which brought us to the conversation of metal-working, then modern art, and then painting. There's no stopping me when I get started on all that.

"I dozed off somewhere over Oklahoma, I think," I say.

She laughs. "Hopefully this blizzard will convince you a transfer to CalArts is a good idea."

"Transfer?"

"Yes. Look, even if you didn't have the grades for it before, you said you're pulling a 4.0 now. And you're talented. I've seen your work."

"Well, on my phone."

"I've seen enough. You have a focus in your paintings that's uncommon."

Focus is what Phoebe saw in my work, too. She said I knew how to use color to draw a viewer's eye to the heart of each painting. That's how she convinced me to take the money she offered and to transfer permanently to my super selective and pricey art school that is across the country from Mom. I'd gotten accepted as a junior, but I came home early when Phoebe got sick, and I had no intention of going back. Especially with the hefty tuition hike that would affect my senior year.

Phoebe wasn't having that. One of the last conversations we had was her trying to convince me to make the move permanent. She'd pressed a check into my hand and held my wrist tight in her thin fingers. Told me she wanted me to go back, and more than that, she wanted me to go senior year, too.

Your work has heart, Mira. You have to follow that. It matters.

I don't know if that's true, but I wasn't about to argue with my dying aunt.

"Anyway," Harper says, bringing my attention back to the present. "No one is going to care that you're at a community college once they see your work."

Community college?

I think over our earlier conversation. I showed her photos of my most recent student exhibit. And I admitted I was a little disappointed in my painting instructor. I'm not sure why she thought I was in community college, but a transfer to any college isn't possible. Because I'm still in high school.

I think about clarifying things, but why bother? If a random stranger on a plane wants to see me as a college freshman instead of a sick-to-death-of-high-school senior, who cares?

"I'll think about it," I say.

"You should," she says. "You can text me if you want me to talk to my friend Jude."

The plane dips hard left, a wing catching a downdraft. The crying woman screams, but Harper just sighs and asks me for my phone number so she can text me, still balancing her cup precariously in her left hand. I'm a far cry from a fearful flyer, but this girl is unflappable.

The plane settles into a hard shudder, and now lots of people are making noise. Harper huffs, muttering, "Honestly, if we're going to crash, let's do it so we can all be done with the theatrics."

I clutch my armrests, but grin.

Dear, God, if you can hear me, please let me grow up to be like Harper.

"Anyway, Jude graduates next year," she says. "Music history, which is *such* a trust fund major, but he's had great opportunities. You said you're not loving Everglen—Wait, it was Everglen, right?"

I nod—that's the name of my high school. It feels a little weird, letting her continue on this line.

"You probably just need something more robust. You'd love CalArts. Everybody there does."

"Wait, you don't go there?"

"No, I'm an international relations major at Pomona."

I smirk. "Sounds like a light load."

She sighs. "It would be if I weren't also majoring in Asian Studies."

The plane lists hard to the right, then pops up and left. Others are crying now, and truthfully, I can't remember a worse descent in my long history of flying. But Harper is still chattering on with a distant look in her eye.

"I don't know what I was thinking," she muses. "I could drop it to a minor, but I like a challenge."

"Sounds like it."

She goes on and on, chirping about majors and internships, without a single glance at the window. It's like she's absolutely certain the plane will land without incident because she has things to do and places to be.

And she's right.

We touch down with a squeak of tires and a smattering of applause. Something in my stomach unclenches so I can take a full breath. Guess I wasn't quite as relaxed as I thought. The flight attendant crackles over the intercom while people throughout the cabin gather bags and laugh in relief. As we're deplaning, I open my phone and check my messages. Six of them. Zari, Dad, and three from Mom.

I pull up Mom's messages first, focusing on the last one.

Mom: Text when you land. Working, but weather has me worried.

I frown and run my thumb over the screen, imagining Mom obsessively checking the weather on her phone. Maybe I'm exaggerating. She wasn't always like this, but after I moved... Well, after Phoebe, really. Everything was different after Phoebe.

"Boyfriend?" Harper guesses.

I shake my head. "Mom texts. The weather. You know."

She laughs softly. "And I mom-talked all the way here with that transfer advice."

I snort. "Trust me. You and my mother are polar opposites."

Which is probably why I immediately liked Harper so much.

Or at the least, why I want to *be* like her. Harper is like Aunt Phoebe with a style upgrade and a world-class travel log. My mom, by contrast, is quiet and cautious, a post-surgery nurse who's afraid of infections and airplanes. And, for most of the last year, almost everything else.

Maybe she wouldn't be so afraid if I'd stayed.

No. I can't keep doing this. She wanted me to go. She wrote the check from Phoebe for half of my senior year, for Pete's sake. And Dad jumped in to pay the rest, thrilled to have me on his side of the country a little longer. We *all* agreed this was best for me.

But was it best for her?

I step off the gangway into the airport and take a sharp breath. Every seat in sight is filled, phone cords strung from endless outlets, suitcases stacked in every corner. The walls are cluttered, too—lined with shopping bags and strollers and rumpled-looking travelers half-asleep or holding phones.

Something nudges my right arm. I turn to see Harper push past me, leather duffel rolling tidily beside her.

"Aren't you going to talk to the desk?" I ask, nodding at the airline counter, where the entire population of Pennsylvania appears to be gathered.

"Spending Christmas Eve in an airport hotel? No thanks. I'm getting a car."

I laugh a little, because I'm pretty sure she's not old enough to get a car. And I doubt there will be cars available. Outside, I see the barest wisps of flurries. I'm going to go out on a limb and say canceling our flight isn't necessary. Heck, delaying our flight seems over the top. Harper marches on, all steely determination and clicking patent leather pumps.

She pauses, turning back to me. "You should come. If you want. I can drop you in Pittsburgh."

Yeah. I'm pretty sure optimism can only take you so far. I smile and shake my head. "I should probably take my chances in line. I've got to figure out what I'm doing."

"Well…" Harper pauses like she might argue, and then shakes her head. "Text me about CalArts. And best of luck getting home!"

She heads down the escalator, followed by a broad-shouldered guy with dark hair and a family with three young children. Near me, several airport staff members are moving folding cots into the hallway. One of them is watching over the work, a walkie-talkie to her ear. The TVs overhead look similarly ominous, one weather forecast displaying the word *Blizzurricane* in shimmering type.

My heart sinks. I don't need to talk to anyone to know what's happening here. Weary travelers. Tangles of charging cables. Passengers sleeping under suit coats. Cots being moved into the waiting areas. I spot the Arrivals and Departures sign on a nearby wall but I don't bother getting close. There's no point in checking for Pittsburgh or possible alternate flights. Every flight has the same status. *Canceled.*

I can't get home.

The thought is a needle of panic to the base of my throat. It's not possible. I have to get home. She needs me. She needs me to make her laugh and get her to watch trashy TV. I can distract her from the fact that Phoebe died on Christmas. But not if I'm not home.

I start a dozen text messages that I delete just as fast. There's no way to text her any of this. No careful framing is going to keep this news from reducing her to a nervous wreck.

Finally, I give up and call my stepfather, Daniel. Daniel, a soft-spoken, steady accountant who is the antithesis of my compact, high-energy father in every way, answers on the second ring. Because he always answers on the second ring.

"Mira," he says after the slightest hesitation. "Merry Christmas."

"Well, Christmas Eve," I say. "And it's less than merry. I need you to help me break the news to Mom that I'm stuck at the airport. Like overnight stuck."

"You're stuck at the airport? Do you need help?"

"No, no, it's just weather. It doesn't even look that bad. I'm figuring it out, but I think I'm going to have to fly out tomorrow. I just need you to tell Mom because you know this is a hard day for her."

"I'm not sure…" He pauses awkwardly, like he's distracted. I wonder if I caught him making the noodles. Noodles are his Christmas thing. We have them every year. I painted them once, giant yellow sheets of dough, rolled paper thin over the dining room table. The rolling pin was my focal point.

Daniel coughs. "Maybe you should leave her a message. Have you texted her?"

I cringe. He can't be serious. "Uh, no, I don't want her to hear about this at work. What if you have her call me when she gets home?"

"Home?" This pause is different. He doesn't move or sigh. When his voice comes back, it's tight and sad. "Mira, I'm not living with your mother. Did she not mention this to you?"

I cover my free ear, sure I heard him wrong. "I'm sorry, what?"

"Your mother and I are getting a divorce. I moved out two weeks ago."

His sentence feels like a terrible joke. Bits and pieces of questions swirl in the corners of my mind, but I can't catch hold of anything. Someone pushes past me with a suitcase, and the bang into my knee kicks my words loose.

"What are—I don't—a divorce?"

"I'm so sorry." He sounds like he is. But it doesn't matter.

My words vanish again. It's too sudden and weird. Was there anything—any *clue* that this was coming? I've only lived with Dad in San Diego for eighteen months, and I was back for six weeks when Phoebe died. And I've visited! Nothing has seemed different. Nothing.

I start forward, suddenly desperate to be in motion. I march without direction, past Arrivals, the Information Desk, the suitcases, cots, and families. Daniel is telling me that he still cares about me and of course my mother, too, and he never meant to hurt anyone, and I'm down the escalator and halfway through the lower level, past baggage claim carousels and rows of plastic chairs in a random curving path to nowhere.

"Mira?" Daniel's voice cuts through the fog of my brain. "Are you all right?"

Funny that he'd ask, but I don't laugh. "I'm... I've got to call my mom."

"I really am sorry. I'm surprised that she didn't talk to you about this."

"Yeah. That makes two of us."

We hang up with him making promises to stay in touch and me agreeing that of course I'll reach out if I need him. And yes, Merry Christmas. And a Happy New Year. My hands are so shaky I can barely press the button to end the call. I stop walking just short of smacking into a concrete pillar, my body thrumming with a strange electric buzz. Energy with nowhere to go.

Daniel is leaving my mother.

Correction. Daniel *left* my mother. Past tense. Old news. But not old news to me.

The world feels sideways, but nothing is different. Passengers pace. Dire weather warnings continue to scroll across every screen in sight. I check through the last three weeks of my mother's texts, a blathering collection of love you, honey and can't wait to see you and do you think a ham will be okay instead of a turkey this year? Why the hell would she not tell me something like this?

Unless she *can't* tell me. She could be in that place where she shuts down. Like when Aunt Phoebe was sick. At the end.

Except *that* time Daniel was there, making her soup and toast. And I was there, holding her hand and forcing her to talk. What is this going to look like when she wakes up alone on Christmas day? Christmas, which was the ultimate holiday in our family—not because of presents, but because we had a list of traditions that we added to and laughed about every year. Mom had to start taking time off work to fit in all the ice skating and cookie decorating and hikes through evergreen forests. We were a ridiculous trio.

And now we are a duo.

Except we aren't even that, are we? I'm here and she's there, completely one hundred percent alone.

Something rattles softly behind me, and I turn to see Harper with something held high in her hands. Her eyes look red and her face is pale, but she's grinning. "Hey stranger. Change your mind?"

She did it. She has keys to a car.

"I thought you had to be twenty-five to rent one," I say.

"There are a couple of places that let you do it at twenty-one. If you pay practically double," she says, checking her phone with a frown. She pockets it decisively. "So, are you coming with us?"

"Us?"

"Meet my friends, the fellow castaways from Flight 3694." She looks back at three people behind her. They're around her age, and they're all looking glazed over and rumpled with that shitty-travel-day expression I'm sure I'm wearing, too. Harper, however, is still perfectly put together, a little twitchy and tense maybe, but unwrinkled.

She turns for introductions like we're meeting at a fancy lunch and not at ground zero of a travel nightmare come to life.

"This is Josh." A blond with sleepy eyes and some kind of injury—guessing from the intense-looking brace on his knee and the crutches he's using—meets my eyes and gives me a slight nod.

"Kayla." A willowy girl waves. Her hair as pale as mine is dark. I think I saw her on the plane. She boarded near me.

"And Brecken." Brecken steps forward with an extended hand and a wide and inviting smile. Maybe a little too inviting, but who knows. Maybe that's just how college guys are.

I pull my beanie off my head and finger comb my hair back from my eyes.

Harper gestures at me, her bracelets jangling. "And, everyone, this is Mira. We're going to drop her in Pittsburgh with you, Brecken. If she agrees to come."

I open my mouth to argue, because this is ridiculous. I do not climb into cars with a group of strangers or jaunt off into a snowstorm. The window reveals the same unimpressive flurries. Maybe snowstorm is a stretch.

Ridiculous is a stretch, too.

Right now, my mom needs me. This isn't something I'd normally do, but to get home to Mom? I'll do whatever it takes.

TWO

THE AIRPORT DOORS SWISH CLOSED BEHIND US, AND the air outside is all exhaust fumes and smelly engines. Plus, it's cold. I'm ready to get in the closest car we can find, but Harper has to wait in line for the attendant to do a walk-through or whatever. The line is not short.

For a minute, the remaining four of us look at each other like maybe we'll try to chat. I try to imagine this as an adventure, but we don't look like happy travelers. We've got Kayla, pale and limp with a fifty-yard stare; Brecken with his too-tight shirt and nervous hands; and Josh with his pained sighs and sad crutches. And what about me? On the outside, do I look like a girl whose world is smashing to pieces?

Finally, Brecken says something about calling his mom, and the spell is broken. Obviously relieved, we all nod, wandering in different directions to make calls or look through our bags.

I dial Mom automatically and remember when her voicemail picks up that she's at work. I hang up without leaving a message.

I don't even know what I'd say to her. A divorce is *not* something I can ask about over the phone. Certainly not when I tell her I'm not going to be at the airport as expected and am instead driving through the mountains with total strangers, but *hey, enough about that, Mom; tell me about your supersecret divorce!*

I look at Zari's text instead—When do you land?—and pull up her number.

I pause before I dial, allowing myself a brief existential crisis over the potential complications here, too. This is hardly the time to worry about our very painful friendship breakup, but it's also not a great time to miss another one of Zari's concerts.

Zari was *not* a fan of me moving across country. Especially when it meant missing her cello audition for the Pennsylvania Youth Orchestra, a highly selective orchestra she'd been trying to get into for years. She didn't make it, and, though she didn't technically blame me, it started a fight. Things were said, and a few months of silent treatment followed. We made a slow, tentative patch-up effort this summer that was supposed to culminate on December 26, when I'd be attending her postholiday breakfast concert.

Except now I'm not sure I'll make it. When I *do* get home—whenever that will be—my mom and I have a lot to talk about. The Phoebe stuff was one thing, but now that I know about Daniel…

Ugh.

Zari and I have been best friends since we were kids. And the whole fight was completely dumb and ancient history now. But

Zari can be tense about stuff like this and—you know? I probably shouldn't call her.

I call her.

And—*dang it, Zari*—she answers.

"Black pants or gray?" she asks instead of saying hello.

"Gray," I answer with a grin.

"Hang on," she says, covering the mouthpiece and yelling at one of her brothers.

I missed this. We met when we were nine and our moms started working the same shift at the hospital. Most of those years, we shared what felt like an endless conversation—a rapid-fire back-and-forth with no need for hello or goodbye or small talk. We'd just pick up at whatever random place we'd left off the last time we talked.

And then I moved, and the long pauses made the conversation weird.

And then Phoebe got cancer, and there were more pauses than conversation.

And then there was the missed concert and the fight. She said I was distant, acting like nothing mattered. I said the things that mattered to me were bigger than cello concerts and finding the right New Years' dress.

We were probably both a little bitchy and a little right. But that's what distance does. I didn't see her in the hallway at school. We didn't bump into each other at the coffee shop. It was just radio silence until a few texts this summer.

And now…maybe, finally, a reunion.

The speaker rattles, and Zari huffs into the phone. "Sorry. You said gray?"

"Definitely."

"Good, the black pair is too tight."

"It's probably not." I'm determined to keep us back in this verbal volleyball match.

"Eh, I don't know. Wait—are you here? I thought you landed later."

I sigh. "Yeah, well, guess whose flight was canceled?"

"Ouch. Getting rerouted?"

"Since they're practically setting up campfires in the terminals, I'm guessing no. But that's not even the good part."

"There's a good part?"

"Did you know my mom and Daniel are getting a divorce?"

"What? A divorce?"

"Yep."

"When? Like now?"

"Like two weeks ago. It already happened. The moving out at least. Did your mom say anything about it?"

"No. And God knows she would." She inhales.

"It's not great," I say.

There's an awkward pause "Mira, with your aunt last year…"

"Yeah, the timing is less than excellent. Plus, she hasn't said a word to me."

"Sounds like you need to get home."

"I am. I'm hitching a ride with some college students I met on the plane." A stretch, since I didn't meet anyone but Harper, but whatever.

"You're getting in a car with a bunch of strangers?"

"Do I have a choice? Anyway, the girl driving is nice. She sat next to me on the plane for like, six hours."

"And the rest of them?"

"I don't know, but if they're Harper's friends, I'm sure they're fine. I just have to get home."

"Yeah, you do. Unless you want to miss the second most important musical moment of my life."

She means it as a joke, but my laugh falls flat, and the stupidity and the fight all bubble up. I feel the simmer of old wounds beneath the silence on the line. It's ancient history. We talked about it on one awkward phone call at the end of summer. We were going to start fresh this Christmas. Just get back to being friends.

She sighs. "I didn't mean…"

"I know, I know," I say in a rush. I'm cutting her off because I don't want to talk about this. I don't want to think about it. I want to get home, and I want to find out what the hell is going on with my mom.

"Hey," I say, jumping on that idea. "Is there any way you can talk to your mom? Ask her if she knows anything about what happened with Mom and Daniel?"

"Sure, of course," Zari says. "Hey, Mira? Be safe, okay?"

"Definitely."

"Maybe call me at a gas station. Tell me how weird they are."

I laugh. "I will."

As soon as I hang up with Zari, Harper waves us over. We follow her around the back of a parking space. A sleek, white SUV lights up as Harper presses the key. I guess that's our ride.

We stay back as she pops the trunk, settling a pricey-looking leather duffel inside.

"Here, let me get that," Brecken says, taking my giant backpack. I roll my aching shoulder.

"Thank you," I say. "Be careful—the latch is all wonky. Sorry."

"I totally get it," Brecken says, but his matching black bags are so pristine they look like they were purchased in the airport, so I doubt he does.

Josh goes through a miserable-looking process of balancing on one crutch and then the other to remove his cross-body messenger bag. I gesture vaguely in case he'd like help, but he moves faster, his neck flushed. I hope he doesn't think I was rushing him.

"They let you rent this?" Kayla asks Harper. Brecken has her frayed floral duffel bag now, too.

Harper—texting furiously on her phone—doesn't look up. "For enough money, they'll let you rent anything."

"Miss Chung?"

Harper glances at the approaching attendant from the rental car company. He's holding a large black duffel bag and loops of silver chain. Snow chains for the tires. I glance outside of the parking garage, where I can still see flurries. It isn't even sticking, so this feels like serious overkill, but the attendant is all the-apocalypse-draws-nigh about it.

He explains how to put them on the tires and then points out a shovel and flares. Where the heck does this guy think we're going? Northern Siberia? Wherever it is, the dude is quite determined to get us there safely. Plus, he's fawning in a way that makes me wonder exactly how much money Harper dropped on this rental.

Still, it looks large and safe and—most importantly—free, so I keep my mouth shut.

Brecken adjusts my backpack beside his bags and Kayla's, and then he shifts Harper's duffel in for the best fit. And Brecken might have a nice bag, but Harper's has an emblem that tells me hers cost more than my car. It's all buttery leather and smooth brass hardware.

Finally happy with the luggage arrangement, Brecken steps back, but Kayla leans in to shove something in her backpack and make her own rearrangements. I watch, wondering how I'd paint her. She's like an overexposed photograph: white skin, pale eyes, and hair so blond it looks silvery under the strange gray parking garage lights.

When she turns around and catches me staring, I offer a brief smile and hope I don't look embarrassed.

"You're from San Diego?" she asks me.

"Pittsburgh originally. My da—" I cut myself off with a

cough. Harper thinks I'm in college. If she finds out I'm not, I don't know if she'll keep her offer standing and I'm not taking chances. "Sorry. I'm in school out there. You?"

She shrugs, looking off to the side. "Something like that."

"Where do you live in Pittsburgh?" Brecken asks me once the luggage is all arranged.

"Beltzhoover. You?"

"Edgeworth," he says, which makes sense given his high-end jeans and pristine shoes. But if he's judging my inferior zip code, he doesn't show it.

"Harper said you're an artist?" Kayla breezes in, pale hair fanned out over her long coat. "Like a sculptor or…"

I relax. "I'm into painting, mostly. Landscapes and cities."

"What's your inspiration?" Josh asks quietly.

I shift on my feet, feeling keenly aware of the fact that two attractive college guys are looking at me, waiting for a response. I'm grateful art is the subject. Art, I can talk about. Art is the center of my universe. I know I probably can't make money creating it, but I want it in my life. I can teach it. Or curate it. Or restore it. Art itself is the thing that inspires everything else. But I know that's not what he's looking for.

"My biggest influences are Gustav Klimt and Jacob Lawrence, but for entirely different reasons. They're nothing alike, but they both move me."

Josh tilts his head. "That's what moves you? I thought art was inspired by real life, not other artists."

I laugh. "Well, yes, but most of the artists I know are inspired by better artists. When we connect with someone else's work it inspires our own. Those connections are everything."

"Connections," Josh says slowly, smile widening. I can't decide if it's cute or if he's teasing me, and I don't really care, so I smile back and turn to the car.

It's pretty swanky for a rental. Leather seats and cup holders in so many places that we'd probably need three drinks apiece to fill them. We load in without much discussion. Harper fiddles with the emergency kit, unzipping and zipping before she slides into the driver's seat. Brecken sits beside her in the front, and Kayla gets in the back next to me. Harper's back to texting, and Brecken pores over a map on his phone. Josh is rearranging his bag in the back, so I could get out and force him to take the middle, but honestly it feels like a crap thing to do to a guy on crutches. When he gets in next to me, I shift over to make a little more room for him.

It's weird, being in a car with four strangers. I'm instantly glad Brecken's up front. He's all nervous energy, talking fast about alternate routes and weather forecasts. He sounds dire, but honestly the roads are beyond fine. And Brecken strikes me as… intense. Maybe it's his eyes. Or all the jittering. Either way, I'm glad we're not rubbing elbows.

My seatmates are low key in comparison. Kayla's propped against the window like she's ready to nap, and Josh is fiddling with his crutches. They're making the cramped back seat even more cramped.

"Here, I can take them," I offer. He fixes me with a long look before reluctantly handing them over. Okay, then. Cute, but a little odd. I stack them on top of one another in the back on top of our luggage.

"Thank you," he says, but he looks nervous. Like he thinks maybe I'm trying to flirt with him. Whatever. He probably has a pretentious girlfriend back at college anyway. A poetry and women's studies double major with tragic bangs and anti-establishment stickers on her laptop.

Still, when he adjusts his leg and groans, I wince in sympathy.

"This couldn't have been fun at an airport," I say, nodding at the hefty brace on his knee.

He frowns. "It had its moments."

"So, what did you do?"

"I'm doing a social experiment on that," he says with a chuckle. "What's your guess?"

I tilt my head. "Pardon?"

"What do you think happened to my knee?"

"Sports thing," Harper says, though he was asking me. "I'm also going to guess that you're a psychology major based on that comment."

Given that comment, I'm not sure I'd classify Josh and Harper as friends. She must be one of those popular girls who introduces any person they've ever met as a "friend."

"It's not sports. No way," Brecken says, without looking to Josh for verification. "My vote is something involving stairs?"

"Both wrong, but both noted," Josh says with a grin. "Mira?" he asks, prompting me for my answer.

"I'm going with a rogue bear attack," I say.

"Rogue bear." His smile widens. "That's my favorite yet."

Okay, maybe not totally pretentious. And definitely coffee shop cute. Like half the guys at Perkilicious in San Diego, he's tall, blond, and in dire need of a meeting with the business end of a pair of scissors. I can't see the rest of his clothes, but his gloves are sporting holes in a couple of fingers. When Harper starts maneuvering out of the parking spot, he pulls out Kafka's *Metamorphosis* and a red pen. All we're missing is a mug of some bougie dark roast and a sulky guitarist in the corner.

"This could take forever," Harper says softly as she eases into the lane leading out of the garage.

Brecken twists in his seat, looking left and right and then squaring his shoulders like it's time to make decisions. He reaches for the radio first, scanning through the stations. "We should listen to the news. Try to find out if there's some sort of traffic report. There might be road closures."

"It's not bad at all so far. And we have the emergency kit," Harper says. "Snow chains and flares—everything we need to get home for Christmas."

I touch my phone, grateful that we're moving. This is it. Six awkward hours in the car with strangers, and I'll be home with my mom. It's going to be fine. We'll talk. I'll gripe about her not telling me. She'll explain. We'll get over it.

"So, what's *your* major?" Josh asks me. He's smiling like he already knows. I think that's the Kafka talking. Coffee shop boys are pretty sure they know everything.

"Undeclared," I say quickly, and I manage not to flinch at the lie. "You?"

He shrugs. "I'm on a business track, but lately I've been interested in other things."

"Heads up," Brecken says. "Looks like the storm is coming."

I look ahead to an electronic display sign over the highway. It's blinking out a message in orange digital letters.

Blizzard Warning from 1:00 p.m. Saturday until 8:00 a.m. Sunday.

I look around at the mostly dry roads and flurries. Are they getting heavier?

I check the clock on the dashboard. 11:28 a.m.

It doesn't look like a blizzard yet, but that might be because the blizzard hasn't hit.

THREE

WE SLIP FOR THE FIRST TIME ON A PATCH OF HIGHWAY
that doesn't look bad at all. It's nothing big—a quick sideways
shuffle of wheels that's more surprising than scary. Before my
heart can even speed up, some high-tech traction system gets us
back under control. The road looks mostly dry.

Black ice?

Maybe just a slick spot.

I check my seat belt, making sure it's snug across my hips.
Planes are safe, but cars are a different matter. I've spent a lot
of time in these mountains.. And I can't remember the last
Pennsylvania winter storm that didn't involve a news story of an
awful crash.

Not that the roads are bad like that. Just some icy patches.
And we don't seem to be going very fast, but the snow is falling
harder now, and ice is collecting on the windshield. All the
electronically sprayed blue cleaner in the world doesn't seem to
be wiping the glass clean.

"Dammit," Harper says, her voice high and tight. "I can barely see for all that ice."

"I can drive if you want," Brecken says. "I learned to drive in upstate New York, so this is nothing."

"I've got it," Harper says. "I just wish I had clean glass."

I stare out the window, pondering a lazy stream of internal questions. Is this really a blizzard? How fast are we going? Is Mom doing okay? Is someone in this car watching me?

I straighten, because it's a strange question to pop into my mind. Stranger still is the chill that rolls up my spine, the prickle of the hairs on my arms standing on end. I look around, because it's exactly the kind of feeling I'd get if someone was watching me.

But they aren't. No one is paying me the least bit of attention.

Harper sighs in the front seat and hits the washer fluid button. The wipers—clogged with ice—drag cloudy turquoise streaks of fluid and road salt across the windshield.

"I can't see very well," Harper admits, slowing.

"Just follow the car in front of you," Brecken says. "I really can drive if you want."

"I'm fine," Harper says, but she grips the wheel hard. "I spent six months with my mom's family in China. I drove on the Sichuan-Tibet highway. Multiple times. I can handle this."

Brecken laughs. "The Situ-what?"

"Sichuan-Tibet. In China. You know, that country in Asia." I think she's teasing but there's an edge to her tone.

"I know where China is," Brecken says quietly.

"I'm sorry," Harper says, slowing even more. "This is just… really annoying."

I pull out my phone, because this is obviously not going to be a quick trip. So, it might be a good time to let my parents know I wasn't kidnapped and stolen away to some remote corner of the globe.

Of course, telling either of them I volunteered to drive with a bunch of strangers probably won't fly. But neither will ignoring the six text messages that have been vibrating my pocket for the last hour.

Dad: Weather looks nasty. Text me when you're there.

Mom: Missed your call, but I know the flights are grounded.

Mom: Call me when you know what's going on.

Dad: Your mom called about the flights. Did they get you a hotel?

Mom: I'm done with lunch, but I'll step out to call you during break. Or you call me!

Mom: Mira? Why are you not calling?

She won't be on lunch now. I could try to text, but she'll call anyway. Unless I tell her *I'll* call and I give her a time. What time, though?

I chew the corner of my lip and create a message for both of them. I need something that's close enough to the truth to keep me from bursting into guilt-induced flames. But far enough from it that my mom won't alert the National Guard.

My fingers move over the touch screen with purpose.

Me: All flights canceled, but I found a ride home. Seatmate from San Diego and her family live near Pittsburgh and rented a supersafe SUV. Mom, I'll call when we stop in a few minutes.

Mom's *typing* bubble pops up almost instantaneously. Of course it does. She lost her sister last Christmas. Daniel a couple of weeks ago. And now her only daughter is driving through a snowstorm that news outlets are treating like the blizzard that drove people to cannibalism on Donner Pass.

The message appears.

Mom: Who are you with? What kind of SUV? I don't know that I like this.

Me: Don't worry. The roads aren't even that bad. Seriously, it's mostly flurries. I'll call in a few. I can't wait to see you!

Mom: You too, but this storm is getting bad. Please call.

The SUV slows and I look up from my phone to see a smattering of brake lights. Outside, the snow has started to stick, but just barely. Tire tracks ahead leave wide dark trails through the white.

"The traffic is going to get worse," Brecken says.

"I think you're right," Josh responds, the light from his phone illuminating his face. "It's nothing but red in ten miles. It looks like traffic hits a dead stop."

"Maybe the road is closed?" Brecken asks.

"Could be," Josh says. "Maybe an accident?"

"It's not even that bad," I say.

"Can we take another route?" Harper asks. "I don't want to be stuck in traffic until Christmas morning."

"Maybe we should," Josh says. "All that red probably means an accident, right?"

"I'll start looking for an exit," Harper says with a sigh.

"Let's do the travel plaza," Brecken says. "My phone says it's eight miles up, just past a big bridge."

Harper's shoulders inch closer to her ears. "Bridge? Don't bridges ice over?"

"They do," I say, because even though the snow isn't bad, it is sticking.

"Don't worry," Josh says. "We won't let anything happen."

Really? It's a nice sentiment, but unless he's going to call on some sort of mutant ice control powers, I think the roads are going to do their own thing.

"Whoa," Kayla says.

Her voice is a jolt. She's mostly slept since we've been in the car, so I'm surprised to see her upright, her slender hand pressed to her window. There's something out there on the road that she's looking at. A wreck, I think. Harper slows, and Brecken curses softly under his breath, but I can't see what they're watching.

I strain against my seat belt, trying to piece together the scene obscured by the snow and Kayla's foggy window. Then the pieces come together. A sports car sits on its roof in the ditch. It's like a flipped over turtle, four tires like curling legs, the dark underbelly exposed to our gaze. My stomach tightens.

I know what this is—it happens every year in Pennsylvania. A dozen snowflakes hit the road and all common sense pours directly out of drivers' brains. Half of the people drive fifteen miles an hour and the other half weave in and out of lanes doing seventy-five.

The weavers are often the ones that end up like this, but Dad always told me the slowpokes cause it. As we pass, I see a dazed-looking twentysomething behind the car with a cell phone to his ear and—I'm betting—a newfound appreciation for seat belts and airbags. Another car is parked on the curb, a broad-shouldered man heading toward the car to assist.

"They seem okay," Brecken says. "Just keep going to the exit."

"That was crazy," Kayla says. She's bleary-eyed when she grins at me, still half asleep and seemingly delighted by the accident. It's creepy.

"Ugh," Harper says. "I still can't see anything."

Brecken reaches like he's going to take the wheel. "Hey, stay in your lane already."

"I can't *see* my lane, okay?"

"It's the windshield," Josh says it at the same time I think it. "It's getting worse."

He's right. Ice is building up on the wipers, so every arc across leaves a narrower section of clean glass. I have no idea how Harper can see the road at all through those tiny clear sections.

"Try the cleaner again," Brecken says, pointing out the right control. Blue liquid dribbles weakly from the top. Clearly ice has clogged the sprayer.

"Shit."

"Do the smacking trick," I suggest. "You know, pull back the wiper blade and whap it against the glass."

Brecken rolls down the windows, and the air is arctic. He does his wiper first, gripping the blade in his glove and pulling it back hard. It hits the glass with a perfect smack, but though snow sprays, it's nowhere near clear enough.

"Okay, try to do mine," Harper says. "I can't see like this."

"I can't reach your window. And it barely worked on mine. We need to pull over."

"No, we can do this." Harper rolls down her window, and I cross my arms. The wind is a weapon. My coat might as well be made of lace.

Even twisting in her seat, Harper can't reach the blade. "I don't think I can."

Brecken shakes his head. "Try again."

"She's not going to be able to do it," Josh says simply. I shoot him a glare, but he shrugs. "Her arms are too short."

He's right—she'd have to stand up in her seat to reach it. But I hate that he said it when I'm sure she's already stressed enough and painfully aware of the limitations of her reach.

"Just pull over," Brecken says. "It'll be okay. This will be easier if you can see."

Josh leans forward then, straining against his seat belt to get closer to Harper. "He's right. You can pull over. You can do this."

No response.

Josh reaches over the seat, slow and hesitant. Then he pats

her shoulder, once. Gently. "Harper? Trust Brecken. Let him tell you what to do. Just follow his directions. You can do it."

"She definitely can," Brecken says. "She's killing it."

"I don't need directions." Harper sounds nervous. Really nervous.

They keep encouraging her, but it's part patronizing man and part fear, and it's one hundred percent annoying as hell. There might be a sliver of kind intention, so I try to hold onto that instead of grinding my molars at the "follow directions" comment.

"Go right here," Brecken says.

Harper nods and inches the wheel to the right until we're stopped on the side of the road. She fiddles with controls and frowns, presses the wiper fluid button and the two beside it. "I don't know how to stop them."

"What do you mean?" Brecken asks.

"The wipers. They're automatic. They keep kicking back on—I don't know how to turn them off."

Brecken leans over and fiddles with some of the buttons and displays on the high-tech dashboard. Hazard lights start up and then the radio, and then I'm pretty sure the car tries to send a text message to God knows who, but the wipers keep wiping.

"I'll just turn the car off."

"Don't bother, we can do this with them running. Might even work better since it'll clear off the ice we knock free," Brecken says. He turns and winks at all of us in the back. "We've got this."

"I'm a believer," I say with a laugh.

"I knew you would be," Brecken smirks.

Harper follows him outside, her heels traded in at some point for stylish boots that probably aren't providing any better traction. She doesn't close the door completely, and the alarm dings incessantly, a succession of pleasant chimes alerting us that something is not as it should be.

Outside, Brecken demonstrates his windshield-wiper-thwacking technique while Harper watches with somber focus. He pulls back his wiper and smacks it against the glass and says something to Harper while the blade arcs across the windshield. Then he repeats the action, shattering more and more ice off the blade until his side of the windshield swipes clean. He steps around the hood of the car just as Harper grabs the wiper.

Harper doesn't have Brecken's sense of timing. She pulls back the blade just as the motor tries to drag it back from the glass. It jerks from her grip, hitting the glass at the exact moment she screams.

Her sleeve is caught. For a second, I think that's the problem. Then, she rips it free and a crimson drop hits the windshield.

Blood.

Harper jerks her hand up to her chest protectively, cradling it with her other hand. Brecken approaches and the wipers smear that tiny red drop into a thin, grotesque arc across the glass.

I wince. "I think she cut herself."

"Yeah," Josh says. "On the wiper blade probably. They have sharp edges."

"Really? She cut herself?" Kayla asks, leaning forward to get a better look. I ignore her. If this girl starts professing her love of Japanese horror films, Josh is sitting in the middle.

Outside, Brecken tries to examine Harper's cut, but she pulls out of his grip. He shucks his gloves and reaches for her like she's an injured animal. Her hand drips red onto the white hood. Josh sighs and twists in his seat. Maybe the blood is making him squeamish? No, he's looking for something in the back.

Kayla laughs again.

"Really?" I ask her.

She frowns at me, but she stops laughing, so I guess I made my point. Beside me, Josh unbuckles, grunting as he tries to shift around.

"What are you doing?" I ask.

"I need to get my suitcase. I was going to get them something for the blood."

"Let me try," I say.

I unbuckle and twist around so I can reach his bag. It's as sturdy and unremarkable as the rest of him, an oversized navy-blue messenger bag sandwiched between Harper's leather bag and the back of our seat. I tug it free inch by inch, but Josh pats my arm.

"Just unzip the front compartment. There's a little bag in there."

"Shit, she's really bleeding," Kayla says, finally sounding concerned.

"Thanks, Mira," he says. Then, to Kayla, "She's fine. Fingers and heads bleed a ton."

"What am I looking for here?" I ask.

"There should be some gauze in the first aid kit."

"First aid kit?" I laugh. "Are you a Boy Scout?"

He raises three fingers with a rueful grin. "Motto is 'be prepared.'"

I find the gauze, as promised, and pull a couple of individually wrapped squares out of the box. A rush of icy air freezes me when Harper's door is flung open. The car alarm dings in harmony with Harper's whimpers. Brecken ducks his head in around her.

"We need some napkins or something," he says.

"Here." I pass up the gauze and some tape, noticing the smears of crimson on Brecken's hand, too. It's vibrant, shocking red—or maybe it just looks that way because their skin is so pale.

Then there's nothing to see but the sides of their bodies, legs close together and arms and hands out of view. I hear the door's soft alarm. Brecken's muffled voice. Harper's small, mousy sounds.

I turn my attention to the windshield. On the glass, her blood is almost gone, only the faintest trail of scarlet left in one corner of the windshield.

"Make sure you have her put some pressure on it," Josh says.

"Is she okay?" I ask.

"I think she's—" Brecken cuts himself off with a gasp.

And everything happens at once.

Headlights glare from the wrong angle. Not behind us or on

the other side of the road. I realize the danger just before I spot the Mustang cutting the wrong way across the lanes. Over the snow-covered median that separates the opposing lanes of traffic.

My lungs freeze over when the speeding car barrels across the snowy divider, sliding into our lanes. It's coming *right* at us.

Someone screams. That stupid alarm dings away. Harper and Brecken are diving into the driver's seat, headfirst. But I'm frozen like the chunks of snow Brecken knocked off the windshield wiper. All I can do is watch as the Mustang's back end slides left. Swings wide. The car spins, and it's still coming.

It's going to hit us. I can see it—the image of it painted in clean, bold strokes in my mind—Brecken and Harper's legs pinned between the white leather seat and that wide metal fender. There will be so much blood then.

I close my eyes, waiting for the impact. Any second now.

Any second.

December 26

Mira,

Do you know that your name means wonder? I looked
it up after we met yesterday. But even if it meant
something else, I knew in that moment that's what I
was seeing. I think you might be a true wonder. Living
proof that the universe is good and right.

That day in the hospital coffee shop—I thought it
would be a nothing day standing in line for overpriced
coffee with a bunch of gossiping nurses. But it wasn't
nothing for us, was it? Do you believe in fate? I suppose
I don't even have to ask. After the connection between
us, I know you must. I felt it the moment our eyes met.
Did you know even sooner? Did you feel it when you
heard my voice, offering to pay for your coffee?

You were so sad, eyes red and swollen. You had that
crumpled tissue in your hand, and the clerk had to ask
you for payment three times before you realized she
was speaking to you. Before you checked your pockets
and realized you didn't have money.

It was nothing to pay for your coffee, sweetheart.
I would have paid for much more. But you treated it
like the most wonderful gift. I felt like an angel, the
way you looked at me, with tears welled up in your
beautiful, dark eyes.

I don't think it's an accident that we met in a hospital, a place where lives begin and end. It all happens so fast, doesn't it? First, I'm just going along, and then, you were there. It was like the sun coming out after a long rain.

I'll never forget anything about that day, Mira.

I'll never let you forget, either.

Yours

FOUR

INSTEAD OF THE CRUNCH I EXPECT, THE SOFT SOUND OF Harper crying cuts through the roar of blood behind my ears. Kayla is dead quiet now, but Josh breathes in and out loudly. My heart thumps hard and fast, a strange contrast to Harper's slow, steady sobs.

I open my eyes. The Mustang is nestled against the concrete highway divider. It isn't even bad. It looks like a gentle bump against the wall.

And we're okay.

We're okay.

We're okay.

"We're okay," Brecken echoes my thoughts aloud, the same words in a soothing loop, like you'd use with a frightened child. He sounds certain of it. Then he takes a deep breath. "We're completely safe. It's over."

I swallow hard, my whole body shaking. Maybe we're okay for now. But there are a whole lot of miles left before I'd call us safe. And this sure the hell isn't over.

Things change after the Mustang incident. I guess it's hard to laugh it all off after something like that. Brecken checks the driver who wrecked—he's fine—and then checks Harper's finger. It isn't too bad, now that the bleeding has stopped. So, we settle back into driving mode, buckling belts and zipping bags. Harper quietly asks Brecken to drive and he agrees.

No one talks anymore about how the roads aren't that bad. They're bad enough that Harper and Brecken almost got killed.

I don't know what it looks like to get hit by a car, but it's hard not to think about it now that I have a mental image of them diving into the driver's seat. I can't shake that image. And I can't shake that awful feeling from earlier—the creepy-crawly sensation that someone is behind me. It makes zero sense. I'm not walking down a dark street alone, I'm in a car with four people, none of whom are even looking at me.

Still, for the first time since I boarded the plane in San Diego, I feel frightened.

Fortunately, the next few minutes are blissfully quiet. No one speaks or plays music.

Harper pulls out an expensive-looking notebook and beautiful pen and starts writing, holding her book awkwardly with her injured hand. Josh is reading again. Proust now, but he's still got his brow furrowed and his thumb running under the lines as he reads, like a conscientious student trying to absorb every word. Kayla slumps back against the window and starts to softly snore as Brecken pulls onto the highway.

Harper is in her own universe with her journal. Josh highlights passages here and there in his book. Kayla moans softly in her sleep, caught in dark dreams, I guess. Only Brecken and I seem present, both of our gazes fixed on the road, the view interrupted by the soft *shh-thum, shh-thum* of the windshield wipers.

Traffic grows heavier, and the three miles to the next exit take fifteen minutes to drive. It's not a real exit or the travel plaza Brecken wants, but he pulls in anyway. It's a no-frills rest stop with a dark-windowed building situated at the top of a small hill. Two sidewalks lead up from the different sides of the parking lot, and a smattering of snowy picnic tables sits off to the right. We pass the first section of the lot—for tractor trailers and RVs. There are two tractor trailers there, but our automobile lot is empty.

Brecken parks and Harper closes her book, checking her phone. The dashboard clock says it's already 1:08 p.m. Great. It's mid-afternoon and we can't be more than 75 miles from the airport. Hopefully we'll pick up some serious time on the next leg.

"We should all try to go," Harper announces. "To the bathroom, I mean."

"Thank you, Mommy," Kayla says.

"Play nice," Brecken says, but his tone is too flat for teasing.

"Are you doing okay?" Harper asks. She's looking at me, so I glance around, but her gaze doesn't shift. She's not asking anyone else. Just me. And everyone else is watching, too, four sets of eyes pinned on me like it's the most obvious question in the world. But only for me.

I give an awkward half laugh. "I'm fine." Then I look around at everyone pointedly. "Do I not look fine?"

"No, no," Harper says. "You're just quiet."

By the time I glance back, everyone is already busy with their own phones or bags or bathroom plans and who knows what else. It's almost like they weren't all looking at me just now, but I'm sure they were. I didn't imagine that.

Stop it. Stop being paranoid.

Josh twists, looking for his crutches, and I squirm, suddenly desperate to get out of this car. This is probably my best chance to find some privacy so I can call my mom in peace. I want to climb over Josh or Kayla, who are both dragging their feet, but the civilized part of me that actually remembers manners and human decency knows it's best to help people who are injured.

"I'll get them," I tell Josh, twisting to slide the crutches out of the back, where they're wedged between our bags. Staying with my trend for manners, I ask him if he needs anything else. Then I ask Harper about her finger. I even ask Brecken if he needs anything.

Eventually, we all exit the car, but I'm the first one up the sidewalk, and I take my time. The day is blissfully quiet and still. It's nice to not be crammed against strangers. There is nothing but me and the cold, clean smell of the air. I take a breath and think, *I could be with Mom right now.* She loves winter. She used to force Daniel out for a walk every morning. Now, she's walking alone.

She's been walking alone for a couple of weeks. If they were having problems, probably a lot longer than that. A twinge pulls at my middle. I should be home with her. I should have ignored her promises that she'd be fine. She wasn't fine after Phoebe. I was fine; she was too devastated to be fine.

But Phoebe begged me to go back to school before she died.

I pull open the door to the rest area, and it's like I've stumbled onto the set of a dystopian society. Muddy trails of footprints lead across the tile in a dozen directions, ghosts of travelers long past. There's been a stampede, but now the building is empty and silent.

All the normal rest area staples are here—the giant wall map flanked by bathrooms with wide entrances, the bulletin board with travel notices and traffic laws. I move past a mostly dark alcove with a sign promising VENDING and then past a tiered rack of tourist attraction brochures for things like whitewater rafting and zip-line canopy tours. Every advertisement is summery and bright, a stark contrast to the bleak, gray landscape outside.

If the entrance was dismal, the bathroom is worse. The pale yellow walls and dark brown tile leave the long, narrow room with a jaundiced glow. Past the empty row of sinks, a line of beige toilet stalls flanks the opposite wall. A single fluorescent bulb strobes on and off above the second sink, a rhythmic flicker that sets my teeth on edge.

I have that same feeling I had in the car, but I don't think anyone could walk into this room and not worry about a serial killer lurking in one of the stalls.

Still, who knows when I'll have another chance to pee? I

march forward, forcing my eyes away from the twitchy light and the dark familiarity of my reflection in each mirror. Even when the stall door is closed, I feel strange and exposed, my arms prickling with goose bumps.

I finish quickly, and the flush diminishes some of the creepy vibes, as does the hiss of surprisingly warm water from the faucet. I shake my head at myself in the mirror. Clearly, I've been watching too many horror movies. Usually, I'm mellow like my dad. Mom, on the other hand, is still convinced a kidnapper could come for me at any moment. She'd laugh about it but would actually be totally wigged out in here.

Once upon a time, my mother laughed a lot.

Outside the bathroom, I pick my way back across the dirty wet floor. I'm still alone in the rest stop, but Josh is approaching the door. I push it open for him, careful to leave him space for his crutches.

"Watch all that water," I say, gesturing at the floor.

He nods, but doesn't really look at me. "Are we the only ones in here?"

"Yes. It's completely creepy. Where's everyone else?"

"Checking the forecast and looking over the emergency kit. Brecken wants to put on the snow chains."

I frown. "He can't. There isn't anywhere near enough snow."

"Yeah, I tried to explain that."

Maybe I'm imagining the superior edge to Josh's voice, but I don't think so. He doesn't wait for me to answer, just moves on slowly toward the bathroom. Yeah, I'm not imagining it. He's cute, but he's nowhere near cute enough to be this big of an ass.

I look out the windows where I can see the SUV trunk popped open. Harper, Brecken, and Kayla are beside it. I'm not ready to deal with the cold just yet, so I call my mom. She picks up quickly enough to tell me she was holding her phone, waiting on me to call.

"Mira." Mom pauses after my name like she's trying to hide her worry. "I'm so glad you called. Where are you?"

"At a rest stop," I say, keeping my own voice as cheery as possible. "Merry Christmas Eve!"

"Merry Christmas, honey. Where are you *exactly*?"

I laugh a little but it's forced and tight coming out. She's stressed and sad and is probably staring at a map of Pennsylvania, plotting a way to rescue me from the big, bad blizzard. I wish I wasn't causing this drama. Because I don't want her worried. I want to show her some of my newest work—I've been experimenting a lot with shadow and light—and drink hot cocoa and ask her why the hell she kept the divorce from me.

But I don't go into any of that. "We are at a rest stop on I-78. The roads aren't too bad, but it's very slow going. I think I'll be later than I thought."

"They're not bad?" She doesn't sound like she believes me.

"It's weird. There's not much snow," I say. "I think the forecasters overdid it."

"Mira, the storm is probably just starting to hit you. It's a mess here. We probably got ten inches."

"Well, it's less than an inch here. Maybe it petered out."

"I really don't think so. Should I call this family you're with?" Mom asks. "I could speak to one of the parents."

"Mom, I'm okay," I say with a laugh. "I'm technically an adult now, remember? Eighteen since the ninth of August and all. And the parents are super careful. You'd totally approve."

I should flinch at the lie, but we're both lying now, aren't we? How could she not tell me about Daniel? Did she think I'd flip out? Or not come home? Or is she in such a bad state she can't talk about it? In those first days after Phoebe, she'd stand around with a vacant stare while her cereal went soggy or the eggs in the skillet in front of her smoked and burned.

She sniffs softly and my chest twinges. I can picture her right now, in her faded Mickey Mouse scrubs, her hand at her throat. Like she's trying to hold in her panic.

"How are things at home?" I ask. A gentle probe.

"Home is fine. I'm worried about you," she says, not biting.

"I told you, I'm completely okay." I flinch again, but forge on. "I'll be home by tonight. Is Daniel working or is he eating with us?"

There's a catch in her breath before she answers. "We'll figure it out once you're home. When you're safe and sound."

"Mom, I know you have to be thinking about Aunt Phoebe. I'm worried about you."

"Mira, we're both thinking about Phoebe. Sometimes the anniversary of a death can be harder."

"Okay," I say, unsure of what she's getting at.

"But right now, I am concerned about your safety." Her voice wobbles. "Are you sure you're okay with these people?"

"One hundred percent." The lie falls easily from my lips.

"Okay. I trust your judgment. Now, let's get you home and we'll talk. Pay attention to where you are. Be smart. Keep your eyes open, right?"

"My eyes are open," I say softly.

And that's it. I don't tell her I know about Daniel. I don't tell her I can sense she's upset. I say I'll be home soon and that I love her, and both of those things are true. But they land in a heap of lies that leaves me queasy when we disconnect.

The second I hang up, I fire texts at Zari.

Me: Did you talk to your mom?

Zari: Where are you? All good?

Me: Somewhere on 78. Roads are fine—this is totally overblown. And my mom STILL hasn't told me.

Zari: Mom wouldn't talk to me about it, but something's up. I could tell by her face.

Me: Did she say anything?

Zari: Mom's glad you're coming home. That's all she'd say.

Me: Shit. She's in bad shape again then.

Zari: Don't know. Maybe she just misses you. How long is it going to take to get here?

Me: Six hours in normal life. God knows in this mess. Also? These people are weird.

Zari: Who are they?

Me: Two guys, two girls from some fancy southern California college.

Zari: USC?

Me: Pomona, I think. It's a bizarre friend group.

Zari: Are the guys hot?

Me: Not hot enough to be as weird as they are.

Zari: HA! Ok, be careful. I was thinking maybe you could come over. After the concert. You have to make it to the concert, Mira.

Me: I will. See you soon?

Zari: Soon.

I tug my beanie on and decide I'm going to need caffeine to endure the rest of this nightmare. I follow the signs promising refreshments. The lights must be malfunctioning, because the only illumination comes from the panels of the vending machines. I follow the glow and decide immediately that REFRESHMENTS AREA is a stretch, because from what little I can make out, there are a few tables situated in darkness and four sad-looking vending machines. Not exactly a bustling food court.

I fish in my pockets for a few dollars, approaching the blue glow of the soda machine. After the right combination of cash and buttons, a plastic soda bottle tumbles down. I stoop to retrieve the bottle and see something reflected in the plastic door. Something behind me at one of the tables.

No, not something.

Someone.

FIVE

I WHIRL, PANIC THROWING ME OFF BALANCE. MY BACK bumps the machine and my hand presses into my chest. Someone is seated at one of the tables. It's a man, stooped in the shadows. I can barely make out battered work boots and straight shoulders under a thick flannel coat. I can't tell where his hands are, and his face is entirely lost under the brim of a battered yellow baseball hat.

"I didn't see you," I say, sounding breathless.

He doesn't respond. Maybe he's sleeping. He's just sitting there in the dark, no drink or snack near him. I inhale and smell disinfectant. Strong disinfectant that's eerily familiar. My skin crawls as I crouch to get my soda. I do it with my body at a strange angle because every fiber of my being resists turning my back on this man.

My eyes adjust, finally picking up the line of his right arm where it rests on the table. His hand looks gnarled and twisted and I hope it's a trick of the light, but when I tilt my head it's clearly not. It's scarred. Burned, maybe. My chest winces in sympathy, but maybe it's not necessary. The breadth of his shoulders tells me his hand hasn't kept him from hard work.

He looks strong. Capable.

But…something about him being here feels wrong. Why would anyone sit here in the dark, not moving or speaking? Is he sick?

"Are you okay?" I ask softly.

Nothing. The soda machine kicks on, the soft purr of the chiller interrupting the silence. I hear the shuffle of footsteps from the restroom. Harper or Kayla, probably. My eyes don't move from his yellow hat, from the dark smear beneath where his face hides.

"Sir?"

Nothing still. Why the hell isn't he saying something?

"Mira?"

I jump, hand flying to my throat as my eyes search the room.

Josh. He's in the doorway, leaning heavily on his crutches. I was so engrossed in my thoughts, I didn't even hear him.

"Are you coming?" he asks.

"Y-yes. Sorry."

I give yellow hat guy a single backward glance as I slip out of the alcove. The doors to the rest stop are already shutting behind Harper and Brecken, so I guess it's just us. I hurry to push them open, a blast of icy wind hitting me square in the face.

Outside the snow is worse, blowing in a spray that slithers into the collar of my coat and creeps up my sleeves. I duck into the wind and pick up speed for the car. When I get there, everyone is shivering and bitching about the cold. Brecken has crouched down again by the chains, but Harper and Kayla are leaning against the open trunk, covered by the small shelter of the open hatchback door.

"This place is a ghost town," Harper says.

I open my mouth to tell them about the guy, but then I see the parking lot is empty. The two trucks I saw earlier are gone, leaving the smell of diesel and nothing more. I twist around, searching. There aren't even recent tire tracks, unless you count the ones leading directly to our car.

We're the only ones here. Which means I don't know where that man came from.

"We can head out," Brecken says.

"Chains didn't work out, huh?" Josh asks.

"They're busted. All four of them if you can believe that," Brecken says, gesturing at the chains on the ground.

"There really isn't enough snow," Harper says absently. Her gaze is fixed to her phone and from her grave expression, I don't think she's reading anything good.

"How could you even tell?" Kayla asks Brecken, sounding like she doesn't much care.

I crouch down, crossing my arms against the cold. Brecken holds up one of the chains, pointing to links that are twisted and pinched. They look like someone's taken vise grips to them. Did some amateur think pinching them was how you tighten them on the tire?

"Those aren't broken, they're pinched together," I say.

"Maybe the last car that used them put them on wrong," Josh says.

"No," Brecken says. "It looks like someone intentionally wrecked them. These are the exact links you need to hook to attach the chains to the wheels."

I let out half a laugh. "You think someone sabotaged our snow chains? On Christmas Eve? I think this is a wee bit paranoid. Someone probably tried to tighten them and screwed them up."

"Is it?" Josh asks. "I'm not a snow chain expert, but I'd think anyone would see tightening them like this would make them unusable in the future."

"Maybe somebody couldn't get them off," Harper says. "If they got frustrated…"

I nod. "That totally makes sense. They could have tried to pull them off, not realizing they were smashing the links."

"Maybe," Brecken says, but he doesn't look convinced.

Harper checks her phone and her face goes tight. She shoves it into her purse. "It doesn't even matter. We've wasted enough time here already."

We load back into the car in the same order, and I wish things were different, that I didn't end up next to the girl who sometimes slumps onto my shoulder in her sleep. I wish, too, that my optimistic words to my mom would have held off the weather, but things are changing fast.

Back on the highway, snow is collecting on the road and we're crawling with the rest of traffic through lanes that are growing slipperier by the mile. We follow a narrow set of tire tracks through the thick snow pelting the windshield. Brecken drives slow and steady, scrutinizing the road conditions with narrowed eyes. His grip on the wheel stays tight, hands at the prescribed ten and two.

He exhales hard. "I think we need to cut north at Easton and head up one of the county highways to I-80. I think we're heading directly into the storm."

"Agreed," Josh says. "The snow must have shifted south."

"Weather said it would probably take one track or another," Brecken says.

"I'm no expert," Kayla says. "But don't the mountains get bad?"

"Only if it snows. At all," I deadpan.

"That's always what I've heard, too," Harper says, scratching away again in her leather book. She closes it with a thoughtful frown. "I wonder if he has a point. Heading away from all of this."

"I-80. It almost sounds scary," Kayla says.

I tilt my head. "Uh, that's because it's a death trap painted with pretty yellow lines."

"It's not a death trap." Brecken drums the steering wheel with his thumbs. "There will be some snow, sure, but look around us. The storm is hitting right here. We need to get out of it, or we'll be driving through it the entire way."

Harper smiles at me. "Don't worry. I won't let anything happen to you."

"You'll stop the storm from hitting the mountains?" Kayla asks. "Impressive."

"It won't hit the mountains," Josh says.

I shake my head. "The storms *always* hit the mountains."

"Even if the storm *is* in the mountains, I-80 will probably be clear, right?" Josh says. "It's a major trucking route."

"So is this," I say, jerking my thumb toward the highway where semis crawl steadily along. "This isn't clear."

"It would be clear if they predicted it right," Brecken says. "This has all the looks of a classic meteorology screwup. The forecast said the mountains would be worse, so all the plows and salt trucks are up there. This piece of shit will wind up closed because they thought it'd be fine. Mark my words."

"If anything, there will be too *many* snow plows up on I-80," Josh says. "We'll probably end up with more salt than snow on the car up there."

"I'm not seeing it," I argue. "I've been on I-80. My aunt lived in Philadelphia for a while, and, I'm telling you, that highway is notorious for being utter crap. Traffic. Wrecks. Closures. There's always something going on, and that's *without* the snow."

"There won't be that much snow," Brecken says. "Just calm down and trust us. Or wait until we get there, and I'll say I told you so."

"No, you won't," Josh says, and then he pats my knee with a smile that he probably thinks is friendly. "I promise, I really believe I-80 is a good idea. We'll be safer there."

"Then let's do I-80," Kayla says with a sigh. "Whatever. Let's just stop talking about it."

Harper, who's writing again in the front, murmurs in agreement.

"I still say it's insane," I say. "Eighty is insane in good weather."

"Oh my God, you're like my damn mother back there," Brecken says, then he looks at Harper. "Are the girls at Pomona like this, too?"

"It's women, not *girls*," Harper says. "Which I'm sure the *women* at your school would have told you."

"Where do you go to school?" Josh asks.

"Premed at UC Berkeley," Brecken says stiffly, his dark eyes flicking to the rearview mirror to Josh. "What about you?"

My brain fizzes as the conversation unfolds. I feel like a laugh is stuck in my throat, half choking with this new, impossible development.

They don't know each other.

"Carnegie Mellon," Josh answers.

"For psychology, right?" Harper says, turning to wink at Josh. "So, we have a doctor, a psychologist, whatever international business rock star I'm going to be, we have Mira the artist, and… what about you, Kayla?"

"I'm not in school," she says breezily, "I was out there… visiting."

The laugh finally makes its way out, and I shake my head, cutting it off short.

"What's so funny?" Harper asks. Josh and Kayla are looking at me, too.

My cheeks go hot. I shouldn't have assumed they knew each other. How would that even make any sense?

I wave my hand at each of them. "Okay, this is really dumb, but I thought you all were friends."

"That's adorable," Brecken says, and maybe it's a jerky thing to say, but his smile in the mirror is friendly, revealing perfect white teeth.

Josh ignores me, but Kayla shrugs. "Maybe we all know each other in another life or some shit."

"I like that," Harper adds. She turns to look over the back of her seat with a smile directed at me. "Maybe this is all fate."

"Or maybe it's nothing and fate doesn't exist," Josh says.

"Wow," Harper says. "Way to be a pessimist."

Josh puts up his hand and forces a laugh that sounds worn. "I'm sorry. Rough day."

"It is a crap day," I say, feeling a twinge of mercy. "And I don't even have crutches."

"I was next to that crying woman on the plane. My knee was killing me, and the flight attendant wouldn't let me get my meds out of my carry-on."

Kayla looks on with interest. "I heard that! She was pretty pissed at you. Did you get them?"

"Not until we landed," he says.

"So, I still don't get how you found us all, Harper," I say.

"Yeah," Kayla agrees. "Do you always collect strangers at airports?"

"It all just worked out. Brecken was in line with me at the car rental place. I met you two on the escalator heading down there, and Mira and I hit it off on the plane, didn't we, Mira?"

She's so earnest, the way she looks at me. Like I'm some poor orphaned girl she's compelled to befriend. My answering smile feels flat. "We sure did."

Harper laughs. "See? I think it's serendipity. Five total strangers connected over Christmas. For all we know this could be the start of some brilliant, lifelong friendship."

"Sure," Josh says, but he doesn't sound like he buys it. "Have we seen any signs for I-80 yet?"

"Right," I grumble. "I forgot our two resident meteorologists think we should head into the mountains in the snowstorm."

"Wow," Josh says, and he looks stung for the span of a breath. But he laughs again. "Okay, I see."

I turn, and I don't know if I'm angry or maybe flirting a little when I fire back. "Really? What exactly is it that you see?"

"Well for starters, you're…high spirited. I didn't notice that about you at first."

"Oh, I did," Harper says. She winks at me. "I saw all kinds of things in Mira."

"Well, I'm high spirited, too," Brecken says. "Just watch."

Harper looks at him. "What are you doing?"

"Driving to I-80. This is a ridiculous mess. I'm over it."

"We didn't all agree to that," Harper says, looking at me. "I want everyone to feel like they have a say."

"It's your call," I tell her. "You rented the car."

"I helped pay for it," Brecken says. "So I say it's a democracy."

"I say just get the hell to whatever highway you want and stop talking about it," Kayla whines.

I see Brecken's grin in the rearview mirror. "So, sounds like a vote for us."

"It's three to two, isn't it?" Josh asks softly. When I turn back, the edge to his expression is gone. "Kayla's fine with this plan, and Brecken and I both thought of it."

Harper checks her phone. Her face goes pale and her fingers hover over the screen. But then, without touching it, she shakes her head and slips her phone back into her purse. She looks stricken in a way I remember from last Christmas in my aunt's hospital room, which tells me something is going on at home. Something that isn't good.

I lean forward from my middle seat to view her better. There is a row of blood droplets on the front of her shirt, three perfectly round, gruesome red blotches. I touch her arm gently and she startles, looking up at me.

"Harper?" I ask quietly. "Are you okay?"

"Shit," Brecken breathes, slowing the SUV. We drive past a line of cars off in the ditch. Nothing terrible. No twenty-car pileup. But it's more proof that this road is not fit for driving.

"We're never getting home this way," Josh breathes quietly.

That seems to jar Harper. She turns to Brecken. "How far away is Easton?"

"Three or four miles to the route north that we'd take."

"And you really think that will get us home?" she asks.

"Yes." Brecken's voice is strange. Gentle. "We can get you home. I believe that."

"Then we can't keep doing this. We should try I-80."

"Harper's in," Josh says warmly. "Okay, Mira. Is that good enough?"

I don't answer, because the vote and the slowdown are reminders that the weather is getting worse. This isn't a joyride with some cool friend group of college kids. This is a Pennsylvania snowstorm with strangers, and we need to be careful.

I look long and hard out the window. It's easy to forget what winter means in Pennsylvania. Bad roads can do much worse than slow us down. And I've got several hundred miles of bad road to go.

SIX

Zari: How goes it?

Me: How I'd imagine riding shotgun with Satan in the 9th level of hell.

Zari: That good?

Me: Keeps getting better.

Zari: Yikes.

Me: It's fine. I just need to get home. Mom needs me.

Zari: We've all needed you.

I hesitate because my chest tightens up whenever Zari goes here. That's the thing about moving across the country. You're not there to fix the big blowout. And you're not there for the new outfits or the is-this-flirting or the painful breakups. It's just a weird, slow fade, and after a year and a half of so-so art school friends, I miss Zari. I miss having a best friend.

It's making my stomach hurt, or maybe that's the drive. Brecken changes lanes more than Harper, and it's making me nauseous. I need to reply to Zari before I'm too sick to look at my phone at all.

Me: I have to go. Be home soon.

I pocket my phone and watch the snowy road slowly slip by. I could paint this. Some part of me wants to—all the blue-gray shadows and headlights glinting off silvery snow. And my focal point? Easy. Any one of the cars wedged into the ditches, flashers blinking and drivers cold and likely in for a long wait.

To his credit, Brecken is a good driver. He handles the road conditions with quiet, calm determination. We slide a couple of times, but Brecken's focus and the car's seemingly endless safety features keep us on track. Given the number of cars I've seen in ditches, I think we're lucky.

I don't know, maybe they're right about the storm. It does look pretty bad here. But when is it ever better in the mountains? Daniel used to tell me all the time, when it gets bad in Pennsylvania, stay as far away from I-80 as you can.

Then again, Daniel used to tell me that he'd always be here for Mom and me, so what does he know?

When we get off the highway, the roads are much worse, slush spraying under our tires and the wipers bumping over a ridge of snow building up at the bottom of the windshield again. Brecken follows the signs through town to I-80, and every stop and start rolls through my middle unpleasantly. I'm getting carsick.

The light turns yellow at an intersection ahead and the van in front of us hits the brakes hard, fishtailing in an instant. Brecken swears softly, and Harper yelps as he hits the brakes. The antilock brakes shudder with a rapid *thud-thud-thud-thud* that doubles the tempo of my heart. Outside the windshield I can see the red, salt-stained side of the minivan. There could be kids inside. They could be watching us coming right at them.

I don't know if we will stop in time. My stomach and hands clench as the car slides slower and slower, finally coming to a halt a few inches from the van in front of us. I let out a breath that shakes.

"This shit is getting old," Kayla says, seeming antsy in her seat.

She squirms against her seat belt, her forehead shiny with sweat. I have no idea what that's about, because I'm still a little chilly.

On my other side, Josh winces, tugging at the side of his brace. The starts and stops can't be comfortable for him, either, with that contraption on.

"Is there anything you can do?" I ask him. "For your leg?"

"Get a new ACL?" he asks, looking up from his book. He chuckles. "Not much anyone can do. Unless you're an expert on lay healing in addition to Pennsylvania highway conditions."

My cheeks feel like they've caught fire. I look down, and Josh laughs softly.

"I'm sorry," I say. "I'm tense. I should have just shut up."

"You know, you're allowed to admit when you're wrong."

"They're recommending no nonessential travel on I-78 through that entire county," Harper says, her face bathed in the blue light of her phone.

"Hm, sounds like we're maybe right to head to a different route," Brecken says. He winks at me in the rearview mirror.

I don't know if I'm more angry or embarrassed, but every surly thing in me wants to shoot the middle finger at this whole car.

"Are you always this uncomfortable when you make a mistake?" Josh asks.

I jerk my gaze to him, but there's nothing mocking about his expression. There's nothing sympathetic, either, really. He looks at me like I'm a tricky math problem.

I am really losing it here. He's not looking at me like that, and I have zero reason to be angry with anyone. I'm upset that Mom's alone tonight. I'm upset that I didn't take an earlier flight. Hell, right now I'm upset that I moved across the country, even though Phoebe begged me to stay in this school and Mom agreed with her.

But no one told me that if I went back to San Diego, Mom would end up divorced and alone on the one-year anniversary of her twin's death.

No, not twin—*Phoebe*. Twin is an impersonal word. Four letters, one syllable, no smell of incense or ginger snaps or oil paints. No long dark hair coiled in a haphazard knot at the back of her neck. Twin could be anyone. But no one else could be Phoebe. I press my hand to my chest, where a fresh ache is blooming.

God, if I'm this upset, what is Mom going through?

The tires spin as Brecken takes off from another light, pulling me back to the present.

"We're going to wreck before we even get to I-80," Harper says when the tires grip.

"It's going to be fine," Brecken says.

"It's not fine. None of this is fine." There's a hysterical, desperate edge creeping into her voice. I think it's of all those messages on her phone. All those hints that something isn't right.

"Hey," Brecken says. His voice is low and soft. Pitched for Harper alone. I see his shoulder move, like maybe he's touching her arm. "We're going to be fine. We are."

"This isn't the plan," she says, her voice soft and panicky. "I can't get in a wreck. You know I have to get home."

"I hear you," Brecken says at the next stop. Then he does touch her, fingers slipping down the white fabric covering her shoulder. "We're not going to wreck, okay?"

There's a long, loaded pause between them that makes me feel intrusive. I glance at Josh, who's watching them, too. He looks away, checking my response, I guess. I bite back a grin, but he just looks at his book. He definitely needs to stop taking himself so seriously.

"You better?" Brecken asks Harper softly.

I'm not looking, but I can hear the soft hiss of his fingers on the fabric of her shirt. The *thunk-shhhh* of the wipers. The soft sighs of Kayla's snores. Again? Why is she asleep so much? Is it some kind of medical condition?

"Okay," Harper whispers.

For lack of anything better to do, I check my own phone.

The battery is getting low, and I burned my backup battery in San Diego when my flight was delayed. I have a charging cord in the back, but there's no point in calling my mom right now. I'm not talking to her in front of these people because I will end up asking about Daniel, or she will end up embarrassing the crap out of me with her panic. It's going to have to wait.

I shut my phone down and try to adjust my seat belt so it isn't cutting as painfully across my stomach. When the signs for 33 North come into view, my shoulders relax. My cramping stomach has ratcheted into real queasiness on the local roads, so I'm more than ready for a larger highway again.

Even if I know where that highway is headed.

On the entrance ramp, the plow has carved a clearer path than any road I've seen thus far. Once we're on, things look even better, wide scraped sections of pavement trailing out before us like gray ribbons under the confetti of snow.

It's definitely clearer here. The snow is falling, but the road crews are keeping up.

Brecken sighs loudly, slouching back a little. "See? It's already clearing up."

I settle back, trying to shake that itchy feeling that's been plaguing me all day. Maybe I just need to take a breath. Things are turning around. I'll be home before I know it, and this whole bizarre trip will be a thing of the past.

I try not to notice Josh's thumb tracking across the pages, over and over. Or Harper's endless scratching in her notebook. Or the way Kayla twitches and shakes next to me, her forehead still shiny, shadows like bruises under her eyes. And Brecken, always looking. Always dragging his eyes from the road to one of us.

This is ridiculous. There's nothing sinister about any of this. None of this is abnormal and I shouldn't be unnerved.

But I am.

Fortunately, the uneventful miles eventually calm my stomach and my nerves. The mountains loom ahead, stark, gray shadows behind the mist of snow, but they're too far away to feel like a threat.

The highway, clear at first, grows a little snowier as the miles pass, but it's fine. Brecken slows down. The other cars stay in their lanes. This isn't the documentary-worthy nightmare of spinning cars on I-78. I wait fifteen minutes and then twenty, but nothing changes. Everything is fine.

Until it's not.

I don't know I've fallen asleep until I wake up to us sliding. My eyes drift open in time to feel the tires catch. I sit up, looking around to see the mountains, once distant shadows, are all around us now, steep and shrouded in a fog of snow.

I must have slept longer than I thought.

"Where are we?" I ask, voice scratchy.

"We're on I-80," Harper says. I notice that her notebook and phone are nowhere in sight, her gaze fixed on the road. Tension thickens the air, making it hard to breathe.

"A little past Old Furnace," Josh says, voice tight. He's staring ahead, too.

The car slips again, and I take a sharp breath, looking around. Kayla sniffs, her eyes watery like she's been crying.

"Are you okay?" I ask her.

She looks at me, sniffing again and clearly annoyed.

"I'm fine." She's not crying—not in a something's-wrong way, at least. Maybe she has a cold. Did she have a cold before and I didn't notice?

"Are you sure?" I press.

"I said I'm fine," she says, tossing a tangle of her pale hair behind her shoulder.

I try not to watch, but her hands are visibly shaking. Like medical-condition or high-fever shaking.

"There's one on the other side," Harper says. She looks afraid. Everyone does.

"I see it," Brecken says, his knuckles white where they grip the steering wheel.

What do they see? What the hell happened while I was sleeping?

I check the other lane, but the snow is blowing hard against the window, making it difficult to see anything at all. We found the storm. We definitely found the storm.

"They're losing control," Josh says softly.

Finally, I spot a pair of headlights the others are tracking in the lanes moving the opposite direction. They swing wildly left to right. Then they spin until I can only see one light. Then no lights. Then the taillights as the body of the car comes to a stop facing the wrong direction. My stomach churns.

"I thought this was supposed to be better," I say, and I instantly regret it.

"This isn't really a good time for an I-Told-You-So," Josh says very quietly.

"I'm sorry," I say, because he's right.

I can't imagine being Brecken right now. What little I can see of the road is nothing more than two narrow tire tracks in a sea of white. The incline changes, the SUV shifting to a different gear as we begin to climb.

"I don't like this," Brecken says.

"Who does?" Kayla says with that weird manic laugh.

"Somebody look at the downhill on this mountain," Brecken says. "Check the traffic."

Harper taps on her phone. "I'm trying. It's slow."

"Try harder."

Harper whirls to him. "Stop barking orders at me! I'm not your secretary."

Josh makes an annoyed noise, his jaw clenching.

"I can try," I say, trying to power on my phone.

The SUV shifts again, the incline even steeper. My stomach clenches, an ache blooming in the center of my forehead. Looking at my phone is making me sick again.

"Can you do it?" I ask Josh.

There's a furrow between his brows. "What's wrong?"

"My stomach," I say. "I'm a little carsick. Maybe I shouldn't look at the phone."

He nods and takes it, tapping in a few things.

"Don't bother," Harper says. "I think we're over it."

She's right. We're coming over the top of the hill, the road leveling out. The engine shifts again, tires slipping. My stomach rolls and I take a slow breath. It's just my nerves. I just need to breathe.

"How long do I have until we're heading down again?" Brecken asks.

"Maybe a mile," Josh says, eyes lit by my phone screen. "There's an accident alert."

"I see it, too," Harper says, looking up from her own phone. She turns in her seat. "Brecken, it's bad. Lots of cars."

"Where?" I ask. Josh hands back my phone and points at the map on the screen. I'm too sick and too panicked to focus. I shove my phone into my pocket.

"It's supposed to be right up ahead," Harper says. "Mile marker 204."

"I haven't been able to read a mile marker in miles," Brecken says, clearly agitated. "I can't see shit!"

The road dips down unexpectedly and a flashing yellow sign at the bottom tells me there is a curve. Another sign announces something else, but it's covered in snow. There's nothing—nothing beyond the fifteen feet in front of our car on the road. It's just the tracks we're following.

And then I see it.

Lights. Red and white and pointing in what seems like dozens of strange, awkward angles.

"There!" I say, pointing. "Do you see it?"

"I already said I can't see—" Brecken sucks in a breath and the hill gets steeper.

"It's the bridge," Harper says, her voice a high, frightened whine. "There's a bridge at the bottom of this hill."

"I see it." Brecken's voice is low. Serious.

"Slow down," Josh says. "Just ease back so you can see."

The engine slows, but the tires slip. And they keep slipping.

"Slow down." This time Josh's voice makes it sound like a command.

"I can't," Brecken says. "We're sliding."

He steers right into the slide, and then left. He's good, but the tires have broken loose, and no amount of fancy driving seems to be saving us. The car is fishtailing wildly in both directions, my stomach sloshing with each iteration. I realize we are sliding down the hill, toward the wreck. And it is no minor wreck. It's the kind of pileup they show on national news.

Dozens dead.

Holiday tragedy.

There is screaming all around me, but I stay quiet. My stomach curls in on itself as we slide faster down the hill, the tires kicking out hard to the right so that we're moving sideways down the mountain. The bridge is a hellscape, cars spinning and wrecked in so many directions I can't count them. I can't even make sense of what's happening.

But we're going to be part of it. That much is crystal clear.

Thump!

My head snaps forward at the impact, not from the bridge ahead, but from behind us. Harper screams and Brecken starts a litany of *Shitshitshitshitshit* as our car spins in a wild circle. I see headlights and taillights and snow and a menacing concrete guardrail. It plays out in an endless loop, a merry-go-round of horror.

I hold on tight, but the impact slams me forward like a rag doll, the seat belt hard across my neck and my ears shredded by a concrete metal scraping that feels like it will never end.

February 4

Mira,

I knew you were a wonder and I was right. When I
moved to California, I believed our moment in the
coffee line might be all we ever shared. Do you know
how that tortured me? The idea of never seeing your
face or hearing your voice again. We don't need to
worry about that now, do we?

I don't care for art usually. So many artists get
it wrong, and when I stepped inside the show that
day, it wasn't because I wanted to see what was being
exhibited, it's because I saw you. Through the window
with your eyes gleaming and your smile so bright. You
were talking to someone else, but I recognized that
glow.

It's the same glow you had when you thanked me
for the coffee, the glow I'm drawn to like a compass to
North. The moment I saw you, saw your face, I knew I
had to come inside to talk to you. So, I did.

But why did you pretend not to remember me? Why
bother with shyness? Two thousand miles and we still
found each other, Mira. That means something. You
can't deny it.

I came back after you were whisked away from our
brief conversation. I wanted to see you again, but

you were only there for the show. It doesn't matter, though, because the woman there gave me this address for you. Fate is still bringing us together.

So, take your time. If you're afraid to speak the words, write them. I can wait. Because I know as well as you do—this is destiny.

I'll be waiting,
Yours

SEVEN

THE IMPACT IS NOT EXACTLY A CRASH, MORE LIKE A hardcore graze. The right front fender wedges against the wall and continues forward with a terrible metal-against-concrete scrape that seems to shred the air and my eardrums both. I squeeze my eyes shut as we shudder along the barrier, the vibration rippling through my spine. It's the kind of noise and feeling that sets your teeth on edge—the car-crash equivalent of fingernails on a chalkboard.

The car rolls to a stop, engine still running.

"Are you okay?" Brecken says, looking at Harper.

She's breathing hard and fast. We all are. But she nods, and we check ourselves over. Looking for broken windows, or maybe injuries we didn't notice. It doesn't seem that bad. I think we got lucky. I open my mouth to say as much and—*crash!*

The impact is in the lane to our left. I whirl in time to see the car rebound from the impact, bits of glass and metal tinkling to the icy pavement. I look around, realizing that our crash wasn't just lucky. It was downright miraculous. There are cars flipped onto their sides and lines of cars crunched tightly together. We are the only car I can see that isn't crumpled beyond driving.

"We have to get out of here," Harper says, and by her expression I can tell she's putting together what I have. We're in serious danger.

"We're going to get hit," Josh says.

"Shit," Kayla says. She's not looking at the wrecks ahead of us. She's twisted to look out the back window.

I don't want to look, but I do and there they are—a volley of cars spinning and sliding their way down the mountainside. This only ends one way. And if we don't move, we're going to be part of it.

Brecken swears and throws the SUV into reverse, pulling back from the concrete barrier with a grinding noise that jolts through my teeth like a shock.

Harper starts to cry. I don't blame her. I'd be crying, too, if I had any breath left in my lungs, but I feel like all the air has been kicked out of me. The first car hits—far to the left—the sound of glass and plastic breaking shatters the quiet. Some of them slip right off the road, landing in the ditch before the bridge.

They're the lucky ones.

The unlucky ones are coming right at us. Fast.

"Go," Harper cries. "Just go!"

I don't want to watch, but I can't look away. My eyes are glued to a Volvo whirling around end after end, close enough to our side of the road to make me wonder if I'll live. To make me wish I'd sent one more text to my parents. Maybe to Zari.

It's just about to hit when I squeeze my eyes shut. Our car lurches forward and I hear a terrible smack. The Volvo hit the concrete, just behind us.

"There's another one coming," Josh says, still calm.

"Go!" Kayla says. "Keep going!"

"I'm trying! There's no room!"

"Hit the wall if you have to," Harper says. "Push your way through."

There's a horrible hissing shriek behind us, a terrible noise that I know from rest areas and truck stops. It's a semi. Brecken's eyes widen in the rearview mirror and he punches the gas. We are scraping the barrier again, but he doesn't stop.

He's swearing softly, pushing his way between a large truck with no one inside and the concrete wall. I don't want to look behind us. I don't want to know why he's swearing over and over under his breath.

But I do.

My stomach shoves itself into my throat, perches there so tightly that I can't breathe. There's a tractor trailer at the top of the hill, and it's coming down sideways. My lizard brain shoots adrenaline into my limbs—pushing me to get out of the car. To run.

Because this truck will hit everything on this bridge. It'll destroy us.

"Go!" I scream, even though he's already going. I can hear the strain of the engine, the awful push/scrape of concrete on one side and metal on the other. Everyone is shouting. I don't know who is saying what. I don't recognize my own voice in the mix, but I know I'm screaming, too.

Finally, we punch through, our car sailing forward, free of the truck and the wall. The tires slip and catch and spin a little until he adjusts the acceleration. We are halfway across the bridge when the truck hits the cars behind us.

Brecken does not stop.

I see an explosion of plastic and metal and unfathomable damage. My throat goes tight. A sickening certainty settles in my gut; a lot of people won't walk away from that wreck. Fifteen seconds ago, I would have been one of them.

I watch the bridge for movement, but all is still. Calm. There is no smoke or fire. As we cross the seam where the bridge meets the highway, I see a few drivers stumble from their vehicles, moving toward the front.

There are people to help. Lots of people in the back and they don't all look injured. I should be relieved, but instead I feel nothing but guilt.

I don't know how we would help. I don't know what we could possibly do. But driving away from this bridge feels like a crime. Everyone else seems unmoved. They are still worried about us getting out of here. Getting to safety. How can I fault them for that?

Brecken drives slower for the next mile than he has the entire trip. An exit sign, green and inviting, promises gas and not much else in half a mile. The snow hitting our windshield is changing, the flakes turning small and icy. It's probably making the roads worse, but the visibility is better. In the distance, a symphony of blue and red lights flash. Help is coming. It should have come a while ago.

We round a slight bend just before the exit and more lights— cruisers and ambulances and fire engines—surround a giant wreck I hadn't seen on both sides of the highway.

"That's the wreck the app warned about," Josh says softly.

"What was that one?" I ask, referring to the nightmare we just escaped.

"A new wreck," Harper says, voice flat.

Traffic inches along, and we are just one more piece of the mess. We start and stop. Start and stop. It takes us twenty minutes to reach the exit, and, by the time we do, my insides are squirming miserably.

Brecken stops at the end of the ramp, and my stomach sloshes, a flash of heat rolling through me. Saliva gathers in my mouth. I sit up, the reality of the situation hitting me. I'm more than nauseated. I might vomit. I fist my hands, swallowing hard and trying to breathe.

It's so hot in here. Hot air blasts from every vent, and my armpits feel damp inside my coat. My neck is on fire, and I can feel a bead of sweat drip between my shoulder blades.

"Can we turn down the heat a little?" I croak out.

Brecken complies, and then the light turns green. We lurch forward and make a left and my stomach rolls dangerously. A short moan escapes me.

"What's wrong?" Josh asks.

"I feel sick," I say. "Really sick."

"Don't puke in here," Brecken says.

"You're sick?" Josh asks, looking deeply concerned. "Is it bad?"

"I need to get out of this car. It's really hot. I think that's making it worse."

"Are you going to puke?" Harper asks. "Do you want to stop?"

"I'm not going to puke," I say, though the chances are reasonable I might.

Brecken slows, and I'm sure it's a conscious effort, but really, I think it might be too late. Waves of fire are running up my neck and face. I unzip my coat, and then struggle to take it off altogether. Josh hooks a hand in the cuff of my sleeve, helping me tug my arm free.

"Thank you," I say.

"Let's get you some fresh air," he says, rolling down his window a crack.

His sudden concern is a surprise, but the air that enters the car is the most delicious thing that's ever passed my lips, so I don't care. I drink in greedy gulps of it, my eyes closed and head throbbing in time with the misery of my stomach.

"We need to stop," Harper says. "She needs a break."

"I know she does. I'm watching her," Brecken says.

"Hang in there," Harper tells me.

I don't answer because all of my energy is focused on not getting sick. The crisp air is helping immensely, but I still need out of this car.

"Let's get to a gas station," Brecken says. "We can call a tow truck."

"Something tells me the mess on the bridge will have half the tow trucks in Pennsylvania tied up," Josh says.

"We have to try," Harper says. "I'm calling the car rental company."

"What are they going to do?" Kayla asks, around a breathy laugh. "Make it stop snowing?"

"We wish," I say.

"In normal circumstances, they'd provide an alternate vehicle," Josh says.

Brecken snorts. "Not happening."

"I need to report the wreck at least," Harper says. "I'm not even sure we should drive this."

Brecken sighs. "Unless we want to jog across the Poconos, I think we're stuck with it."

I don't have anything to add, because I'm pretty sure Brecken is right. No one is going to be available, and there isn't a magic wand that's going to poof us onto safe, dry roads. We took our chances and now we're paying for it.

Regardless, Harper is insistent about the call. She keeps her phone to her ear, grumbling about a twenty-minute wait for the customer service rep.

Not half a mile down from the highway, a gas station appears, but it is not the gleaming, neon-encased complex I hoped for. Four pumps line the front of a run-down service station. The building is bigger than most stations, making me wonder if there was a garage component at some point in the past. Now, the whole thing looks like a store, though I can't be sure because most of the large front windows are cluttered with marketing posters for beer and cigarettes and signs advertising live bait and camping supplies.

My confidence in clean bathrooms isn't high, but whatever. It's a gas station and it's open. It could offer an outhouse in the back of the lot, and I'd have zero complaints.

It's also hopping. There are at least twelve cars parked in the unplowed lot and more at the pumps. There are people everywhere—travelers in puffy coats assessing cars, making calls, doling out snacks to bored-looking kids of every age. Most of the cars are sporting some kind of damage. It runs the gamut, from scraped bumpers to a Ford with the entire right side smashed in. One has lost the front and back bumpers entirely. A few fortunate travelers are dealing with more mundane issues like iced windshield wipers and empty washer fluid compartments. Gauging from the maps and phone navigation systems I see around, others are just trying to figure out how to get wherever they're going.

I stare at a wrecked Toyota near the entrance to the lot, its side-view mirror dangling like a sad earring.

"How bad are these roads?" I ask. I try for a search on my phone, but I have zero service.

"Record-breaking," Josh says, then he hands me his phone. "According to the news reports, there are two pileups on I-80. One is thirty-two cars, the other is twenty-one."

I read the headline he just quoted and then hand the phone back, too sick to look at anything else. The gas station lot is crammed, so Brecken pulls back out and parks in line, waiting for a pump to open up.

"Might as well get gas while we're here," he says.

"Good idea," Josh agrees.

He shifts into park and twists in his seat to face us. "That's fifty-three cars in that wreck, and we know they aren't counting us or the cars that spun down after."

"The highway should have been closed," Harper says.

"It is now," Josh says. He's staring out the window and pointing in the direction of the on-ramp for the highway.

Sure enough, through a thin row of bare-branched trees, I can see the curve of the exit ramp. More importantly, I can see the flares and police car parked across it. Josh is right. They closed the on-ramp. We got off the highway thinking we'd make calls. Get a tow or maybe a new car.

But now we're trapped in the middle of Pennsylvania with no major highway to get us out.

How the hell am I going to get home to my mom?

I check my watch. She's going to be off work now, maybe even home in her jammies making hot tea. I take a tight breath, my throat thick with thoughts of our teakettle. The way she always serves mine with a little saucer with a spoon and three sugar cubes. I don't know where she gets them, but ever since I got a book in third grade about proper English tea, Mom has always kept sugar cubes in the house.

I wish I was there, warm and safe and a million miles from this god-awful disaster highway. And when she checks the news, she'll see these giant pileups and have an all-out panic attack.

Wait. Mom still thinks I'm down south on I-78. She probably still thinks I'm safe. Except that when I don't call, she'll start to worry. She might try to track my location, but she'll need Dad's help since I'm on his plan.

Shit, will she think of that? Will she call him? Would she have called already?

The questions are piling up like the cars on the bridge. I need damage control, and I need it now.

I pull up my mom on my phone, and my finger hovers over the option to place a call. I hesitate. I desperately want to talk to her. Even sad and distant, she's my mom and hearing her voice would make this all a little easier. But I need to think this through so I don't make things worse.

If I call and reassure her, she might worry less. If I'm lucky, she hasn't thought about checking my location. But she knows me. If she calls, she'll sense the weirdness in my tone. And that might make her look me up if she hasn't already. Damn it.

"You look deep in thought," Josh says.

"I'm trying to decide whether to lie to my mother," I tell him honestly.

"You can lie to your mom?" Brecken laughs. "My mom could work for the FBI. I can't keep anything from her."

I sigh, pocketing my phone. "Me either. It's like a mutant power."

Harper puts her head back against the seat, her phone at her ear. "This is taking forever."

"They're probably getting a ton of calls," Josh says. "All these accidents."

"We should get snacks and use the bathroom while we're here," Brecken says. "Just in case we can't find another rest stop."

"We don't even know if we can keep driving this thing," Harper says.

"And with the pileups..." My eyes drift to the police car blocking the entrance ramp.

Josh's eyes follow mine, and he frowns. "It is really bad. The back roads are probably worse, but we'll have them to ourselves I bet."

"Exactly," Brecken says. "We can go as slow as we need to. This thing has incredible traction. I had no problems until we got on that downslope, and *that* only happened because I was on a highway and couldn't take it really slow."

"I don't know," Harper says, sounding uncertain. "But I know I can't stay here. My signal is terrible, and I *need* to get home."

"I know," Brecken says softly. "I have no desire to stay here."

Well, that makes several of us. My mother needs me, and my phone has crap signal too, so staying in this parking lot for the twelve hours it might take to clear up the wrecks is not an option for me. I'll strap on cross-country skis or steal a horse or something if I have to.

"Well, I think I'd rather take my chances going slow than waiting for the highway to reopen," I say. "That could take all night."

"Agreed. I'm sure the hell not spending Christmas Eve night in some redneck gas station," Brecken says. "There aren't even card readers on the pumps. Want me to pay inside?"

"No, I've got it," Harper says, waving him off.

"I'm going to hit the head," Brecken says, stepping out.

"Good plan." Josh reaches for his crutches and Kayla abruptly sits up, wiping drool off her cheek.

"Where are we?" she asks as Josh gets out. He slowly follows Brecken toward the gas station.

"A gas station," I say. "They closed the highway."

I do a double take because I can't fathom being able to fall asleep again after the bridge. But Kayla is groggy and disoriented. She doesn't look good. She's pale and shaking, her forehead sweaty. She looks twice as sick as I feel.

I tilt my head, which isn't hurting the way it was before. My stomach is settling, too. But Kayla looks much worse. Like she has a fever. Maybe the flu.

"Are you feeling okay?" I ask.

"I'm fine," she says, but her eyes are darting nervously around the car, and she doesn't look fine. She doesn't look anywhere near fine.

She fumbles with the latch several times before managing to push the door open. Then she ambles toward the station, following the boys. She's almost as slow and awkward as Josh on his crutches.

"That girl is weird," Harper says the moment she's out of sight. Then she turns to me, still holding the phone. Her brows scrunch in concern. "How are you holding up?"

"I'm better," I say, still watching Kayla. "Do you think Kayla is sick?"

"Carsick like you?" she asks.

"Maybe bubonic plague sick," I say. "She looks terrible. And she's slept most of this trip. Do you think she has something?"

"I don't know," Harper says, watching her. "Maybe."

Josh holds the door for Kayla, who shuffles into the station. He follows her in, and the door closes behind them, mostly blocking my view. It looks like they stop briefly near the register, chatting. Maybe they're looking for the bathrooms. Or maybe Josh is asking Kayla if she has Ebola because she looks like she's about to fall over dead.

Ugh, this is exactly what I need. I'm stuck in a car on Christmas Eve, and I'm riding shoulder to shoulder with Typhoid Mary.

"You sure you're okay?" Harper asks. "We've got a lot of mountains left. That won't be easy if you're nauseated."

"I know. Maybe I'll get a bottle of water."

"I feel responsible for you," she says, her eyes full of sadness. "I brought you here, Mira. This was *my* plan, and now you're sick and probably scared to death."

"I'm fine, really," I say, uncomfortable with this, with her kindness altogether. Why was she so nice to me on the plane? I'm pretty sure I'm not giving off little lost orphan vibes here.

"I'm sorry," she says, clearly picking up on my unease. She adjusts her phone to the other ear—still waiting. "You just…you remind me of someone."

I look back at the gas station, because I don't really want to ask about this person. Whoever I remind her of isn't here dealing with this mess. "Well, I chose to be here. You were really nice to let me tag along, but the choice was all mine."

"Okay, then. No more mother-hen business," she says with a smile. "I promise. You should see if they have some of that motion sickness medicine."

"Okay."

Harper's hand flies up and she presses her phone closer to her ear. "Yes? Yes, I'm here! Hello? Can you hear me?" After a brief pause she nods. "Okay, so I rented a car with you guys from the Newark airport today…"

I slip out of the car while she's talking, making my way past a family passing sandwiches out of a cooler and an older couple with a cell phone held between their faces. It's like a smaller version of the Newark airport, people everywhere trapped by the stupid weather.

I pull open the glass door, bells overhead giving a dull jangle. The store smells like heat-lamp hot dogs and old coffee. The door closes behind me, and I edge past a row of plastic-wrapped snack cakes that a group of women in their twenties are eyeing. There is a glass display case of fishing lures and knives beside a cooler marked Live Bait. The bathroom doors are next to the cooler, so I head toward them, cutting through the aisle that seems most likely to carry a don't-throw-up pill.

Brecken and I pass each other in the aisle, which offers the most bizarre mismatched inventory I've ever seen. I scan the options. A single box of tampons that looks like something my grandmother might have bought in high school. A travel container of diaper wipes, though I see no diapers. There's also a dusty safety razor in plastic packing and a couple of rolls of individually wrapped toilet paper. The medicine options are limited: little packets of aspirin and ibuprofen and a bag of cough drops by a brand I've never seen. Nothing specific for treating nausea, but there is a packet of pink multi-stomach-symptom tablets. The price tag makes me cringe, but puking in the back of the car sounds worse, so maybe I should give it a shot.

"Doing a little shopping?" Brecken asks.

I jump, surprised by his voice and his presence. I didn't realize he'd stopped walking. Was he just watching me browse the shelves? I shake my head. "Just looking for something for my stomach. What are you doing?"

"Keeping an eye on you," he says, smirking. "I'm a nice guy like that. You probably sensed it."

"Hm," I say, instead of arguing. "Have you seen any Dramamine?"

He glances at the front counter, where endless boxes of cigarettes tower around the register. "Unless it's a kind of fishing bait or tobacco product, you're probably shit out of luck. Where's Harper?"

"She got through to the rental car company," I say, noticing she's pulled the car forward to the pump but hasn't actually gotten out yet. "I'm not sure what good it's going to do."

He shrugs. "She's a planner. She wants to follow the rules."

I laugh. "There are rules for things like this?"

"She sure seems to think so." He smiles ruefully. "I'm going to go check in with her. Gas up the car so we can get out of this shithole."

"Sounds good," I say.

He walks outside and crosses to the car, then opens the driver's-side door and helps Harper step out. My neck goes hot at the way his fingers linger on her wrist, but it could be nothing. Is this flirting? I've had a couple of boyfriends, but they were awkward stumbled-into-it-as-friends things. I know zero about the world of lingering eye contact and meaningful hand brushes. It could be flirting—it could be friendly. But Brecken moves slower around her. Speaks softer. And she tucks her hair behind her ear before she answers him, looking left and right, like what she's saying is for Brecken alone.

"Do you think something's going on between them?"

I jump, surprised I didn't hear the telltale clunk of Josh approaching. I shrug, giving a half smile. "Oh, I don't know. They just met, right?"

"Did they?"

I open my mouth to answer, but then I close it. Josh and I share a look that settles deep in my bones. He sees it, too—this nameless connection between them. I don't know what to call it, but it smells like a secret. One they don't want us to know.

EIGHT

I SHAKE MY HEAD WITH A LAUGH, DETERMINED NOT TO let paranoia take root. "We could just be jumping to conclusions. I doubt they found their soul mates in an airport rental car line."

"Some people believe in love at first sight." Josh shrugs.

I roll my eyes. "People believe all kinds of things."

He gives a small smile. "It's the most beautiful thing about humanity, isn't it?"

"I don't know," I admit.

I try to smile, but it feels all wrong on my face. I can't read Josh. He's got that heavy intellectual edge of superiority lacing everything he says. Even the way he watches Harper and Brecken makes me think he's taking notes on how he'd do things differently. Better.

Harper starts heading toward the station, and her movement breaks the spell for both of us. I clear my throat. "I should stop in the bathroom. Should we help Harper with gas?"

"She said she had it, and it might be hard. I only have a card," he says.

I relax a little. I'd been worried about this. I probably have nineteen dollars in my account right now, so unless I break out Mom's emergency credit card, and God knows this qualifies, I can't pay for much. And if I use the emergency card, she'll know exactly where I am. I can just imagine the level of panic that will descend on Beltzhoover if she finds out I'm near I-80, land of today's record-breaking pileups. I flip through my wallet and realize I do have a little cash. Not that sixteen dollars is going to change the world, but it's something.

I would have asked Dad for more cash, except I thought this would be a one-layover flight home. I check my watch with a sigh. It's going to be dark soon. By now I should be landed, home, and settled at the table with a giant bowl of noodles and ham. Of course this year there won't be noodles. Daniel made the noodles.

Hell, who cares. Even the divorce is just a thing to move past. Worse things have happened in our world than a couple splitting up. It would be okay if I could just get home.

At the least, we could sit and watch the Thanksgiving Day parade. Mom always records it, and it feels a little silly watching it on Christmas Eve, but since I usually spend Thanksgiving out with Dad, she keeps it every year for me. And we get around to watching it when we're fed up with cheesy Christmas movies. Maybe we'd be planning some of our other traditions. The bowling trip. Christmas lights and hot cocoa. An all-nighter of baking and board games. We used to do so much with Phoebe. It's all different now.

I'm not sure what we'll do when I get there. The only thing that's certain is standing in this nasty gas station in the middle of Nowhere, Pennsylvania, makes me desperate to be home for Christmas morning.

Kayla barrels down another aisle, not even looking up at me. She heads outside, but Harper stops her at the door. From my angle, I can still see Kayla's red-rimmed eyes and limp hair.

"I really hope she's not sick," I tell Josh. "She's been shaky and sweaty most of the trip."

"She's probably just catching up on sleep," he says. "She seems okay. A little tired, I guess."

"A little?"

I laugh and he half-smiles, his eyes fixed on me in a way that I might like if I wasn't an anxious wreck, trapped in the middle of a snowstorm. If he was a little nicer, I could easily stumble into a temporary crush.

"Something on your mind?" he asks, smiling like he knows exactly what I'm thinking.

The superior edge is back, and that crush is looking less likely. I shake my head fast. "No, not at all. Sorry."

"Are you sure?" He's still wearing that smile.

"Very sure," I say, turning toward Harper.

Harper's propping the door open with her shoulder, and she's clearly doing her best to keep Kayla from leaving. For her part, Kayla's trying to nod and edge away, but Harper keeps talking.

Maybe as the driver she feels responsible for Kayla, too. She could be checking on her. And if so, I hope like hell she finds out whether Kayla's mystery illness is contagious. I'm super not interested in getting wickedly sick on top of everything. Kayla finally shrugs off Harper's hand and heads outside, producing a cigarette from her purse and smoking near an ice cooler that feels pretty ironic given the weather.

The door swings open again and I startle. It's Josh walking out. I hadn't even noticed him walk away. God, I hope he doesn't think I like him. I really do not need that. I watch him swing-stumble on his crutches toward the car, where Brecken is pumping gas. They give each other the guy high five, then start chatting like snow isn't clumping in their hair and whipping their pants against their legs.

It's bad out there. Bad enough that whatever road we end up on, it's going to be slow going. And speaking of going—I probably need to stop standing around like a dumb ass.

I head to the bathroom and find Harper inside, furiously typing on her phone. She doesn't even look at me. She just stands in the corner, eyes locked to the screen and fingers moving comically fast.

I linger at the door, wondering if I should say something. Ask something. She looks up briefly, anguish written on her face. But then she looks down and I remember: she might not want to talk to me about any of this. If she wanted to bare her soul, she would. It's not like she was shy on the plane.

She leaves while I'm in the bathroom stall, the door closing behind her with a soft creak. I finish and wash my hands. In the store, she's searching her purse at the counter. Abruptly, she heads back to the bathroom like she forgot something. Keys, maybe?

I snag five bottles of water and five bags of chips from the nearest display. The guy at the register—who can't be much older than me—holds a carton of cigarettes. My eyes drop to the embroidered letters on his name tag. Corey.

Corey turns around, saying something to an older man behind him. The second guy isn't wearing a uniform, but since he's a more weathered, stouter version of Corey, I'm guessing he's related. Maybe the owner. He's slouched in a folding chair watching a small television set on a shelf under the counter.

"Dad," Corey says. "*Dad.*"

The man doesn't look up, but reaches to take the carton of cigarettes from Corey. He pushes it into a row of them under the back shelf without ever taking his eyes from the screen he's watching.

I set down my items and swallow my sudden uneasiness. "Hi."

Corey doesn't return my greeting. He looks at me with vacant eyes, ringing up my purchases. He stops now and then to rub the sparse, overgrown stubble on his chin. His nails are ragged and dirty, and I don't want to look closer. I tap a chip in the counter with my finger and wait for him to give me a total.

"Station closes in twenty minutes." It's the older guy. The dad.

Corey reads me the total and I hand over a ten-dollar bill. I don't want to look at Corey, but looking at his father isn't much better. He's got a wad of something dark in his mouth and a cup next to him I don't want to investigate.

"Your friends better hurry up," he says, nodding indistinctly.

"My friends?"

"That one," he says, shooting a gaze at Kayla, who's come back inside while I've been at the counter, and is wandering the aisles. She looks like she's on another planet. "And the one who can't find her wallet."

I turn around in time to see Harper fly out of the bathroom and directly out the door, panic evident on her face. At the counter, Corey is watching me, his lips chapped and eyes heavy-lidded. I force a smile. Everything about these men unsettles me, but it could be me. I'm beyond on edge.

"How about I pay?" I ask, because I'm more afraid of not paying than I am about explaining all of this to Mom. If anything, I'm suddenly eager to have someone know exactly where I am. "I have my credit card with me."

"Credit card machine is down," the father says. "I told your pretty little friend and she was all fine with it. Said she had *plenty* of cash."

"Until she didn't have her wallet," Corey says. His snicker is broken by the chime of the doorbell and the shuffle of someone else walking in.

"How much is the gas?" I ask, flipping through the not-substantial stack of bills left in my wallet. Six dollars and some change. Plus whatever he gives me back when he finishes the slowest transaction in history.

"Forty-eight twenty."

I wince. "I don't have quite that much. Don't you have one of those backup machines for credit cards during power outages?"

"The backup is *cash*," Corey says, rubbing his chin again. He's clearly enjoying this moment of power. "We got signs outside you could have read."

"Maybe we missed them," I say, bristling. Whatever happened to holiday spirit? "There's kind of an emergency going on outside, and we almost ended up in one of those big accidents, so I'm sorry if we're a little rattled."

The father stands up then, the metal legs of the lawn chair scraping the floor. I automatically take a step back from the counter. He's much broader than his son, with fists that could double as sledgehammers. He looks mean. My animal instinct fires signals through every vein. Danger. This man is dangerous.

The father steps to the counter, and though every cell in my body wants to move farther back, I force myself to stand my ground. I inhale through my nose, smelling tobacco and gasoline and, more distantly, chemicals. Disinfectant. Something that I smelled earlier in the first rest stop, and now I know where it's from.

Hospitals. Whatever this popular-in-Pennsylvania cleaner is, it's apparently used in all kinds of institutions. Rest stops. Gas stations. The building where my aunt died.

I shake it off and look up, noting a sign posted on the wall below the racks of cigarettes.

Attendant is armed and trained.

"Rattled or not, you'd better pool your money together and pay for the gas you already pumped," the father says, pulling my attention from the sign. "There were plenty of signs. Like I said, I'm closing in twenty minutes."

"What if we don't have the cash?" I ask.

"I'll bet kids like you have plenty of cash between you."

I don't know what he means by "kids like you," but his tone makes it clear it isn't a compliment.

"I'll talk to the others," I say. "We're not trying to get away with something here. We didn't see the signs. We didn't know the machine was down."

"Not my problem. We got family to get home to, and you need to pay for what you took."

He doesn't wait for me to respond. He sits down in the folding chair, the metal legs scraping again. My eyes flick up to that sign about being armed. It could be for show. I hope. But this man has knives in a display case and a promise in his eyes that makes me think he's not one to throw around idle threats.

"Will there be anything else?" Corey asks, handing me a few coins.

"Can I return this stuff?" I ask. "That will give me some cash."

"Sorry, no refunds," he says. He's practically sneering. I think he likes this—putting me in my place.

I narrow my eyes and put my cash on the table. "Keep the change. I'll be back with the rest."

I turn around to look for Kayla, but she must be back in the bathroom. Great. Not that I'm expecting her to hand over a bunch of cash. There's a creak, and I notice someone walking down an aisle near me, toward the back of the store. I'm hoping it's Kayla, but it's not. It's a man in a battered yellow baseball cap.

A rush of déjà vu washes over me, and my shoulders tense. I've seen this before. Something about this—the hat. I've seen that hat recently. And I've smelled that scent. It isn't the gas station. It's him. The man from the rest stop.

A chill rolls up my spine with the memory. The man who was sitting in the dark at the tables. This is him. I can't see his face, only the back of his hat and the cardboard-brown jacket he's wearing.

It's not possible. That was a hundred miles from here and an entirely different highway.

But I swallow hard, throat catching as I take in the faded brown coat with dirty blond hair curling over the collar. He stands at the open cooler door, perusing whatever's inside. My body goes cold.

It's him.

But how?

He begins to turn, like he can feel my eyes on him. I see the barest hint of a fleshy chin. A bulbous nose—

"Mira!"

I whirl to the door, where Harper is standing, eyes wide with panic.

"Help me find my wallet?"

"Of course." I loop the handles of the plastic bag with my water over my hand and head for the door. I spare one glance at the coolers, but the man in the yellow hat is gone. Vanished.

Restroom. He's in the restroom. And he's just a guy on the road like us. It happens. But all the same, I feel like he's somewhere in that station watching me. I follow Harper back to the car, because I can't think about some weird man I've run into twice. That's a coincidence, not a problem. Paying the creepy guys in this gas station, though? That's not negotiable.

I pull open the passenger door. Josh is in the back, clearly searching, so I start on the front compartment.

"She's already looked here," Brecken says from the driver's seat. He's contorted, searching the console carefully. "Harper, did you check everywhere back there?"

"It won't be back here." Harper says. She's leaned into the trunk, sorting through every bag. Then she unzips hers. "I don't even know why I'm checking my bag. I had it up front! That's where I got the business card with the rental place number."

"Try to breathe," I say. "I'm sure we'll find it."

"We should have found it already! I had it *on my person.*"

"Try to close your eyes and picture the last time you touched it," Josh says.

Kayla laughs, announcing her return to the car. She's definitely looking more spry. She slings her backpack into the back. "Way to make it sound pornographic, Joshie."

"It's not pornographic." Josh sounds annoyed. "It's a psychological trick. It can work when you're trying to remember something."

"I agree with that," Brecken says. "Try to picture it. It might help."

"I don't need to try," Harper snaps, zipping her bag shut. "I had it in my right coat pocket when I called the rental agency. I haven't touched it since."

"Maybe you're remembering wrong," Brecken says. "You've got a lot on your—" He cuts himself off, and she shoots him an alarmed look.

"We could check the station again," I say.

"I checked every inch of the bathroom and the aisle where I walked," she says. "I had it in the car. I'm sure of it. I remember putting the card back."

Wind blows in through the open trunk, spraying snow onto the seats.

"Close that and get in here," Brecken says. "Let's just sit and think for a minute."

Another blast of wind comes in, and this time Josh and Kayla swear, turning their heads away from the shot of icy air. Harper closes the hatchback with a *thunk* and moves to the passenger door where I'm searching. She opens the back.

"I can ride back there," I tell her.

"No, you should be up front," Harper says. "It helps with car sickness."

"We'll be partners in crime, Mira," Brecken says, winking at me. I think he means to be friendly, but my laugh comes too late and lands flat.

The last thing I want is to sit near this poster boy for old-school fraternities, but what argument can I use? *No thanks, I'd rather be nauseated in the back seat.* I relent, sliding into the front seat and closing my door against the cold.

The leather is warm thanks to the seat warmers. Heat seeps through my coat and into the backs of my thighs, and now that I'm not nauseated, it's nice. I put my bag on the floor and buckle my seat belt. The man with the yellow cap still hasn't come outside. The parking lot has emptied some; travelers moved on, I guess. I look at the station, but it's hard to see who's inside with the snow picking up again.

"We need to pay those assholes. Who has cash?" I ask.

"Don't look at me," Kayla says. "I have like three dollars."

Josh shrugs. "I have nothing. I don't carry cash."

"Right, because you're in the twenty-first century," Harper says with a sigh.

I gesture at the gas station. "And we've slipped into a gas station from 1978, where everyone fishes and the gas stations only take cash."

"Don't you have some money squirreled away somewhere else?" Kayla's question is clearly directed to Brecken and Harper. I get it—they definitely look like they come from money—but it's a ballsy ask.

"Seriously?" Brecken snaps. "Why do you just assume we've got cash? In case you forgot, Harper lost her wallet!"

Kayla snorts. "Your Patagonia fleece tells me *you're* not hurting for money. I didn't think it would be a leap. And don't get me started on that girl's earrings."

"I spent my cash at the rental agency. And lay the hell off of Harper," he says, a muscle in his jaw jumping. Why is he so defensive about a girl he doesn't even know? I turn and catch Josh's eyes from the back. He fires me a look that tells me he's thinking something along the same lines.

"Brecken gave me cash for part of the rental," Harper says. "I had two hundred dollars. I *need* to find my wallet."

"I'm pretty sure Butch Cassidy and the Sundance Creeper are going to be ready to throw down if we don't get this gas paid in the next ten minutes," I say. "I paid them like seven. Does anyone else have anything?"

Josh flips through every pocket. "Nothing. Sorry."

Brecken opens a sleek wallet. "I've got a ten."

Kayla tosses three crumpled dollars. "I've got nothing else. And don't look at me like that, I told you in the airport I couldn't pay."

"Seriously?" Harper says, looking panicked. "We have five people in this car and twenty dollars among us?"

"It's not our fault this place is stuck in the Dark Ages," Brecken says. "I could buy this damn station with the amount of open credit I have in my wallet."

"Don't they have one of those old-school card machines?" Josh asks.

"Apparently not," I say. "And the guy wasn't exactly accommodating when I asked about it."

"I wouldn't mess with that old one," Kayla says. Her expression isn't glazed or sardonic or breezy. She is deadly serious. She's looking at the station, a frown tugging her thin lips downward and I wonder if she saw the same sign I did, about the attendant being armed and possibly ready to pump bullets into people who don't pay for their gas.

"What are we going to do?" Harper asks, her voice small and thin. She is so different than the confident girl she was on the plane.

"Just breathe," Brecken says, reaching over the seat toward her.

A conversion van pulls between the pumps and the gas station. I can hear the music blaring from the passenger cabin, even through the closed windows. Wind howls hard against the glass and I shiver.

Brecken turns on the engine, then tilts his head. "What if we offer what we have? Just explain it to him and offer to send the rest."

"It is Christmas," Josh muses.

"He won't take it," Kayla says darkly. "He won't settle."

She's afraid. And I think Kayla knows something about men like Corey and his father. She senses something. It makes me believe that what she's saying isn't a line of bullshit. I remember what Mom said, about keeping my eyes open. She meant things like this.

"I think she's right," I say.

Josh sighs. "I can't say I disagree. They don't seem overly reasonable."

"He'll call the police and say we were stealing," Harper states. "I *can't* have that happening."

My attention catches on that last sentence. Did I hear her wrong?

"I can't," she repeats, looking only at Brecken.

I stiffen. *Why it would be bad to call the police?*

He nods in reply, decisive. Then he scans the parking lot left and right.

Harper takes a sharp breath. "But I'll talk to him. I'll try."

"No," Brecken says simply.

"It's the only way. I'll handle it. I just need to think for a minute and come up with a plan. It'll be fine."

Brecken shakes his head again, still staring out at the gas station. The cars. The road beyond it. His grip tightens on the wheel and my stomach clenches.

He can't be thinking what it looks like he's thinking. It has to be something else. He's not going to just drive out of here, is he?

Because that *is* stealing.

And if I've ever in my life met a person I'd be terrified to steal from, it's the man sitting on that metal folding chair. Kayla's face is frozen over. It feels like a warning.

Brecken shifts the car into drive and inches the tires forward.

I gasp, looking back over the seat at Josh. The mix of shock and faint fear on his face matches my feelings exactly.

"What are you doing?" Harper asks breathlessly. "We haven't paid."

"We'll send them the money," Brecken says, adjusting his grip on the steering wheel. "If he thinks I'm going to stay here so he can call the cops, he can kiss my ass."

I inhale to argue, but before I can get a word out, Brecken hits the gas. Hard.

NINE

THE SUV'S TIRES BITE AND WE FLY.

Harper grapples for her seat belt and shrieks. "What are you doing?"

I grip the seat as the car's weight shifts hard to the right, swinging back as the tires straighten. "Stop the car!" Harper shouts.

"Stop." I mean to back her up, but my voice is a breathless whisper, lost in the roar of the engine and my pounding heart.

"You stole it." Josh says it flatly, shocked. "You're just driving away."

"Calm down." There isn't an iota of uncertainty in Brecken's voice. He accelerates as we begin to pass the gas station. The tires break loose, the car slipping to the right. Kayla's fear melts into something else, her eyes clouding over. She starts to laugh, and I twist in my seat, my eyes fixed to the gas station windows. They are too cluttered with stickers to see inside. Is there movement?

Am I imagining it?

Maybe he can't see us through all those posters.

The station door flies open.

My blood runs cold. It's the father. He's pulling on his coat, keys already in his hand.

"He's coming after us!" I say.

"Let him try." The friendly Brecken from earlier is gone, and I don't recognize this cold replacement. He is determined to get away with this. "We'll be long gone."

"How?" Josh asks. "We can't get on the highway. The roads are snowy."

"I can't do this," Harper says, breathing hard and fast. "I had a plan. I had a plan and it was working."

"Calm down," Brecken says again. "We're shorting a forty-dollar gas bill. We didn't light the place on fire."

"You think that makes this okay?" Her voice is shrill. "This is stealing! Do you think I can afford—" Harper cuts herself off.

I turn around, looking for the guy again. I can't see him through the snow and pumps and clutter of cars around the lot. And then I do. He climbs inside the cabin of a mean-looking pickup truck just as we cross under I-80, the bridge above leaving us in total darkness for the span of a breath.

We emerge into the waning daylight, and it kicks my voice into gear. "He saw us. He's already in his truck."

"High-speed chase in a blizzard!" Kayla cackles, and Josh snaps his fingers, presumedly in front of her face.

"Kayla. Not the best time. You got it?"

Her giggles quiet, but don't entirely subside. Outside the

snow falls in soft, picturesque sheets. Kayla is wrong about the high-speed chase. We're probably only doing thirty. We can't go much faster. The road has been plowed once, but it's still two or three inches deep with snow. Thirty feels *way* too fast.

"I can't believe you'd do this," Harper says, sounding teary.

"I'm trying to help," Brecken barks.

Behind us, headlights appear. It's the truck.

"He's behind us," I say.

Brecken takes a right onto another side road. "Somebody look up a map. Help me out."

I pat my pockets, but my phone must be in my bag. I open the glove compartment, hoping for the best. There's a folded road map with PENNSYLVANIA printed across the front. Brecken sees it and shakes his head.

"That's not going to help unless we know where we are," Brecken says. "I need navigation."

"I'm already on it," Josh says, his phone casting his face in a blue-white glow. "Make a right in fifty yards."

I fold the map and put it back.

"This one?"

"Just take it!" Josh shouts. Brecken does, the back end fishtailing hard. A few moments later, Josh does it again. "The next left. And then the right just past it."

My stomach is rolling again and my throat is too tight and too full. I grip the seat beneath me, my palms slick with sweat on the leather.

"I can't breathe. I can't breathe." Harper says it over and over.

"You're okay," Brecken says, twisting left and right, sliding and shuddering around each corner and bend. "We're doing fine."

My heart is beating so hard against my ribs, it's a miracle nothing cracks. But after a couple of miles, I think maybe he's right. The truck lights are there, outside the back windshield, but after a few hills and another turn, they're gone. The road stretches behind us, dim and narrow and clogged with snow. There are no lights. None.

Wait.

Headlights appear far in the distance behind us. I fix my eyes on those pinpricks of light, measuring the distance between that truck and ours. If I can see them, can they see us?

"Turn your lights off," Josh tells Brecken.

"I didn't turn them on."

"They're automatic," Josh says. "Turn them off manually and your taillights won't glow."

He does and the road goes grayer than gray, a stark reminder that night is coming. Tall trees on either side of the car leave us lost in shadow. The snow hisses softly beneath our tires.

Brecken heads up a hill and brakes a little at the top. The car slides and my stomach rolls, but I twist around in my seat, searching that back windshield. To the twin pinpricks of light in the distance. I try to gauge things I have no hope of measuring. Distance. Speed. Make and model. Is the truck gaining on us? Is it another car altogether?

"Make a left just over this hill," Josh says softly.

"What?"

"Here," Josh says. "Into that campground. He won't see because we're on the downslope. Stay in the tire tracks so it's not obvious."

Brecken pulls in, past a battered wooden sign that reads: CEDAR HILL CAMPGROUND.

The driveway is nearly overgrown, following a gentle upward slope with a sharp curve to the right.

"Use the hill-climbing button," Harper says, for the moment sounding steadier.

The SUV lurches back and forth, tires alternately slipping and biting. My forehead breaks out in a sweat. I can't sit in this car much longer. I'll be sick. I'm sure of it. I twist left and right in my seat, trying to find the headlights through the tangle of dead trees. I see nothing.

Finally, Brecken makes it up to a small lot, pulling to the right where a closed camp registration booth sits between two gated paths leading in and out of the campground. He parks between two thick groves of brambles. A couple of pines create decent cover.

We will be hidden from the road here.

He won't see us.

He won't.

I say it in my mind, desperate to believe it. Desperate to wake up from this awful dream, so I can be with my mom. Does she even know that I miss her? On all our phone calls, when I ramble on about color and shadow and the next show—do I ever stop rambling about my art long enough to tell her that she still matters? That I love her?

"Tire tracks," Josh says, his tone clipped and matter-of-fact. "He'll just follow our tracks where they turn off the road into the driveway."

"Shit." Brecken flings the door open and sprints for the hill. Desperate for fresh air and high on adrenaline, I throw my door open, too, bolting after him. Snow sprays cold against my cheeks, and I drink it in with relief, feeling my stomach settle. My nerves are another story, but I follow Brecken.

He is trip-sliding his way to the bottom of the hill, already kicking at the snow closest to the campground entrance. He drags a large branch out from the forest, sweeping it in wide arcs. It's working better than I'd have thought. And the wind is helping, too, howling across the road and up the hill to sting my eyes.

I try to stamp and shuffle to help the branch. It's hard. Breathing is difficult out here—every gulp of air seems to drag ice into my lungs. Seeing is nearly impossible unless I shield my eyes. But when I do, I can see that our tracks aren't just covered on the road. They snow has nearly drifted over them all the way back to the top of the hill. Maybe even before that. We should be okay.

Through the trees I see the truck's headlights in the distance before they dip down the hill before ours. He's much closer now.

"He's coming! Hide!" I yell.

Brecken runs back a little way and then flattens himself

against a tree. He's only fifteen feet away from the road, his face tight and eyes closed. I'm farther up the hill, surely hidden by the dead bushes and clustered spindly evergreens. I curl my fingers inside my red gloves and hold my breath as I watch the truck take another hill.

He's getting closer.

And closer.

He's on the second-to-last hill, and my throat is tight and dry. I want to close my eyes. I want to curl up and hide like a little kid afraid of the dark, but I stare even as the snow stings my face and tears stream down both cheeks.

The headlights appear.

Oh, God, is he slowing down? Does he see us?

Brecken looks at me, his dark eyes wide and worried across the snowy drive. We didn't hide the tracks beyond the entrance. There wasn't time. The sound of the engine rumbles into my ears and my heart pounds, a rabbit in a box. Snow peppers my face with cold pinches as the truck rolls to the driveway and moves past.

My held breath comes out in a long heave, and Brecken sags, bending over with his hands on his knees like he might get sick. I know the feeling. Then he looks up at me, grinning, and I go still at the wolfish look of his features.

Maybe Brecken is a boy I should be careful with.

He knows how to smile at girls. And I'd bet he also knows exactly how attractive he is and exactly how he can use it. The ice running through my veins now has nothing to do with the cold.

Brecken pushes off of the tree and the squeal of brakes and sound of hissing snow comes from the road. My stomach clenches again, my throat going dry in an instant.

I search the road, where snow still sprays in great clouds. Two brake lights glare at me, red eyes in a sea of white. I wait for the reverse lights, for the inevitable return of panic, but they don't come. The truck turns right, moving down another road. Chasing us down a path we didn't take.

I lean against the nearest tree, weak with relief, my breath steaming in the cold.

The branches crisscross overhead, black jagged lines against a gray sky. It's either later than I thought or more snow is coming.

Brecken crunches his way up the mountain, his cheeks flushed, and his dark hair tufted up in spikes.

"Close call," he says, looking exhilarated. "We make a good team, Mira. If we stick together, we'll be fine."

"Maybe," I say.

He winks. "Don't worry. Destiny's on our side." His smile doesn't fade when I don't answer. He looks triumphant, breathing hard and pink-cheeked. "You ready to go?"

"Are you sure he's gone?"

"We're safe now."

I nod and watch him retreat to the car. But I don't believe a word he says.

I'm not safe now. I haven't been safe since I accepted this ride.

TEN

HARPER AND BRECKEN TAKE A WALK WHEN WE GET BACK. And by *take a walk* I mean Harper drags Brecken off into the trees so she can scream at him. I don't know why she bothers with the wandering. All of us can hear her tearing him a new one. Also, she's not the only one who's pissed about his little felony stunt. This trip has been a nightmare since we started, and having a criminal behind the wheel is making it worse.

Maybe if someone else could drive, things would calm down. I settle back into the front passenger seat and flex my fingers in front of the heater vents. Josh mentions his phone getting low and asks if I have a charger. For once, I can actually help out with this. Dad always sends me with more chargers than devices. My cordless charger is dead, but I offer up an adapter with two cords. He plugs his into one.

Kayla is fast asleep in the back seat, her head flung back now that she's in the middle with no window to lean on. Josh watches out the window with his eyes narrowed. Harper and Brecken aren't visible from here, but I know that's who he's trying to see.

"There's something going on with them."

I laugh. "Yeah. Probably the fact that Brecken stole gas while illegally driving a car rented under her name."

He doesn't laugh like I'd expected. "No. They have a secret. Can't you see it?" He meets my eyes and holds my gaze. "I mean, why is she letting him drive? Why should she trust him? She's not asking any of the rest of us."

"I don't know," I say, squirming in the seat. I turn off the seat heater, suddenly feeling faintly sick again.

Josh twists around, searching the ground in front of him and around his legs for something. I bite my lip and watch, trying to assess whether or not he could drive. He seems *sort of* mobile. Maybe he could take over?

"Can you drive with your leg like that?"

He does laugh then, neck going pink. "I can barely use the bathroom with my leg like this."

I exhale. "I'm so sorry. I just hate the idea of him driving. Maybe Harper will drive again."

"Maybe," he says, sounding a little distracted. "Have you seen my book by chance?"

"No." Through the windshield, I spot Brecken coming through the trees with Harper at his heels. He's striking in that moment, tall and broad-shouldered. Good-looking in a way that has probably turned a lot of heads. Confident in a way that makes me nervous.

But is that nervousness really about Brecken?

I don't know. It could be this trip in general. The weather.

The wreck. My mother at home spinning herself into knots. The creepy guy in the hat.

"How could I misplace a five-hundred-page book?" Josh asks absently. I frown, looking around my seat, though I know it can't be up here. Josh has been in the back the whole ride, and I've seen phone books smaller than the thing he was reading.

Brecken wrenches open the back door while Josh is still looking for his book. Kayla startles at the blast of air and the sudden cabin light.

"Cold," Kayla complains groggily, crossing her arms over her chest.

"Scoot over," Brecken says, "I'm joining you." He looks at Josh. "Did you lose something?"

Josh sighs. "Yeah. One of my books. I don't get it. It was right here."

"Maybe it's with Harper's wallet," Kayla mumbles, not bothering to open her eyes.

"Not funny," Harper says, sliding into the driver's seat. "Can I charge my phone?" she asks, looking at the cord.

"Yeah, I think I still have decent battery left," I say.

"Great. Mine's dead." She plugs hers in. "Can you pull up the map on your phone until my battery charges a little?"

"Oh, sure!" I reach into my coat pocket, but it's not in there. I check my other pocket and then my jeans, and then I laugh.

"What is it?" Harper asks.

"Now I'm the one missing something."

Harper frowns. "You lost your wallet?"

"Maybe she lost a book," Brecken says, a thin, mocking edge to his tone.

"Just my phone," I say. "I'm sure it's in my bag or something."

"It's probably back here," Josh says.

He hands me my bag and starts looking, and I check through each compartment, unzipping zippers I haven't touched in weeks. Nothing. I double back through my bag and then my coat pockets and then check all around my seat. Panic pushes through me, hot and electric. I was sure I put it in my pocket on the hill. I remember Josh showing me the traffic.

"Josh?" I ask, turning to the back seat.

"I'm looking," he says. "It might have gone flying during the wreck."

He's right, so I check under my seat and between the console and everything else. I close my eyes, trying to remember the last place I saw it. When Josh handed it to me? No. When we got off the highway. I tried to check for traffic, but I had no signal. Did I set it on the seat by Kayla? Oh God, did I leave it at the station?

"Does anyone remember me having it after the gas station?" I ask.

"I can't be sure, but I think you were carrying it when you walked back to the car," Brecken says. "Check the chips and water bag."

I do, and come up dry. "No dice."

"Don't be nervous," Josh says. "I'm sure you have it. Everybody check your seats."

"Let's just call her," Brecken says.

I sigh. "My phone is on silent."

"It'll still light up," Harper says. "Give me your number."

I do, and she calls as promised. Of course, it doesn't light up. My panic ratchets into something spectacular. I can't lose my phone. Not out here. Not with a bunch of strangers and not with my mom at home, possibly losing her mind.

I *have* to find my phone.

Everyone is searching, between the seats and inside pockets. There's nothing. It's a rental car, so it's not like there's much to rifle through.

"Something is going on," Harper says. "My wallet *and* her phone?"

"And my book," Josh adds.

"This isn't normal," I agree. "We haven't gone anywhere. We couldn't have lost all of these things."

"And yet…" Kayla trails off with a chuckle.

"It's not funny," Josh snaps.

"Come to think of it, you've been pretty quiet through all this," Brecken says.

Kayla's eyes narrow to slits. "I'm not the only one who hasn't lost anything, rich boy, so don't start with me."

"Both of you need to knock it off," Harper says.

"She's right," Josh agrees. "Maybe we should check outside? Could you have dropped it running around with Brecken?"

I perk up. "Good point!"

"We should check under the car and near the doors, too," Josh says. "Maybe it fell out of your pocket."

We all make our way into the snow, forming a circle around the car, inching our way out around it. I search every inch of my path down the campground driveway, stepping directly in my own footprints on the way there and back. It's nowhere.

Brecken checks his path, too, which feels stupid, but I'm desperate. I'm at the place where you look for car keys in the fridge. It has to be somewhere.

"Any luck?" Harper says, appearing at the top of the driveway.

Brecken shakes his head.

I take a breath and a strangled noise comes out when I release it. "Oh my God, it's really gone. I must have left it at the station."

"Don't say that," Josh says, leaning heavily on his crutches. "It has to be here. Let's check the car again, okay?"

"We need to go," Brecken says. "This sucks, but it's just a phone. You can use mine if you need to call anyone."

Harper touches my arm again, leaning in. "I know this is scary, but I promise I'll take care of you. You can call from my phone whenever you need."

"Yay, we're a giant support group," Kayla deadpans. "Can we go now? I'm freezing."

"Look, I can't just leave. I have to try," I say. "I *need* my phone."

It's my only tether to the real world—*my* world. The one where Christmas is happening, and Zari and I might be okay, and my mom… I just need to get there and all of this will make sense.

"Let's just look a little longer," Josh says.

"We've already looked. Maybe it's time to see the writing on the wall on this one," Brecken says. Harper gives him a look that could wilt lettuce.

He takes the hint and we keep searching. Kayla's efforts are cursory at best once her space is checked over. As soon as we stop paying attention, she curls up in the middle of the back seat and watches everyone else—everyone who's still outside in the cold, mind you—in silence.

In the end, Josh and I are the only ones who won't give up. Even with his leg immobilized, he manages to awkwardly search under the driver's seat and all three of the back seats. Twice.

He even makes Brecken check the back, where our bags are, and, to Brecken's credit, it sounds like he's doing a good job of it back there. He wrestles every bag in and out, searching every possible inch of space.

And then there's nothing left to check. Everyone has retreated to the warmth of the car, and it's just Josh and me, staring at each other over the open back passenger door. Josh's flashlight turns off and he frowns.

"Sorry. I think my battery's still low."

"It's okay," I say. And then I look at the car, where Harper is checking her watch. My stomach squeezes. "Maybe we should go."

"Maybe," Josh says. But when I move to pass him, he touches my sleeve, taking a little breath.

I shiver, either from the cold or the strange feeling I'm having—danger or interest or some other emotion I'm too wrung out to identify. "What is it?"

"It feels weird, right?"

"Getting into the car knowing my phone is lost?"

"No, the fact that we've all lost something," he says. And then he leans in, his eyes bright as he whispers, "It's scary."

I look at him, but he's distant, pensive, his fingers on my sleeve seemingly forgotten. If I were to paint this scene, I know how the canvas would take shape—stark white and gray lines of snow-covered hills, his face turned away. But his strange grip on my sleeve—that's what matters here. That's the focus.

He shakes his head like maybe he's rethinking it. "I'm sure it's coincidence. But Harper's wallet. Your phone. My book. Are we really all so clumsy that we'd lose these things and have no memory of it?"

I open my mouth to answer, but I'm not sure what to say. My pulse is suddenly racing, tendrils of dark possibility unfurling in my mind.

Josh shakes his head. "Forget it. I'm probably imagining it."

He ducks to get back in the car and the wind gusts, whirling my hair around my face. I push it back when the wind dies, but the chill running over my skin remains.

April 8

Mira,

I thought you'd write by now. I believed in that. In you. I'd hoped my letter would give you time to admit your feelings. To accept what we are. But even if you won't write about it, I know the truth. I know what's in your heart.

It's my turn to play shy, sweetheart. I have a confession, too. I found your painting. The new one. I saw it online. I knew right away it was yours, even before I saw your name. I understand the shadows and sadness in your work, Mira.

The clock tower reads 3:30 p.m. That's exactly when we met in the coffee shop. And the woman you painted in front? In a white sweater and dark jeans. Just like you wore that day.

But of course, you know these things. And now, you know that I see them too. I only hope that you'll find it in yourself to put down your paintbrush and pick up your pen. Write me real words this time.

We can't deny this thing between us any longer. You can't keep me waiting forever.

Yours

ELEVEN

JOSH AND I SETTLE INTO THE BACK, AND HIS FACE IS RED from the exertion of the search and the discomfort of getting into his seat again. Guilt surges through me. It's my fault he was up moving around. I take his crutches and feed them back into the cargo area.

"I'm so sorry, Mira,'" Harper says.

"It's okay." I take a breath, trying to steady my voice. "It is just a phone."

"You'll be home with a new one before you know it," Brecken says. Of course he does. In his neighborhood, he'd probably end up with an extra Christmas gift over a lost phone.

"Maybe we'll find it when we're unloading in Pittsburgh," I say. "Josh, do you want me to plug your phone in again?"

Brecken pulls out his phone. "We can use my phone while theirs charge. I've got like twenty percent and a backup battery in my bag."

After plugging in Josh's phone on my two-cord charger,

Harper turns back to touch my arm. "Do you want to use my phone to call home?"

"I'm okay for now," I say, waving her off. "We should get going. I've held us up long enough."

"All right," Harper says and then she shakes her head. "No, you should come up here. Brecken can move to the back seat."

He scoffs. "You want the two biggest people in the back?"

"I want the person who's carsick and upset about losing her phone up here. And I'm still not thrilled with the fact that you committed a crime while driving a vehicle rented in my name."

Brecken moves, but it's clear he isn't happy about it. When Harper asks about directions, he offers a vague "Head south and west" and refuses to engage in more detail. So Harper pulls out, turning south on the road that brought us here.

Five minutes into the drive, I'm not sure if it matters that I'm in the front seat. Brecken gets over his silent treatment and embarks on an endless journey of back-seat-driving commentary. His constant nagging is making me just as sick as the drive did earlier.

"You need to watch that hill," he says.

Harper nods. "I've got it."

"Try tapping the brakes. Just light taps."

"We're fine," she says.

"Maybe *you're* fine. I feel like I'm being driven around by a fourteen-year-old."

"What the hell does that mean?"

Brecken thrusts his hand between the front seats between us, gesturing back and forth at the windshield and the road beyond. "You're all over the road here."

"I am not."

"You're hugging the outside of every corner and accelerating into the turns. We're going to wind up in a ditch."

"*You're* going to wind up in a ditch," Harper mutters.

Josh and I laugh, and Brecken bristles. "Yeah, ha ha ha."

"Ease up, man," Josh says. "She's not the one who's already been in a wreck."

"What are you talking about? Do you seriously think what happened on the bridge was my fault?"

"It wasn't your fault," Harper says quickly. "It could have been worse."

"It could be better, though," I say, a sigh slipping out with my words. "Like if we were home. That would be better."

"What would you be doing if you were home right now?" Josh asks.

"Kayla would be sleeping," Brecken mutters. "You?"

"Reading probably."

"Reading on holidays?" I ask him.

Josh shrugs. "On all days."

"We watch holiday shit," Brecken says. "Old ones. *National Lampoons*, *Elf*. If it's got jingle bells or Yule logs or anything like that, Dad will force us to sit through it. Which is ridiculous."

"Why is it ridiculous?" Harper asks.

"We're Jewish."

"Wait, don't you celebrate Hanukkah?" I ask.

"Hell, we celebrate everything. Mom has decorations for Saint Patrick's Day. She'd invent holidays if she could."

Harper laughs and Brecken nudges her seat playfully. "All right, what about you?"

"I'd be writing cards and letters. I do it every holiday."

"Like real letters?" Brecken says. "Handwritten?"

"The best kind," she says.

I chuckle. "I hate to break it to you, but they're probably not going to get there in time for Christmas this year."

"It doesn't matter," Harper says. "People don't write letters anymore and they should."

"I've written letters," Brecken says softly.

Stunned silence descends, and Brecken's face shutters, his shoulders going back like he's been caught admitting to collecting doilies. "What? Hasn't everyone?"

Josh holds up his hands. "Sure, I mean, a few."

"Because girls like them, right?" Brecken asks. He looks at me and Harper and even Kayla, who's either asleep again or still ignoring us. "Am I wrong?"

Harper's smile is small but genuine. "You're not wrong."

"It's overrated," Kayla says, her voice unexpected. She's got her thin arms crossed over her chest, and it makes me wonder how long she's been listening.

"Mine weren't too successful," Josh says, scratching the back of his neck. "But I'll take it you had a different response?"

Brecken's face goes red. He pushes a hand through his hair. "I didn't say they worked. I said I think girls like them."

Kayla shifts in her seat. I don't turn, but I imagine her burrowing her head against the window again. "I just think most people don't mean it. I think if you write a letter like that, you should mean it."

"I meant every word of mine," Brecken says seriously.

"Me too," Harper says.

"Well, yeah," Josh says. "That's the point, right?"

"So what's your verdict on letters, Mira?" Brecken asks, bumping his chin at me. "Overrated or extra special?"

I shrug. "I wouldn't really know. I mean, unless you count cards from my parents, I've never gotten one."

There's a lengthy pause in the car, a silence that makes my neck go hot. This time I can feel everyone's eyes on me because they *are* on me.

"Never?" Josh asks softly.

"Not that I can remember," I say. "And it seems like something I *would* remember."

"You would," Harper says, reaching to stroke my arm. She looks stricken. "The right letter can stay with you for a long time."

"Maybe you'll get one this Christmas," Brecken says with a smirk. "If we ever manage to get home to a mailbox."

"Maybe," I agree, though it doesn't seem likely.

Still, the idea of it sounds a little bit wonderful. I try to imagine someone writing a letter on thick, white paper. Folding it up and sliding it into an envelope like the words mean something. What would I say in a letter like that?

I turn to look out the window, where the snow seems to be slowing. It's beautiful out there, the entire world dipped in a thick, white glaze. It looks the way Christmas should look. Except that I'm in a car, and my mother is alone. This will be another awful Christmas and why? Because I just couldn't miss the last day of my art show? I couldn't fly home on the 22nd like I always do, but instead had to push it until now.

I should have known better. I tempted fate, and fate is making me pay.

"Watch your—"

Whatever Brecken is going to say is cut off when the car shimmies to the left, snow spraying around the left tires. Harper lets out a little shriek that feels a beat late, and my pulse jumps into overdrive at the same moment.

Harper steers right but overcorrects. The right tires bobble out of their lane and into the trail of plowed snow at the side of the road.

The car shudders to an abrupt halt, the front tire deep in a rut and spinning uselessly. She tries to pull forward, to steer left and then right to pull out, but the car doesn't budge.

"Try backing up," Brecken says.

She does. She tries half a dozen tricks called out from all over the car. But none of them work.

We're stuck.

TWELVE

JOSH GRUNTS AND I TURN AROUND, WINCING WHEN I SEE both of his hands on either side of his leg brace. His foot is wedged awkwardly behind the driver's seat.

"Are you okay?" I ask.

He lets out a tight breath, his face red when he looks up at me. "Yeah." Then he pulls his foot loose and bites back a cry. "Okay, I've been better."

"What can we do?" I ask. "Do you want to sit up front?"

Josh groans. "Maybe let's revisit that when I'm not in agony?"

"And when we're not stuck in a snowdrift on the side of a mountain," Harper adds.

"I have no idea what we're going to get out of here with," Brecken says. "We're going to be digging out with the ice scraper."

"No, we have a shovel," Harper says. "In the back in that emergency kit."

"The kit with the busted snow chains?" Brecken asks, pushing open his door. "Superconfident about that shovel, let me tell you."

The shovel is actually okay. It's about the only useful thing in the kit. There are a couple of flares, one of those orange, reflective triangles and a matching vest, and a pouch of cheap-looking tools. It's the lamest emergency kit I've ever seen. Still, I'm glad to see the shovel.

I cross my arms, feeling a little silly for getting out at all. There's one shovel and three of us, and Brecken clearly has the upper-body strength to get the job done quicker than Harper or me.

"What can I do to help?" I ask.

Brecken shrugs. "I don't know. Stand over there and look pretty or something."

"Is it 1972 in your mind?" Harper asks, barking a laugh.

"Made you laugh, didn't it?" Brecken asks.

"Not even a chuckle here," I say.

"Come on partner," he says. "You and I have been through things. Help me lighten the mood a little, will you?"

Harper shakes her head like she's dealing with a younger brother who doesn't know better. But Brecken *should* know better. And I can't help but wonder if there's a vein of truth running underneath all these shitty comments.

Harper sighs. "Good intent or not, you'd be wise to check that kind of chatter at the door in medical school."

Brecken tenses, looking down. "It's not going to be a problem."

I laugh. "Just don't call us when you end up in an HR office one day."

"Duly noted. Let's start digging."

Harper frowns, the wind blowing a sheet of her dark hair across one eye. "I feel like we're never getting home. Do you think I should have…"

"No. You're doing the best you can and you know it." Brecken squeezes her shoulder. "Okay?"

"Okay," she says.

I feel like I've gone invisible and wish it was true. I hold my breath, hoping they don't notice me, because the long look they're sharing feels private. Maybe Josh is right, and this *isn't* the first time they've met.

But why the hell would they hide it?

Brecken pulls out his phone to hand it to Harper. "Hold this so I don't drop it?"

I brighten at the sight of it, realizing this could be a good opportunity to call home. It's been a while since I called, and I'm sure my mom is having a nervous breakdown.

"Brecken, can I use your phone to call home?"

"Help yourself," he says. "Battery's low, fair warning. And I'm going to need the charger when we're back in the car."

"Of course. Thank you."

He unlocks it and I start dialing my mom's number, freezing before I finish the last two digits. I can't leave her hanging like this, but calling her? What happens then? Do I tell her about the route change? The pileups? The fact that the highway is closed?

My stomach curls in like a fist. Two years ago, I wouldn't have hesitated, but now? She was still skittish the last time I saw her. On the phone she seemed better, but I know her. I can't stand here on Brecken's phone talking her off the ledge for thirty minutes. I need her to be calm. And most of all I need her off the phone in five minutes flat.

Which means I can't call my mother.

So, I call my dad. He doesn't answer the first time, or the second, probably because he doesn't recognize the number. But after the third try, he picks up. His voice makes my shoulders sag with relief. That single hello is an open window, allowing my real world to spill through like sunshine.

"Dad," I say, exhaling in a rush.

"Mira," he says, clearly alarmed. "What's going on, kiddo? I've been trying to reach you since they grounded the flights. Are you okay?"

"Relatively speaking, yes."

"So, fill me in," he says. "Where are you?"

I sigh, relaxing further. "I don't even know where to start."

He chuckles. "Well, you're calling from someone else's phone. Start there."

"There's a lot that happened before that." I fill him in on the weather delays and me taking a ride, and the disaster detour up to I-80. I don't invent a family because Dad doesn't hit the panic button easily. And he doesn't now. He does a lot of uh-huhs and a few pauses that tell me he maybe doesn't love my choices here.

Not that I blame him. I'm loving my choices less with each passing mile.

At some point, I start rambling about the I-80 pileup and then I'm all over the map. Talking about the rest stop and the weird guy in the hat. My lost phone. Kayla sleeping all the time. I trail off before I talk about Brecken stealing gas. Some things are just too much, even for Dad.

"So, where are you now?" he asks.

"I don't know. We're on some county road. It's really awful. We're driving through a ton of snow."

"I've got to say, I'm not a big fan of this."

"That makes two of us," I say honestly.

"Why don't you stop at a service station or a truck stop? Hunker down and call the police. They'll take you to the station and you can stay warm and safe until the roads clear."

"I can almost guarantee the police are wrapped up with all the accidents. Plus, we're in the middle of nowhere. I don't even see houses."

"So, what's the plan from here?"

"We're trying to head west so that we can get back to I-80 where it's open," I say.

"Do you feel comfortable with that? Do you feel safe?"

I take a deep, pine-scented breath and curl my frozen toes inside my boots. "Mostly. I don't know."

"Talk to me. Are they driving recklessly?"

"No, no, it's nothing like that." I pause, trying to figure out what it *is* like. "I don't know, they're just strangers. And they're a little…"

"Strange?" Dad supplies.

"Yeah. I guess that feels right. They're just kind of weird."

"Weird dangerous or just weird?"

"Probably just weird," I say, feeling a little silly now that I'm talking to him. "Honestly, I'm so tired I can barely stand up. I'm probably being dramatic."

"I'm sure you're exhausted. Not to change the subject," Dad says, sounding sympathetic, "but have you talked to your mom?"

"Only a little." I bite my lip. "Actually, that's my other main reason for calling. Did you know that Daniel left Mom?"

He pauses, so I'm guessing he didn't hear me.

"Daniel and Mom split up. Did you know?"

Another pause, but this time I'm sure he heard. Which means he did know.

Before I can ask about it, he exhales. "Mira, we can talk about all that later. Right now, you need to focus on getting home safely."

"You knew and didn't tell me? It's the anniversary of Phoebe dying, Dad! Mom needs me."

"I know things weren't good when Phoebe died, but your mom is doing better. She's okay. We're both worried about *you*."

My laugh comes out sounding sad. "I'm fine! And I know she's not. There's no way. Also, I didn't realize that moving in with you meant I'd be the last person to hear things."

"That's not fair. We had our reasons, and we can talk about them later," Dad says. "What your mom needs is you and these other kids getting home safely, so that's what you need to do right now."

These other kids. Sure. Except she thinks these other kids are a responsible, well-insured family of four. I wince.

"Yeah, about that…" I trail off, stamping the snow under my boots. "Okay, so you really aren't going to like this part. Mom knows I'm with Harper, but she also thinks I'm with Harper's parents. And she thinks we're still driving on I-78. I may have fibbed a little."

"You know I don't condone lying to your mother."

"I know that, I do. And you can ground me until I'm forty when I get home. But please. Will you call her? She doesn't know I lost my phone, and I'm sure she's really worried and if I call her…"

Dad sighs. "She'll never let you off the phone."

"Yes. That. Also, she'll probably send out the National Guard and the Royal Canadian Mounted Police."

"Not sure she has those kinds of strings or that Canada would come to your aid," he says, but his chuckle on the other end of the line is reassuring. I can almost see his crinkled dark eyes and wide smile. "And let's be clear that I might do it, too, if things don't turn around."

"Dad, please," I say softly. "I just need you to try to help her stay calm."

"Look, I'll call your mom, but you can't worry about her anymore. Take care of *yourself* and get home safely."

He makes me promise to check in with him at the next gas station. And informs me he won't hesitate to call this number back, and maybe the police, if he doesn't hear from me every couple of hours.

"One more thing, Mira."

"What's that?"

"You trust your gut, okay? If you feel unsafe, for any reason, any reason at all, trust it. Just get out of the car at whatever gas station you can get them to stop at. Stay put and stay warm. It might take a while, but we will get you home, so don't worry about that."

"Okay."

"And your mom? She's going to be fine."

I resist the urge to disagree with him before we hang up. Dad didn't see how terrible it got. He didn't endure the weeks after Phoebe died when Daniel and I would find her in the kitchen in the middle of the night peeling potatoes for no reason. Or standing in the laundry room sweeping the same spot over and over. It was bad.

Bad enough that maybe I should have never left.

I try not to think about how she'll react to Dad's call. I try not to imagine her standing in front of the Christmas tree in her bathrobe, with that strange, closed-off expression on her face. Like she's sleepwalking even though she's wide awake.

Maybe Dad's right about her doing better. But what is Christmas supposed to be without Phoebe for us? No more off-key Christmas carols and eating cookie dough straight out of the fridge, salmonella be damned. It's just...empty.

"Just get me home," I whisper to no one in particular. "I need to get home."

It's as close to a prayer as I've uttered in a long time, and there's a faint layer of desperation in my tone.

Brecken's phone buzzes, and I notice the battery is at 8 percent before it powers down. I crunch my way down the hill to the car, where Harper is in the driver's seat with the door open. Brecken has shoveled out the tires and wedged a flattish log underneath the two that are sunk in the worst. In the driver's seat, Harper guns the engine, and Brecken pushes hard into the front bumper. He's trying to help her get it backed out.

"Here, I'll help," I say. "I'm sorry—I think your phone is about out of juice."

"No big." He laughs through his strain. "And I appreciate the offer for help, but I doubt all ninety-eight pounds of you is going to do much."

I ignore him and take position beside him, bracing my hands on the car. I dig my heels in and lean forward. The bumper is smooth and cold and solid, and I like it. It feels good to brace myself for physical work, to know exactly what I need to do to move forward from here.

Brecken smirks. "Push a lot of cars out of ditches, Mira?" I don't know how he makes it sound like a dirty joke, but he does.

I cut my eyes to the windshield, where Harper watches from behind the wheel.

"Try it again," I yell to her.

She does, and Brecken and I push. The car rolls back a few inches. We can tell the second the tires gain traction. The engine's power kicks in, and the car accelerates, motoring up and onto the pavement in a smooth rush.

"See? We were made to work together," Brecken says, winking. "Partners in crime."

He doesn't wait for me to respond, just heads back to the car to confer with Harper at the wheel. I don't know what transpires, but Brecken goes to the trunk and opens it.

"What's going on?" I ask.

"I'm going to grab my backup battery," Brecken says.

He unzips the front compartment of his smaller bag and instantly frowns. "Not funny. Who the hell has it?"

"Who has what?" Josh mutters, his voice muffled from the interior of the car.

"My backup battery. It was in the front compartment of my backpack."

He picks up the backpack and looks underneath it. Checks the side pockets, too.

"Check the main compartment," Harper says. She's behind me now, having gotten out of the car.

"I don't need to. It isn't in there. I never put my battery anywhere but this pocket."

"Well, it looks like you did this time," Harper says, but as he searches the front and side pockets again, ice rolls up my spine like a wave.

He's frantic, rummaging through the top layer of the main compartment and jerking Josh's bag out of the way to grab his second bag. I take a step back and Harper looks at me, the reflection of my own unease in her eyes. Because we've already done our own frantic searches. We've already lost something.

"You must have misplaced it," Josh says, but he doesn't sound like he believes it.

None of us do.

Harper's wallet, Josh's book, my phone, and now this? Our stuff isn't going missing—someone is stealing it. And there are exactly four people who could be responsible.

I take a sharp breath and look at my fellow travelers with new wariness.

Someone in this car is lying.

THIRTEEN

BRECKEN THROWS HIS BACKPACK DOWN, FACE RED, THE tendons in his neck stretched tight like cords beneath his skin. "Everyone out of the car."

"What?" Josh asks.

"*Now,*" Brecken says. "We're searching bags."

"What are you talking about?" Kayla asks, sounding groggy.

"Brecken lost something," Josh says, tugging his crutches free of the cargo area. "He wants to search the bags."

Outside, I stay quiet and still, watching Brecken root around the trunk and check his pockets, inside and out. He's angry, but thorough, unzipping every zipper, fishing around each pocket with his large, wide hands.

Josh is at the back already, but Kayla is slow, shuffling in the car for what seems like an hour before she finally emerges.

"So, what are you missing?" Kayla asks, frowning.

"A backup battery for my phone," Brecken says.

Though I'm freaked out by another missing item, I can't help but roll my eyes. "The world comes to a halt over that, but you thought my *actual* phone wasn't a big deal."

"Let's just say it's not the damn battery I'm after." Brecken looks at Kayla and all of our eyes turn to her.

"What do you mean?" I ask.

"I don't give a shit about it, except that it's high end. It'd fetch more than a few bucks at a pawnshop, just like a phone. Or a wallet."

"Uh, probably not a book," Josh admits, scratching the back of his neck. "I mean, I guess it looks old, but it's not valuable."

"Well, as far as I can tell, there's one person in this car who hasn't had something turn up missing," Brecken snaps. "I say it's well past time we check Sleeping Beauty's bag."

If Kayla's surprised by the question, she doesn't show it. She crosses her arms over her chest and glares. "Bullshit."

"Bullshit why?" Harper asks calmly. "He's right. You're the only one who hasn't lost something, and—correct me if I'm wrong—but you don't seem super keen on us looking through your bag."

"Maybe that's because I'm the only one keeping track of my things."

"We're searching your bag," Brecken says.

Kayla reaches for it, snarling. "You're not touching my bag."

"What do you think you're going to do about it?" Brecken asks. Goose bumps rise on my flesh at the confidence in his tone. He knows she can't stop him. He knows none of us can. He tilts his head. "We're not going to have a thief sitting in the car with us."

Kayla's eyes brighten. "Newsflash, Brecken. We already have a *thief* in the car."

"That's different," Harper says, but her voice wavers.

"I don't know that it is," I say.

"Thank you," Kayla says.

"Don't thank me." I put my hand up in the universal sign to stop. "It looks shady as hell. We don't know you, and you haven't lost anything."

"None of us know each other, asshole," Kayla says.

"Watch your mouth with her," Harper says. "She's right."

"It's a fair point," Josh says. "But I don't know if it's right to search her bag."

Brecken whirls on Josh. "Why the hell are you defending her?"

"I'm not. I just think we should be fair. We all dump our bags or none of us do. If we have nothing to hide, it shouldn't be a problem, right?"

"Fine by me," I say, shivering. "Let's get this over with. I'm freezing."

I open my bag from the good latch. The busted one is getting so rickety it might break completely if I use it anymore. I pull two sketchpads, my laptop, and a large tin of Prismacolors out first, followed by a zippered pouch of toiletries and another zippered pouch with a single change of clothes. I always have a few outfits at Mom's house, so I don't need much.

"You have colored pencils?" Kayla laughs, momentarily

forgetting her anger as she points at the Prismacolors. "What are you, six years old?"

Harper lights up and reaches for them, but I can't afford a new set of these right now, so I open them briefly before she can touch. I reveal the worn pencils in their metal nest, shocked by their vibrancy. It's been a long time since I've touched these. It's been nothing but charcoal for sketching for me this year.

"Is that it?" Brecken asks.

"Check for yourself," I say, nudging my bag forward.

He does, but not with much enthusiasm. My bag is small, and, besides, it's pretty obvious I didn't do this. I wouldn't have stolen my own phone.

"I'll go," Josh offers, opening his canvas messenger bag.

Josh's bag is about what we'd expect. The kit he'd pulled out earlier when Harper cut her finger, some wrinkled clothes, the paperback of Kafka, a few pens, an energy bar, a binder stuffed with notebooks, large envelopes, and a couple of folders. Classic college-student detritus. Nothing is sinister. Nothing is even particularly interesting.

Harper's bag is the surprise of the hour. Inside her buttery leather duffel that probably cost more than everything I own, she produces two equally gorgeous toiletries bags, crammed so full that both of the zippers bulge. There's a wad of clothes, some battered-looking notebooks, a hair straightener with a tangled cord. In general, the bag is such a mess, I'd think she only had ten minutes to pack for a last-minute flight.

"Wow." Brecken's face reflects my surprise. He reaches gingerly, pushing at a leather pouch with a mother-of-pearl button holding it closed. Everything else is a disaster, but this case is immaculate. Sleek and spotless.

Harper opens it, her cheeks flushing lightly. Four pens, heavy and expensive-looking, are lined up in the pouch. It's as lovely as the sleek journal she was writing in.

"They're Parkers," she says. "They have a nice feel in the hand."

Brecken cocks his head. "They have a nice *feel* in the hand?"

Her flush deepens. "I told you I write letters. My grandfather loved good pens. I get it honest."

"You're next," Brecken says, looking at Kayla.

She dumps her bag without saying a word, and I wish instantly she hadn't. Clothes similar to the dress she's wearing now fall out, folded faded dresses and a pair of jeans that make it painfully clear how thin she really is. A broken hairbrush sits atop the mix, next to a ziplock bag with a toothbrush and a sliver of soap. She's got a couple of lighters and a small sleeve-style wallet that lands faceup. A picture of Kayla—a younger, healthier Kayla—stares up from behind the plastic ID sleeve. There's no phone. No cords. And certainly no wad of cash stolen from Harper's wallet.

"Wait a minute," Kayla says, apparently to herself.

Her brow puckers as she unrolls dresses, shakes out a sweater. She's looking for something, and by the way her shoulders tense, it's clear she's not finding it.

Harper lifts a hand, maybe misinterpreting Kayla's actions. "That's okay. We've seen enough."

But Kayla doesn't stop. I don't think she's doing this for our benefit. She lost something, too. She pauses, hands shaking and her mouth a thin, hard line. Whatever she's looking for, she is not happy she lost it.

"I guess that's that," Brecken says. "I'm sorry. I just... It's weird."

"We're not done," Kayla says, her voice sharp.

I nod at Brecken. "We haven't seen your bag yet."

He unzips each of the compartments on his backpack, and Josh starts half-heartedly checking. Brecken tugs forward his duffel bag, too, and gestures at it. "Have at it. And if any of you want lessons on how to properly pack a bag, I'm happy to help."

Harper reaches for the zipper, her manicured hands pushing the two sides apart. "Whoa. Obsessed much?"

I lean forward to see that he wasn't exaggerating about knowing how to pack a bag. Every visible inch of space is filled with tidy, black zippered cubes, the kind you see on late-night infomercials and in-flight advertisements. This is how organizational freaks stow their clothes so nothing rolls around in their luggage. Brecken pulls out two small cubes and unzips them revealing neatly rolled socks and folded boxers. The shirts are even crazier. I've seen shirts in store displays folded with less precision.

"That's...a lot," Harper says simply.

"I like things neat," he replies. "It's efficient."

He reaches into his bag again, pulling out a larger cube, but his fingers stall on the zipper.

"What the hell?"

His voice is soft and breathy, the disbelief stark on both his face and in his tone.

"What is it?" Harper asks.

But Brecken doesn't answer. He reaches into his bag reluctantly, giving Harper a faintly horrified look before he pulls a thick, heavy-looking book free of the bag. I don't need to read the cover to know it's Proust. I don't need anyone to say a thing.

Josh's book is buried in the bottom of Brecken's duffel bag.

June 12

Mira,

What kind of game are you playing? Do you really believe you can continue to ignore what this is? What we are? Some nights I walk around your block a dozen times, waiting to see you in a doorway. A window. I want to find you so I can force you to look into my eyes and explain why you haven't written back.

I'm trying to be patient. I know you are painting things for me. For us. I saw your newest work. The carnival and the crowd.

At first, it didn't make sense. The painting is bleak and gray—nothing like the carnivals I remember. And the title—The Darkest Ride. None of it made sense, but then I saw myself. There I was in the crowd. White shirt and black shoes and a smear of hair just like mine. When I met you, I was facing to the left.

It's a beautiful tribute, Mira. But I want more.

We can't keep ourselves apart much longer. You're fighting forces that are bigger than both of us.

Do what you need to do. And do it soon.

Yours

FOURTEEN

"WHAT THE HELL ARE YOU DOING WITH HIS BOOK?" Harper asks Brecken.

"Where's my stuff?"

I don't recognize the screeching voice as Kayla's until I look at her. And I *barely* recognize her. The subdued, sleepy passenger is gone. This new Kayla has color in her cheeks and looks ready to hit someone.

"What the hell are you talking about?" Brecken asks.

Kayla scoffs. "Don't act like you don't know. You have his book, so you have the rest of it. Now where's my stuff?"

"I have no idea how the hell his book got in there!" Brecken steps back, hands raised like he's discovered a bomb in his bag.

"So, someone else put my book in *your* bag?" Josh asks calmly.

Brecken is spluttering. "How the hell would I—"

"Did you take my wallet?" Harper asks.

"Or my phone?" I chime in.

Kayla snatches at his bag. "Where's my stuff?"

Brecken pulls it back instinctively, but then flings it at her. It hits her square in the chest, and she stumbles but grabs it.

"Screw all of you!" Brecken's eyes have gone dark with anger, his mouth twisted in a feral smile. He looks at each of us in turn. "I don't need your crappy phone or your pretentious book or whatever *shit* you're looking for." He gestures at Kayla vaguely.

She pays no attention, just flings the bag back into the cargo area and starts rooting through it frantically. I hear a flurry of zippers and rustling. Brecken's eyes flick toward her and his jaw tenses, but he doesn't move to stop her.

"Have at it," he says. "Because you're not going to find whatever it is you're looking for. None of you."

"We already found Josh's book," I say.

He gestures at us again. "Who the hell says one of you didn't plant it in there?"

"Why would anyone do that?" Harper asks.

"We already know you're willing to steal," Josh says evenly.

"That's bullshit. That was a no-win situation," he fires back. "And even if I was a thief, what the hell would I want with your weird-ass book?"

"It doesn't make any sense," I say, and it really doesn't. There isn't a reason to plant Josh's book somewhere else. Or to steal Harper's wallet and no one else's. If someone nabbed it at the gas station, why not take others? They don't know how much cash we have.

"He's a liar," Kayla says, but her rooting has clearly produced nothing. She keeps going.

Brecken throws up his hands. "Okay, why would I let you check my bag to begin with if I'm the thief? Why wouldn't I keep my mouth shut?"

We don't say anything. It's a good point. That doesn't make sense.

Brecken leans in, challenging us with a look. "If I knew Josh's book was in here, why would I let you find it?"

Josh cocks his head. "What kind of choice would you have had, man? We were already searching everybody else's bags."

"It was his suggestion, though," Harper says. I can tell she's doubting this as much as I am now. "And Kayla hasn't found anything else. Have you?"

Kayla shoves his bag away in a huff, saying nothing but breathing hard. Josh takes her hand and mutters something reassuring. She locks eyes with him and seems to settle.

"None of this makes sense." I shake my head. "This is all random stuff. A book. A phone. A wallet. Whatever the hell Kayla is missing."

"Gee, I wonder what that could be," Brecken muses.

"Well, it's all valuable except for the book," Harper says. "Maybe we got hit at the gas station. Someone could have stolen our stuff and shoved the book in that cube while looking through Brecken's bags. It's possible right?"

"Possible," I agree, but it doesn't sit right. What thief would take the time to put everything back *just so*?

"Look, we need to get moving," Harper says. "I'm freezing.

And no offense, but I'm tired of spending Christmas Eve in a car with all of you. I want to be with my family. I need to get home."

"Me too," I say softly.

"Maybe we can stop at the next exit," Harper says. "Sort it out then."

"What if more stuff gets taken?" Josh asks, his eyes drifting to Brecken.

"Don't look at me! I can't believe you assholes think I'd want your crap," Brecken says with a sneer.

"Brecken, stop," Harper says.

"He won't stop," Kayla says, but she's much calmer now. "He's deflecting so we won't think he's behind it."

Brecken throws out a hand. "Says the resident burnout from the back seat!"

"Maybe we need to settle down," Josh says.

Light flickers through his hair, and I shift on my feet to see it better. Headlights. We can't sit here in the middle of the road with a car approaching. We return to our seats, and I don't know how Brecken ends up back behind the wheel or why I end up in the front with him, but before I can protest, we're rolling onward.

The car behind us is a distant presence, a pair of yellow-white eyes blinking now and then through the blowing snow. I feel watched again, so I turn to look over my shoulder and this time, I'm right about the feeling. Kayla is staring at me.

Her pale eyes are rimmed red and her mouth is open just a little. She doesn't blink. Doesn't smile or nod. She just stares.

I shift, uncomfortable under her expressionless gaze. I want her to turn those strange eyes somewhere else so I don't have to look at her. I want to ask her why her eyes are red and why she's sleeping so much, but some part of me thinks I already know these answers. I don't want them spoken out loud.

"What are you looking at?" I ask her.

She smiles that strange, otherworldly smile, but says nothing. The dread in my stomach turns to ice. And then stone. What was she looking for in Brecken's bag? Was she the one who planted the book? Is it possible she's behind this and we just haven't found our things?

Does she have my phone?

Without warning, Kayla's eyelids flutter and she drops her head back to the headrest with a sigh. The snores begin within seconds, and this time I know she isn't sick. Or tired. This is something else.

"I didn't know," Harper says softly. She reaches over the seat and touches my shoulder. It's light and quick, but it's an indicator that this apology is meant for me. I don't need it. I have no idea why she acts like this with me.

"What do you mean?" I ask.

"I didn't know about..." Harper's eyes flick to Kayla meaningfully. "I wouldn't have asked her to come if I knew she was..."

Harper lets the words trail into nothing. But I can fill in the blanks. Kayla is on something. I don't know what, but everything about this screams *user*.

Brecken sighs, voicing my suspicions in a flat voice. "Girl's got junkie written all over her."

"That's not what I meant," Harper says, but she doesn't disagree. "It's just…you're a sweetheart, Mira. And you're young. I would have never dragged you into this if I'd known."

"Of course you didn't know," I say softly, wanting her to move on. Wondering if she knows how young I actually am. It doesn't matter. I don't want her treating me like someone who needs looking after. "I made my own choice to be here. It's not on you."

"Look, I get what it looks like," Josh says, "but maybe this isn't what we think."

He taps his bare wrist meaningfully and then points at Kayla's arm. It's flopped over her lap like a forgotten rag. A thick, dull silver bracelet sits halfway between her wrist and her elbow.

A medical alert bracelet.

Guilt pricks at the back of my neck. Zari's brother Jayden has a similar bracelet for allergies. I should have noticed that. God, am I so removed from my old life that I miss things like this?

"I didn't even see that," I say.

"Me either," Harper adds.

"I'm staying with my original vote," Brecken says. "She's not a poor terminally ill girl. Or if she is, she's a poor, terminally ill junkie girl."

"How would you know?" I ask.

"My whole family is full of doctors. Both of my parents. My

uncles and older brother. He runs a recovery clinic for addicts, so he talks about it a lot."

"Wow, I didn't know you could learn medicine through osmosis," Josh says, quiet but with a touch of bite to his tone.

"He said he's studying medicine," Harper defends.

"Can we talk about something else?" I ask. "Where are we?"

"On some bullshit county road that no one gives two craps about," Brecken says. "I don't know where the hell I'm going. Here, Mira, can you help?"

He thrusts his phone at me and I take it, ignoring the critically low battery warning. Our signal isn't good, and the map loads one miserably slow inch at a time.

"I need a bigger road," he says.

I nod. "I'm working on it. And your phone isn't going to last."

I trace the routes with my eyes, but there isn't much that doesn't snake us miles into the mountains before moving back to I-80 maybe only an exit or two from where they closed it. I shake my head. "Our best bet is to double back to Route 53, I think. We're in the middle of nowhere."

"So we double back," Brecken says.

I cock my head. "Uh, except that gas station was on 53."

Brecken shrugs. "They're probably long gone."

Josh clucks his tongue. "It feels risky."

"That gas station had a sign that the clerk is armed," I add. "I don't want to be anywhere near that place again."

"Stop being hysterical," Brecken says. "Every backwoods gas

station has a sign like that. And they've probably been home for the last hour. They're likely a couple of beers in."

Anger taps, white hot, at the center of my chest. "I'm not being hysterical," I say. "The man ran to his truck and *chased* us."

"I don't want anyone feeling unsafe," Harper says. "If Mira doesn't want to go back, we don't go back."

Brecken stops in the middle of the road. I turn, but the headlights I spotted before are nowhere in sight. We're alone for now.

"Why are you stopping?" Harper asks.

"I'm waiting for you to tell me what to do," Brecken says. "If this snow gets much deeper, I'm not going to be able to see the road. We could end up driving off the side of a mountain."

"We need a plowed road," Harper says.

"Which means a major road," Brecken replies. "All of these back roads are going to be slow going. Like ten miles an hour slow going."

"He's right," Josh says calmly. "We need to double back. Route 53 is probably our best chance at something plowed."

Brecken's phone buzzes a five percent battery warning.

"I don't know," Harper says, but she's staring out at the road and I think it's because she wants me to go along with it. "We're not doing it until we're all in agreement."

I nod, and try to think it through. Brecken isn't wrong about the road. There is one set of tire tracks we're following. They're the only ones other than the tracks we're leaving behind. If the tracks we're following turn off at any point, the game is up. We won't be able to see a thing.

"Harper."

It's Brecken, and he's twisted around in his seat, his voice soft. This message isn't for the rest of us. Just her. I feel that invisible tether again, winding between them. "I know this is scary, but we've got to get you home."

Harper looks at Brecken and her eyes fill up and spill over with fresh tears. Her chin trembles when she opens her mouth to respond. "Nothing else can go wrong."

"Then we go," he says, and he looks at me. I nod without even thinking about it. What choice do we have? None of our options are great here.

Brecken starts rolling forward again. No one asks for a vote. No one argues. At Josh's next instruction, we take a right, and then another right. The roads grow gradually less clogged as we head closer to Route 53.

A few houses dot the mountains now. Not many, just little blips of color here and there, some festooned with Christmas lights. Some only bearing the faint glow of a lit window.

I should feel relief that we're closer to civilization. We can drive faster and make some actual progress. But I can't think about any of that. All I can think of is the book in Brecken's bag. My missing phone. And Harper's soft confession to Brecken, her words highlighting a fear I can't even name.

Nothing else can go wrong.

FIFTEEN

THE ROAD WINDS AND TWISTS, AND THE GOING IS BEYOND slow. Somehow, we hit Route 53 a few miles east of the gas station, but it's pitch-dark by the time we get there. We have no choice but to drive back past it on our way west. Worse still, we've downed our water and both Harper and I need to find a restroom.

Naturally, this means we don't find an open gas station. Actually, we don't find an open anything, but to be honest, there isn't much to *be* open. It's mostly tree-covered mountains and steep valleys veering into darkness. Here and there, we'll see signs of human life. We pass a closed Dollar General, a handful of houses and—in a tiny, no-name town—a white, steepled church. There's a tree festooned with lights next to a sad-looking elementary school, but nothing looks open or inviting, and certainly nothing looks likely to provide restroom facilities.

"I hate to say it, but I'm going to need to stop, too," Josh says.

"You can pee in a bottle if shit gets desperate," Brecken says.

"That doesn't exactly work for all of us," I grumble.

Brecken thumps the steering wheel. "Can we not make this another feminist argument."

"What are you talking about?" Harper asks.

"Women make everything about gender, and it's bullshit."

I narrow my eyes at him. "Funny coming from the guy who told me I couldn't help push the car."

"Also funny coming from the girl who's currently at my mercy."

It's a joke. It has to be. But cold runs through my veins in a rush all the same. I close my mouth, but Harper opens hers: "Actually, Brecken, it's *my* car. My name, right?" She winks at me and her voice lilts—an effort to lighten the mood. "I think you're all at *my* mercy."

Kayla snorts. I turn to look and notice her smirking, even though she keeps her eyes closed. I wonder how long she's been awake. How long she's been listening. For that matter, is she always listening? Has she been asleep at all?

I turn forward, staring out at the snowy road, feeling a million miles away from everything familiar and safe.

Something isn't right with these people. With all of them.

The thought comes fast and unexpected. I inhale deeply, reminding myself that's paranoid talk. The kind of thing my mom started thinking after Phoebe died. But I'm not like that. I'm not paranoid.

But I'm not obtuse, either. I've learned to pay attention when the hair at the back of my neck prickles—when a carnal, bone-deep instinct tells me something is wrong. And that's what my instincts are saying now.

Something is wrong in this car. With these people. Dad told me to trust that instinct. Hell, he didn't need to teach me. I know to pay attention and to stay calm. That's why I'm good with my mom. It's damn hard to fall apart when you're busy being steady for somebody else.

"A park!"

Harper's sudden cry jerks me out of my own head. I spot it off the side of the road, a sad little picnic area nestled in a cluster of snow-covered trees. There are a few tables and freestanding grills lost under a thick canopy of snow. Two lonely swing sets and an old-school climbing gym sit to the right of a small squat building with two entrances.

Restrooms.

My bladder reminds me of the large bottle of water I downed. Brecken pulls in and we all stumble out without a word. Harper races for the back of the car, rifling through her bag. Whatever she's after, she finds it quickly and makes a beeline for the restroom. Kayla trails after her, her steps wobbly and slow.

When I get out, Brecken is at the trunk again, unpacking, unzipping. Moving things. Maybe he thinks if he rearranges things enough times and in enough ways, all of our missing items will appear.

I head to the bathroom, looking back to make sure Josh is okay getting out. He's crouched awkwardly, his braced leg stretched out to the side, by the open driver's door, reaching just under the car.

"Are you okay?"

"Now I dropped my damn wallet."

"Do you want help?" I ask.

He waves me off. "I'm fine."

I nod and follow Harper and Kayla up the snowy sidewalk. I take a deep breath of cold air, feeling that same, terrible prickling. An indescribable unease that someone is watching me.

But they aren't. Brecken is in the back. Josh is leaned against the car, looking at his wallet. Harper and Kayla are both inside the restroom. I'm alone, but I feel *wrong*.

You trust your gut, okay?

My dad's words thrum just beneath my skin. Because if my gut is to be trusted, I need to get away from here. Away from this car, these people. Every sense I have is heightened and aware— warning me to run.

But how? Where would I go?

Even if there is something dangerous about these people, I can't stay here. This isn't a gas station where I can call my parents and stay safe and warm until someone arrives. This is a poorly lit park in the middle of *nowhere*. No electricity, no heated building, and no phone to call for help.

Gut instinct or not, logic is going to prevail. No one in this car has done or said anything threatening. Yes, I'm riding with a burnout and a thief. But that's not a scary enough reason to risk hypothermia in the Pennsylvania wilderness.

Well, not quite a wilderness.

There's nothing but trees on either side of the restroom building and a mountain sloping up steeply behind it as far as the eye can see. Across the highway, however, there are more signs of civilization—a snowy field and—across that—a single row of well-spaced houses.

I squint at them, feeling a wave of homesickness roll over me. In the darkness, the houses look warm and bright. One bears an evergreen tree wrapped in glittering white lights. Another has tiny glimmers illuminating each window. Electric candles, if I had to guess.

Someone is in those houses tonight. I might be able to get there, running across the field. I could hide in the trees behind the restrooms. Wait for the others to leave and then sprint across the field. Knock on doors until one opens. And then hope that someone has mercy on the strange, bedraggled girl showing up at their house after dark on Christmas Eve.

I shake myself. I am not pounding on a stranger's door over a case of the heebie-jeebies.

I head for the building and use the bathroom quickly, surprised that both Harper and Kayla are still in their stalls when I'm at the sink washing my hands. I move fast, rinsing off the pink soap with water so cold it burns my fingers. With the water off, there is nothing but the buzz of the yellow-tinged light over the sink. My breath steams in front of my face.

Footsteps shuffle in one of the stalls. Someone sniffs.

Crying?

Maybe I should ask, but I don't. Something in me keeps me from saying a word.

Outside the restroom, a wide, flannel-covered chest looms into view. I stop short with a gasp, thinking instantly of the man in the baseball cap. But it's Josh. Just Josh.

He leans on one crutch, his jaw tense. Almost angry.

"Sorry," I say. "You scared me."

He doesn't answer and he won't look at me. He looks lost in his own mind. Or maybe like he's working out a tough math problem. Maybe we're all getting a little nerved out.

The bathroom door bangs behind me, and I turn to see Harper walking toward us. It seems to startle Josh into moving, too. He shuffles toward the bathroom with his squeaky, stilted guy-on-crutches gait—*clink, thump, clink, thump.*

Harper's eyes stay on the sidewalk, her hands balled into fists at her sides.

Everyone is acting weird. And maybe this isn't just the heebie-jeebies. Maybe I need to pay attention. My eyes dart to the houses again, the yellow lights flickering in rectangle windows.

It's not that far.

The thought twists thin roots into my mind. The field isn't that large. I could run through the snow. The only one here is Harper, and my gut tells me she wouldn't chase me. Not in that skirt. She'd call after me and wait for the others. I walk faster without really deciding to do so, and then I'm at the end of the sidewalk. In the parking lot. At the SUV. And walking right past it.

"Where are you going?" Harper asks when I'm near the rear bumper.

"I…"

I don't finish, because what can I tell her? I'm leaving. I'd rather run through that field and bang on the door of a perfect stranger than get back in this car. I'd rather be anywhere else in the world than here with all of you. The panicky flutter in my chest provides no words to make sense of the things I'm considering.

Headlights cut down the road and hope fills my chest like a balloon. Someone's coming. Please let it be the police. Or someone—anyone—who can set my mind at ease and get us help. Please let it be someone I can leave with. Someone who will take me home.

I cup my hand over my eyes to shield myself from the glare of those headlights. I can't see anything else, but whoever it is, they're slowing down.

They're slowing down!

I bounce up on the balls of my feet as the vehicle turns into the park's entrance. I'm ready to run to them when I realize it isn't a police officer. Or a car.

It's a truck. Dread pours through my veins before I even see. My body knows before I recognize the red paint and broken left mirror. But then my mind joins the race.

This is the gas station owner's truck.

Adrenaline fires liquid heat from the center of my chest to the tips of my fingers. My stomach rolls as the truck pulls closer, my feet stumbling backward. I should have gone when I had the chance. My gut was telling me something was wrong, that something bad was coming.

And now it's too late to run.

SIXTEEN

THE TRUCK PULLS INTO THE SPACE NEXT TO OURS, AND I hold my breath. I think of the tobacco, dark and wet in the pocket of the father's cheek. The gruff apathy of his voice telling me they'd be closing soon. Here and now, the deep idle of the truck's exhaust sends the hair on my arms upright.

My gut whispers a new truth, and I trust it: Corey's father did not stop his truck for a chat. He has not stopped looking for us. He's not here for money anymore, maybe hasn't been after money since Brecken pulled out of the parking lot.

This man is here for revenge.

The engine cuts off and the quiet is awful. The breath I'd been holding comes out in a rush, and then I can't stop breathing— shaky, off-rhythm pants that steam in the air and leave me dizzy. The cabin of the truck is completely dark. I can't make out who's driving, but it doesn't matter. I know who's inside.

"Get in the car," Brecken says roughly.

I don't hesitate. Harper's fingers twist in my sleeve and I look for Josh. He's still in the bathroom. I grab Kayla instead, who's appeared like a ghost between us. We shuffle-squirm into the car like a chain of paper dolls. We go to the back, maybe because it's the closest door. I wind up in the middle seat again, Harper's fingers digging into my arm and Kayla's eyes sharply focused on the spectacle outside.

The truck doors open—both driver and passenger sides—and two men step out. I was wrong. He did stop looking for us—just long enough to bring Corey along.

Behind the counter, he'd looked reedy and pale. Weak. But here in the darkness of this parking lot, it's different. Corey's heavy canvas coat could be hiding anything.

Both men have thin mouths and small, mean eyes, and I am afraid of them. Because I am sure they mean us harm.

They approach Brecken, who's standing at the driver's door, his shoulders back like he'll take on both of them if he has to. Brecken isn't small, but I have zero confidence in his abilities against these men. There's something about the way they watch him. Like hunting people down on Christmas Eve isn't all that out of the ordinary in their world.

Brecken moves for the driver's-side door, but Corey steps in front of his path.

"Where the hell you think you're going?" he asks.

"Home for Christmas," Brecken says, and I cringe, because smart-ass is not the card I'd play here.

The father moves closer. "You haven't paid for the gas to get you there, boy."

"Look, if you haven't noticed, the highway is closed, and you aren't really chock-full of ATMs around this county, so I can't *get* your money."

"Bet one of you little rich kids has some cash. Sure the hell don't have any respect, do you? You think you can just walk—"

The wind kicks up, snatching the rest of his words from the air. Harper's fingers are cold and hard on my wrist. She holds me so tightly my skin pinches against my bones. I hiss, but she won't release me. She keeps her wide eyes on the window and leans her head closer to me.

"What are they saying?" I ask softly.

"I don't know. Lock the doors," she whispers.

"We can't. Josh isn't back," Kayla says, the sudden clarity of her voice a shock in the quiet cabin. She is fully alert.

Brecken isn't in the car, either, but I don't say that. I don't need to. Outside the men are muttering, but I can only pick up snatches of words, my brain matching voices to men.

The father shouts, "—little fucking thief!"

Corey interjects, "You don't—"

"—told you I'll send you—" Brecken pleads.

The father interrupts, "Watch your mouth—"

Brecken argues over him: "—forty damn dollars!"

I hear the distant rhythm of Josh approaching from the bathrooms. My heart skips a beat and skids into a new, faster rhythm. Corey and his dad turn. They see Josh, too. They advance, and Josh holds up a hand, saying something I can't hear over the wind.

Harper starts to cry, and the men move toward Josh with an air of intent that squeezes my throat. Leaning so heavily on his crutches, Josh looks vulnerable. I reach over Kayla and grab the door handle, ready to yank it open and go after him, but then everything happens at once.

Brecken pulls open the driver's door, slamming the palm of his hand into the horn. It blares—a loud shock that makes both Corey and his father jump.

"Get his door!" Brecken says. Kayla lurches forward, pushing the front passenger door open for Josh.

"Josh! Haul ass!" she screams.

"He needs help," I yell, trying to clamber over her. She pushes me back with a single fierce look.

"No!"

I try again, but Harper tugs at my arm. "You're not going out there."

"Lock the doors!" Brecken says, and I don't know what's happening up front. There's a flurry of activity. Josh has finally hobbled over to the door. A crutch clatters to the snow-covered pavement and he wobbles. Corey is right there to grab the other crutch. Josh yelps.

"You think you're smarter than me, you little shit." He shakes Josh and Josh half-trips, half-lunges into the seat.

"Don't touch me," Josh snarls, kicking his good foot at Corey.

Corey dodges with a cruel laugh. "Mind your manners or I'll do more than touch you."

Someone cries out. It's Brecken. His nose is streaming blood.

I didn't even hear the punch, but it happened. And now the father has his leg and is pulling, trying to rip him out of the car. Harper grabs Brecken's arm and I lunge over her, reaching for Josh. He's red-faced and breathing hard and we're all tangled up, my body draped over Harper's arms.

"Get the hell off me!" Brecken screams, his legs pistoning at his attacker.

There's a soft *thump* and a strangled *oof.* The father crumples, clutching his stomach.

"Dad!"

Corey releases Josh and his second crutch like they're of zero interest and scrambles around the back of the car. Josh turns to his side, grabbing his crutches off the ground outside his door. Soft cries come out with every breath. I hear Corey's hands slapping at the back of the car. Then he's at the door beside us, his sneer against our window.

Harper screams, but Corey ducks down beneath the glass. He's not interested in us. He just wants to check on his father.

Brecken knows a chance when he sees it. He starts the car, and the engine purrs to life. Both doors are still open and Corey rises, wedging himself in the open door.

"You go nowhere you little shit!"

I want to scream, but the breath I suck in freezes in my throat. Harper yells for me, and we both shrink back, closer to Kayla. Away from the smell of cigarettes and diesel fuel emanating from Corey's canvas jacket.

"Get out!" someone growls, and I can't quite tell if it's Corey or Brecken. They're struggling. Josh is leaning over now, smacking at Corey, grabbing for the wheel. The father is up again, looming outside of the door. The air tastes like sweat and gasoline and violence.

There are punches. Kicks. Terror.

Brecken is getting the upper hand and the father yanks Corey hard. The boy topples out of the car, groaning, and the father is in, one meaty fist immediately clamped around Brecken's throat. Brecken makes a strangled, gurgling noise. Josh squirms with a cry, leaning over the console, one hand on the wheel, one hand trying to pull the father's fingers off of Brecken.

"Stop, stop, stop," Harper sobs.

"Help us!" Josh yells back at us.

Suddenly, Brecken throws the car in reverse. We lurch backward, dragging the father down to the pavement. He swears and crumples.

My heart is leaping. Galloping. I scramble for my seat belt.

Josh's door is still open. One of his feet is dangling outside again. Brecken punches the accelerator and grabs the wheel. Josh is still holding it, too. The wheel twists and there is a horrifying sound. A *thump-thump* like we're going over a speed bump.

Except speed bumps don't scream.

Harper's shriek rises into a wail.

"Shit! Shitshitshitshitshit!" Brecken hits the brakes hard, coughing roughly.

My stomach tumbles end over end as I look out front. Our

headlights illuminate the snow-covered lot and the two dark figures near our tire tracks. One of the men is prone and twitching on the ground.

The father. Please let it be the father. The one who choked Brecken. The one whose bones don't look like they'd snap under a stiff breeze.

But it's not the father. It's Corey.

We hit a person. A guy who can't be much older than us. He's bleeding into the snow because of what happened. Because of us.

I want to look away, but I can't. Corey flails and screams, his upper body writhing in obvious agony. His left leg—jutting at a strange angle—does not move. Slowly my eyes process the scene spotlighted beside our tire tracks. His leg seems pinned to the pavement, his shoe pointing the wrong direction. It's that sight— that impossibly twisted shoe—that almost brings the contents of my stomach up.

"Holy shit," Josh says quietly. He must have seen it, too.

I turn away as Harper makes a thin, keening noise that cuts right through me.

"Oh God," Kayla says, sounding vaguely shocked.

"What did you do?" Brecken screams. His foot must slip off the brake, because the car lurches backward again. Josh grabs the door handle and I gasp. Brecken finally stops the car near the park exit. We're maybe twenty yards away. Far enough that I can't see that shoe anymore, but it doesn't matter. I can see enough. I see a father curled over his son protectively. I see a boy—because he doesn't look like a man now—thin and writhing in a way that will be printed on the back of my eyelids for the rest of my life.

"What did you do?" Brecken screams again, pounding the steering wheel. Harper's sobs are steady and muffled. Her hand is over her mouth. She's shaking.

"What are you talking about?" Josh asks, looking genuinely confused.

The pieces come together over the backdrop of Harper's screams and Kayla's soft swearing. Brecken is somehow blaming Josh for this.

"You hit him!" Brecken says. "I was trying to get away and you grabbed the wheel."

"Brecken, I tried to steer away! *You* pulled it back!"

Brecken sputters. "No! *I* was trying to get away! You hit him! You jerked the wheel."

Josh raises both hands like he's dealing with an armed man in the midst of an angry breakdown. His voice is calm and soft. "Brecken, I know this is scary—"

"It's not scary! I know what you did!"

He sounds hysterical. Frantic. In contrast, Josh moves slower and speaks more softly.

"Brecken, you jerked the wheel to the left," Josh says. "I thought you saw him. I thought you were trying to—" He stops himself. "Look, it was an accident. But it happened."

"No," Brecken says, sounding sick. "No. No, this isn't happening. It isn't."

"It happened," Josh repeats. "It was… You didn't mean to."

He doesn't sound like he believes it. Cold slithers up my spine as I watch Corey in the headlights, his body convulsing in pain. Even over the engine, I can hear his screams, thin and childlike and terrible. Harper clamps her hands over her ears, sobbing.

"Help him!" she cries.

"We have to help him," I say, my voice cracked and weak on my lips.

"They have guns," Kayla says simply. She sounds numb. Distant.

"What?" Brecken turns.

Outside the window, I see the father has a phone to his ear. He looks up at us and I can't read his expression, but I don't need to. He was angry before. He was ready to hurt us before.

He'll kill us now.

He slowly stands, turning toward his truck. He's going to get something. I remember the sign in the service station, and my heart drops like a stone through still water. Kayla's right. They probably have guns.

"Go back," Harper weeps. "Go help him."

"What is he doing?" Josh asks.

The truck door is open now. He's looking for something. Under the seat.

"He's getting a gun," Kayla says. She is cold and certain. "I saw one behind the counter. Under the cigarettes."

"Lots of people have guns," Brecken says, but he sounds afraid. "It doesn't mean anything."

"It doesn't mean *nothing*," Josh says. "He said he'd kill me. You heard him."

"Guys," I cry. "He's coming out."

The man is upright again and he isn't heading for Corey. He's turning to us. Is he holding something? My throat goes tight.

"What do we do?" Harper asks, gasping through her sobs. "What do we do?"

"Go," Josh says calmly.

"We can't go!" I shout. "It's a hit-and-run!"

"No, we will stop," Josh says. "We'll stop and call a little way up the road. We can say we saw a gun. He threatened us."

"Self-defense," Kayla agrees. "It's self-defense."

"I didn't see a gun," Brecken cries, sounding tortured.

"Are you sure?" Josh asks. "Because he's getting closer."

"We can't leave them," I say, my voice small and lost, my eyes fixed on Corey. I think of his patchy facial hair. His lanky limbs. Is he even eighteen years old?

The father puts down the phone and takes another step toward us. The car goes silent. No one moves. No one breathes. Another step, and now there's no missing it. He's holding something metal and he's coming our way. Harper's sobs stop abruptly, her breath ragged.

"Brecken," Josh says quietly.

"What's happening?" Harper asks.

Brecken lets out a strangled sound and punches the gas. The car sails backward, fishtailing onto the road. The father raises his hand, and Brecken jerks the shifter into Drive. By some miracle, there is no spinning or slipping. The tires grip and we move. But I watch that man as we drive by. I watch him until a line of trees separates us and we can't see him at all.

I hope it's the last time I lay eyes on him.

Because if we see him again, I'm sure he'll kill us.

SEVENTEEN

BRECKEN STOPS HALF A MILE DOWN THE ROAD. HE pushes open the door and vomits onto the pavement. None of us breathe a word. Harper wipes her eyes and checks her purse with shaking hands. The bandage on her finger has come loose and it's oozing.

"Your finger," I say.

She shakes her head. "It doesn't matter. I need my phone. It's on the charger."

Josh follows the cord to the charger in the front and hands the phone back to her. She presses the screen. Tries again, turning it faceup to activate. The phone remains dark, and Harper coughs out a noise that isn't quite a laugh.

"It's dead," she says.

"What do you mean?" Josh asks, taking his own phone off the second cord. His voice is soft and confused. "What the hell?"

Cold wind gusts from the open driver's door, where Brecken is still hunched out of view, spitting into the snow.

Harper's voice goes high and shrill. "I charged it for the last hour and it's totally dead!"

"Mine too," Josh says, frowning at his own phone while the open-door alarm *ding-ding-ding*s.

"What the hell is going on?" I ask, checking the cords. I take Harper's phone from her and try plugging it in. Unplugging it. Then Josh's. I unbuckle and lean forward between the front seats to check all the connections, jiggling every potential weakness. The charging indicator refuses to light. The charger is broken. It was working fine in San Diego.

Josh tries them himself. He does all the wiggle, tighten, unplug-replug tricks. We try switching the cords. Nothing works.

Josh pulls the charger out and fingers the connection to the car. "Something's chipped here. Did it get kicked?"

"I don't know," I say.

Brecken leans back into the car, slumping in his seat. I catch a glimpse of his eyes in the rearview mirror. They're red-rimmed and swollen.

"Brecken." Harper holds her hand out. "We need your phone."

He doesn't ask anything, just checks his pockets for his phone and lights the screen to unlock it. He frowns. "It's at two percent. It won't call out on that."

"Damn it. Something's wrong with the charging port."

"Plug it in the back," Brecken says.

I find the port and pull open the flap, but the metal is busted.

A fresh-looking gouge mars the plastic and a chunk of the metal inside is broken off. "It's broken."

I touch the scrape in the plastic, which is still sharp. Jagged. Was it like this before? Wouldn't I have noticed this earlier?

"Are you kidding me?" Josh asks, sounding desperate.

"The whole outlet is busted," I say. "I don't think it's going to work with anything. It looks like it's been tampered with."

Josh leans forward, and I suspect he's checking his own outlet again. He's quiet for a second. And then he swears softly. "One of the metal things is pried off," he says. "Was it like this when you plugged it in?"

"I didn't inspect it or anything, but it seemed fine," I say.

Harper shifts in her seat. "Okay, we need a phone. What about you?"

She's looking at Kayla, who, of course, doesn't answer. Harper reaches over me and nudges her. She isn't gentle about it and Kayla's eyes fly open. Her eyes roll, and something white crusts the corner of her mouth. She looks pale. Sick.

No. I remind myself that she isn't sick. She's on something.

"We need your phone," Harper says.

"I don't have a phone," Kayla slurs.

"What do you mean you don't have a phone?" Harper and Brecken ask at the exact same time.

"That's bullshit!" Brecken adds.

"You went through my bag yourself, Richie Rich," Kayla says, head lolling.

"What the hell is wrong with you, you little piece of—"

"Okay, stop." Josh holds up his hands in a *T* for time-out "Everybody stop."

"Let's find a place to pull over," I say. "We'll see if any of our chargers will work. Maybe we'll get lucky."

"Fine by me," Brecken says, putting the car into drive and easing forward. "Somebody get that map out of the glove box. See if we can figure out where the hell we are. We can compare the highway numbers or whatever. Just get an idea."

Josh opens the glove compartment, reaching for the map. His laugh is hollow. "You've got to be shitting me. It's gone."

Brecken reaches over, checking it himself. He swears. Then slams his palm against the dash.

"It was in there," I say. "It *has* to be in there."

"It's not in there now," Josh says.

I unbuckle and stand up, leaning between them to check for myself. Because I saw that map. I pulled it out and put it back and I *know* it was in there. I feel the top of the compartment, the places where the plastic is joined. The soft vinyl area in the back that allows it to open and shut.

"It's gone." I croak out the words.

I sit back down and I can tell I'm close to tears. My heart is going too fast. Thumping in a way I don't like. This won't stop. Why won't this stop? Everyone starts yelling, and I cross my arms over my chest rocking gently back and forth in my seat.

I see a flash of my mother in the hospital doing this exact

thing. We sat side by side in scratchy waiting room chairs while doctors delivered a litany of terrible news about Phoebe. Lesions. Nodules. Tumors. No longer singular, these terrible word bullets ended in *s* now. Plural versions of a tragedy. And my mother sat the way I'm sitting right now, stony-faced and rocking, her arms crossed tight over her middle. Like maybe she could hold in her insides as her universe blew apart.

I uncross my arms and force myself to tune in. Because that isn't me. I'm the one who's fine through all of it, at the hospital. At the funeral home. Even when we put her favorite flowers on the grave this summer. My mom fell apart, but I held on to my art and did what my aunt asked me to do, and I've been *fine*. I'm always fine. Because I can't let myself be anything else.

"Mira?" Harper's eyes are dark with concern. "You don't look good."

"Yeah?" I force a laugh, then swallow it down, because I can't laugh. What the hell is funny? Someone's stealing things out of this car. Pieces of our lives are disappearing. A wallet. A phone. A map. Who would even want a map?

Someone who doesn't want us to find our way out of here.

Someone who likes us alone and frightened.

"Are you okay?"

Josh this time, his brow creased. Brecken's watching me, too, eyes flicking to the rearview mirror, dark and assessing. *Am I okay?* I don't feel okay. I feel like I'm losing my mind, and the way they're watching me seems to confirm it.

"I'm fine," I say. I learned after Phoebe that if you say it enough, people believe you. Say it even more, and you'll believe it yourself.

"Maybe you should drink some water," Harper says.

"Maybe you need to stop babying her," Brecken says.

"Watch your mouth," Josh snarls. I startle, surprised that he'd care.

"Brecken's right," I say. "Really, I'm fine."

"Wait!" Harper shouts, pointing ahead. "There! Stop there!"

"What are you talking about?" Kayla asks.

"Pull in up there," Harper says. No more scared little girl now. This is her confident all-business tone I heard on the airplane when we were bobbling down to the ground like a yo-yo with wings. She's pointing to a small parking lot maybe a hundred feet up the road, with a squat building behind it.

"Yeah, I don't think that's a gas station," Brecken says.

"Obviously," Harper says. "But it's open." Red light shines from a neon sign near the door, a four-letter confirmation of Harper's claim.

Brecken pulls into the lot, the car crunching over snow-covered gravel.

There are two cars parked and no windows on the building unless you count the glass door. It's beige and featureless, with an unlit sign hanging over the door. The wind blows it back and forth, but when the gusts die, Josh reads the name aloud.

"*The Cock 'N Bull Bar*? Really?"

Brecken sniggers. I swallow, my throat clicking.

We park beside a newer Honda with file folders scattered across the back seat. Even before the engine is off, Harper thrusts a hand between the front seats, her palm facing up.

"Keys."

"What the hell? Do you think I'm going to—"

"Give. Me. The. Keys." And then her voice softens. "We can't afford to have anything else go missing, Brecken."

"Let's just remember we already searched bags. I didn't steal any of this shit," Brecken says, but he drops the keys in her palm all the same.

"Uh," Josh scratches the back of his neck, looking as uncomfortable with this turn of events as I feel. "Are we sure this is the best place?"

"It's the only place. I'm beyond done with this adventure. We need to call the police," Harper says. "We're going to tell them what happened. Then we're going to wait here for them to come and pick us up."

"Look, we can do whatever you need to do," Brecken says, lowering his voice. "But are you sure the police are a good idea? I mean, with everything?"

With everything? My ears prickle at that comment, but I'm careful not to look too interested. Josh doesn't play it so cool; he watches Brecken like an armed bomb.

"You ran somebody over," Harper says. "It doesn't matter what I think now."

Kayla sits up with a groan and rubs her eyes. "What's this place?"

"The Cock 'N Bull," Josh says, completely deadpan. "Harper wants to go inside."

"Cool. I could use a drink," Kayla says around a yawn. She's sweaty and dazed.

"Does this strike you as a good time to stop for a drink?" Brecken asks.

"Stop deflecting," Josh says.

"We're stopping to call the police," Harper tells Kayla.

"This feels like an opportunity to pin everything on me and pretend you all had *nothing* to do with it," Brecken says, sounding more annoyed than afraid.

"We need to tell them what happened," I say. "If we don't, we all look guilty."

"How stupid do you think I am?" Brecken snaps, a muscle in his jaw jumping. "*I* look guilty, not you. Just me, because I was the one behind the wheel."

"No one's accusing you of anything," Josh says, and he's using that soothing tone again. It makes me think of preschool teachers. The cold look that crosses Brecken's face tells me he doesn't appreciate it. But Josh goes on, undeterred. "Harper just wants to be honest. I think that's what we all want."

"Like you're being honest?" Brecken asks, eyes narrowed. "About who pulled the wheel?"

"I *did* pull the wheel." Josh says each word slowly. "I pulled it because I didn't want *you* to..." He trails off shaking his head. "Let's just explain what happened. It was an accident, right?"

Brecken shakes his head. "You guys really don't think it was, do you? You think I did this?"

"I don't know what to think." Harper opens her door. "And it doesn't matter, does it? We hit him and just drove away. Whatever the circumstances, we can't ignore that. Let's go in."

Josh and Harper are already heading that way, but my body tenses looking at the neon sign.

"I'm not twenty-one," I say quietly.

Kayla laughs. "Hell, they're not going to check ID. Merry Christmas, Mira. You're stranded in the middle of Hellhole, Pennsylvania, but hey—you can probably get drunk."

She leaves with her strange, wispy laugh trailing behind her, and I feel suddenly terribly alone. I don't like to get drunk. They don't know this—no one knows this, other than Zari and Phoebe. Zari knows because she was the one who held back my hair when we snuck into her mom's liquor cabinet and drank most of a bottle of some awful peach nightmare. I cried and puked and confessed the next morning to Phoebe, who washed my clothes and fed me some weird herbal tea that eased my hangover. Kayla doesn't know any of that, but her comment makes me hate being here. I don't want to be with these strangers. I want my mom. My best friend. I want to go home.

Maybe this bar will help us get there. But as I watch Kayla's thin body wobble-sway across the snowy parking lot, I can't help but feeling like it's a step in the wrong direction.

August 30

Mira,

You post that you're single and searching—you make jokes with your friends like you think love is a myth. What we have is sacred, but you treat it like trash. Who do you think you're fooling?

You belong with me.

You know it in your bones.

You paint it on every canvas.

The student gallery. What a surprise to find you're only in high school. But the rest was no surprise at all. Another clock with the same time. All is dark except for me. White shirt. Dark pants.

I'm the one turned away in the painting, but you're the one who turned your back on me.

You can't keep running from this, Mira.

I will make you see.

Yours

EIGHTEEN

AT THE BAR DOOR, KAYLA PAUSES, HER REFLECTION illuminated in the glass. Her eyes and mouth are dark blue smears of shadow in her pale face. It's unnerving.

"Are you staying outside?" she asks with a smirk.

I slip in behind Kayla, and Harper doubles back to the door. She stops to hold it open for Brecken, but for a split second I don't see him. Maybe he decided to wait in the car. But then, he's there, loping across the lot with his chin up and eyes glittering.

Harper doesn't pause in the tiny lobby, but turns left into the main bar area like she's been here a million times. I follow her in, my senses reeling at an onslaught of unpleasant odors. Spilled beer and old cigarettes. Deep-fried food and a blend of sweat and cheap perfume that makes me think of my school locker room.

Twenty seconds inside and I know enough about the Cock 'N Bull to know it's not a place any normal person would choose to spend Christmas Eve. It's dark, cramped, and almost entirely empty. A plain, nondescript bar stretches across the longest wall in the room, dotted with a dozen red-topped barstools and two men on them. Eight round tables sit in a haphazard scatter around the rest of the room and Josh, clanking his way in—heads straight for one of these.

Harper walks directly to the bar. A gaunt woman stands beside the register, a white towel slung over her shoulder and a hard look on her face that doesn't match the tiny, glittery Christmas trees dangling from each ear.

"Merry Christmas," Harper says, smiling widely. "Wow, are we glad you guys are open."

"Not for much longer," the woman says. "Closing early tonight for the holiday."

"That's okay, we really just need to use your phone," Harper says. "There was an accident, and our phones are dead. And of course our car charger is messed up. It's been a complete nightmare. Do you have a charger?"

"At home," the bartender says.

"I'm sorry, I don't carry mine, either," the man on the stool in front of her says. "Were you in the accident?"

He looks much friendlier than the bartender. He has dark, wide eyes that radiate concern and a collared shirt that looks expensive. The guy at the other end of the bar is a silent lump in a flannel shirt. He's hunched over a glass of something amber-colored, not even sparing us a glance.

"No. Well, yes. Sort of. It's been an unbelievably terrible day."

"You shouldn't be out driving in this," the woman says.

"Anybody out in weather like this is looking to cause accidents or end up in them."

"Believe me, it wasn't the plan," Harper says, and then she turns to the friendly man. She holds out her hand.

"I'm Harper," she says. "Harper Chung."

He hesitates at her all-business approach, but then grins and offers her a wide, brown hand. "Mitch. Smitty to my friends." He narrows his eyes, looking curious. "You weren't in one of those pileups, were you?"

"Almost," she says. "We were on the bridge when it was happening, but we got pretty lucky. But we were just in another accident and we need some help. We're not hurt, but is there any way I can use your phone? We just need to call nine-one-one."

"Because your car's banged up?" the bartender asks, looking suspicious. "Look, the police have real problems to worry about tonight."

"This is a real problem," Josh says, sounding sad. "A person got hit. We need to make sure the police know what happened."

The concern in Smitty's eyes deepens to worry. "Where? Is he nearby? Is he all right?"

"Yes, I think he's fine. I know they called the ambulance, it's just..." Harper trails off, chewing her lip like she's not sure how much to say.

I pick up where she left off. "We were there. We witnessed it. One of the people on the scene was threatening, so we left, but we still want to call the police."

"But you left," the bartender says, her arms crossed and her lips pursed like she isn't sure about our story. And it makes sense, because we're being shady as hell. "We're not a phone service, we're a cocktail lounge. So, if you aren't ordering something—"

"Joyce, for heaven's sake," Smitty says, shaking his head and reaching into his trousers to produce a worn leather wallet. He pulls out a couple of twenties and lays them on the bar. "Get them some drinks and a pizza and give them the phone."

"Oh, you don't need to do that," Harper says. "Just the phone would be—"

"It's Christmas," Smitty says, shaking her off. "Plus, this weather is the worst I've seen in a decade. Both of those situations deserve a drink, and *every* situation deserves a bit of decency, don't you think?"

Harper pauses, letting out a slow breath that shakes before she answers. "I think I can agree with that."

"Good." Smitty smiles. "Then tell me what you're having."

Harper doesn't ask anyone for preferences. She orders three draft beers and two Cokes. Joyce interrupts right away to tell her they don't serve Coke, but something called RC, and Smitty laughs and cuts her off.

"You are missing the *joy* in your name, friend. Now put something wet in front of these kids and shake off that grinchy spirit. It's the holiday, and I do believe you're getting a gift."

"You didn't need to do nothing," Joyce says. The way her mouth softens isn't a smile, but it's not far off. She looks at us like we're trouble, but Smitty clearly gets a pass.

"What about that gentleman?" Smitty asks, nodding down at the end of the bar. "He need a refill?"

"No." Joyce's voice is low, but serious. She cuts a swift, hard glance at the flannel lump. Given her expression now, her earlier attitude toward us seems positively magnanimous.

"Joyce—"

"He don't need another drink," she repeats. "If he does, he can buy it himself."

Chills run up the back of my spine as my gaze drifts to the end of the bar. I can't see the man's face because of the way he's hunched forward, but the drink in front of him is almost empty now, only a thin layer of brown liquid left in the bottom of the glass.

"If he does want another, he best be ordering it soon," Joyce says.

Smitty just laughs, but I feel chilled, even though it's warm and dry inside. I don't know what's making me cold now. Maybe nothing. Maybe everything.

I have got to knock this off. I'm acting like the boogeyman is hiding behind every corner, and it's ridiculous. My eyes drift to a painting in the far corner of the room, a Monet print, light and airy and full of movement. I used to work with colors like that. My paintings used to dance.

Do they still?

I think about my recent paintings. Themes of time and darkness and shadows. Maybe I lost the colors when Phoebe breathed her last.

I make my way to the table where the others are waiting.

They pepper me with questions about the other three occupants of the bar. There's not much to say, but I recount whatever I can while Harper calls the police. I can't hear her part of the conversation, but I can watch her talk.

Joyce watches on, her head tilted as she lingers over every word Harper says. Even Smitty quiets at a point, his wide smile vanishing at something Harper mentions. I don't have to ask. I know she's talking about hitting Corey.

I can only imagine what this looks like to them. Would I believe our innocence if it was my bar and five strangers walked in admitting they took part in a hit-and-run? Hell, I don't know if I believe it, and I'm one of us.

I don't think this looks like a harmless accident. It looks like a crime.

Harper returns to our table, but my eyes drag to the bar where Joyce and Smitty are speaking. They've got their heads tilted toward one another, creating a private space where they can confer—no doubt about the phone call they overheard. At the other end of the bar, the stranger remains utterly still, his body curled protectively over his now-empty glass.

Harper slumps in her chair with a heavy sigh, looking uneasy.

"Well?" Brecken asks.

"I told them the basics," she said.

"Which basics?" Josh asks.

"I told them there was an accident, and that we hit someone but that we were worried about the father being armed, so we left."

"You told them about the guns behind the counter?" Kayla asks.

Harper nods.

"How about the stolen gas?" I ask. "Did you explain that we tried to pay?"

"I didn't talk about stealing the gas," she says, and her eyes land on Brecken. Her gaze is softer. Hesitant. And her voice follows suit. "When they get here, we can explain. I know what it looks like, but we all know it's not that simple."

"Oh, it's plenty simple," Brecken says, face hard. His eyes flick to Josh. "And I'm looking forward to talking to the police."

"That's not going to turn out how you want," Josh says softly.

Kayla scoffs, pushing her chair back and rising. "Yeah, they'll simple that shit up real fast. And I'm not sticking around to get busted."

"Sit down," Josh hisses. "Where are you going to go?"

I look up, shocked at his sudden anger. "She can go if she wants."

"It's not smart," Harper says, her expression flat when she turns to Kayla. "There isn't anywhere to go. There isn't anything open."

"I don't give a shit," Kayla retorts. But, other than swaying on her feet, she stays put. Her red-rimmed eyes and slack mouth tell me she's got enough chemicals in her system to have reason to be afraid of the police.

"You're not going to get in trouble," Brecken says. "The cops aren't going to care about whatever shit is running through your veins. They care about what happened to that kid."

"Corey," I say, because it feels important. "His name is Corey."

"They might care about the stolen gas, too," Josh says.

Brecken bares his teeth in a sharp smile. "They'll certainly care about my version of things."

"Can you both knock it off?" Harper asks. "We just need to get our shit together and handle this. Do you understand? No one is going to try to pin this on anyone. Because it's an *accident.*"

There's something clinical about the way Harper phrases this. Like she's discussing a class project that's gotten a little out of hand. She glances around and notices our collective tension.

"I'm sorry," she says. "I'm just... I can't be held up here. I have things going on. I can't..."

"Well, *you* won't be held up," Brecken says. "You weren't driving when it happened."

"Brecken," Harper says softly.

He gets up and wanders to the far end of the bar. Harper follows. Joyce arrives with a tray of drinks. She sets them down hard, her gaze drifting to Harper and Brecken, their heads ducked in intense conversation.

"I don't want any trouble," Joyce says.

"No trouble," Josh says brightly.

I don't know if I believe him, but I still pull myself together and smile up at Joyce. "There won't be any trouble at all."

NINETEEN

I AM DESPERATE TO BE HOME, DESPERATE FOR SLEEP, and desperate to be away from these people.

Joyce brings us a rubbery pizza and delivers it with a quiet reminder. "We close in forty minutes."

"How long do you think the police will be?" I ask Josh.

He sighs. "No idea."

So much for sticking around here. I take another sip of my mostly flat definitely-not-Coke and try to avoid Kayla's eyes.

At the bar, Joyce slides another drink to the man in the corner. He hasn't said a word. Hasn't looked up from the second tumbler of whatever he's drinking. With the way she looked at him earlier, I'm surprised he's getting another drink.

"Hey, Mira?" Kayla says.

"Yeah?"

Kayla gives me the smile of a girl who's only half here. "Are you afraid to look at me?"

Apparently, I've been staring so much at everyone else in the bar that Kayla, who's been on the verge of a coma most of our trip, thinks I'm avoiding her. I can't imagine why she'd care about it, but I frown.

"Why would I be afraid to look at you?"

She leans in and I fight the impulse to flinch. She shrugs a slim shoulder.

"Maybe you're afraid that whatever bad, bad stuff I put inside my body might somehow rub off on you? That you might be bad, too."

"Stop," Josh says.

Kayla whirls, her eyes narrowed. "Why do you care?"

He glares. "Because we don't need any more drama on this trip."

Kayla laughs, but to my surprise leans back, crossing her arms over her chest. Her sullen swagger melts away. She pushes her thumb into a crack in the tabletop, and her chin trembles.

"It's not what you think," she says. "It's not—it's not like I'm some stupid party girl who just craves the high."

"I didn't think..." I don't know how to finish, so I trail off with an awkward shrug.

Kayla gets up with a laugh that pinches at my chest. "Yeah, it's best when you don't think about people like me at all. So, keep it up."

She walks toward the RESTROOMS sign on the side of the room.

I shake my head at Josh. "Why did you have to snap at her?"

"I didn't mean to snap. I've got other things I'm worried about," Josh says. He doesn't look at me, though. His brow is furrowed and his gaze is fixed on Harper and Brecken at the end of the bar.

I walk to the bathroom to check on Kayla. Maybe I can't control what's happening here, but I can decide who I am. I can be a person who cares enough to pay attention.

Kayla is sitting on the counter, her back to the mirror. There's not much to the bathroom—two stalls and a single sink with a roll of brown paper towels set in the corner beside the faucet. I stand across from her, leaning against the wall she's facing.

Kayla doesn't say anything or acknowledge me at first. Her eyes are glassy, and her hands are wet like she's just washed them. When she finally looks up, I can see myself tense in the mirror behind her. Embarrassed at my reaction, I try on a smile. It fits like it belongs to someone else.

"Come to check on the burnout?" she asks.

"That's not how I think of you."

"You think of me?" She smiles back and it isn't soft or real. Whatever tender, honest thing I saw a few moments ago—it's gone now. "I'm touched."

I feel that familiar unease again, but I shove it down hard. I won't let everyone else's emotions continue to throw me into a tailspin. If I can handle burying my aunt, I can handle an awkward conversation in a bathroom.

"Do you honestly think you're the only one in the car that's used drugs?" I ask.

Her expression is predatory in that moment, like she knows

exactly how to strike for the kill. "Oh, you're a bad girl, are you? Maybe you've hit a joint or two at a party. Or maybe that one time, when your friend's mom was away, you snuck one of her Valium, because you were just *so* stressed."

"You don't know anything about me," I say.

"I know you're not a user. You might dabble. You might play. But you don't *use*."

I don't even dabble, so I don't argue. Instead, I lean back against the wall. "Well, I'm not going to talk to the cops about it, if that's what you're worried about."

"You're not my problem, Freshie."

My reflection in the mirror frowns, my mouth a bracket. Kayla tilts her head, her long hair a tangle against the glass.

"What is your problem, then? What are you worried about?" I ask.

"I'm not worried about any of you. You're all too messed up to even know how to watch your own backs."

"I'm watching my own back," I say.

She laughs like it's the funniest thing she's heard all day. "Oh, sure. You're tough."

I shrug. "Okay, fine. If not me, what about Brecken? You really think he doesn't know how to look out for number one?"

"I think he's got a lot on his mind," she says evasively.

"Like the fact that he was the one behind the wheel when all this happened? Or the fact that he stole the gas, which started this whole mess in the first place?"

"Calling the police is stupid," she says.

"They need to know the truth."

She laughs again. "Yeah, you're all qualified to give it, right?"

"What's that supposed to mean?"

"It means I'm the only person in that car that isn't a liar."

"I'm not a liar," I say, but the words come out a little flat and dry.

"Aren't you?" she asks, the smallest smile playing at her lips.

And I don't answer, because she's right. I am a liar. I lied to my mom about who I was with. I lied to everyone in the car about being in college.

"Look, everyone lies about something, but that doesn't mean we're going to lie to the police."

"Maybe." She shrugs. "I'm just saying, we're all implicated in some of this shit. And when things like this go down, the police don't go for the truth. They go for the easy targets."

Kayla sighs then, pushing her hand into her hair. The medical bracelet on her arm jangles. It looks old and heavy on her delicate wrist.

"What's your bracelet for?" I ask point-blank.

I can tell my directness surprises her, but she still answers. "Type 1 diabetes and a seizure disorder."

I'm opening my mouth to respond when she shakes her head.

"It's not mine. It's my brother's. Jonah."

"Oh," I say. "Wait. Why are you wearing his medical bracelet?"

"Because he's dead. He died three years ago."

I hate my reflection in this moment. After Phoebe, when I'd

tell people my aunt died—they'd make a face like the one I'm making now. It's an awkward mix of sadness, discomfort, and regret, and I remember so clearly wanting to punch everyone who wore this expression.

But you can't do that. Instead, you have to—

"You don't have to say anything," she says.

Do *that*. You have to smile or say something reassuring exactly like Kayla just did. Somehow, even though you're the one with the trauma, you become the comforter to the person fumbling through an attempt at sympathy. Usually you end the awkwardness with a thank you, but Kayla doesn't.

She looks at the wall like she's a million miles away. I thought her drugs—her shit, as she called it—was missing. But she looks like something is kicking in.

I feel differently about it now that I know about her brother. She isn't doing this to have a good time. She's probably just trying to dull out every awful, hollow thing she's been drowning in for the last three years.

My mom could have ended up like this. Desperate and addicted.

If she didn't work in the emergency room. If she didn't have a thousand stories of overdose victims suffering unspeakable pain and life-shattering consequences, she might have gathered up all those bottles of pills on Phoebe's end tables. On one of the bad nights, maybe she might have tried one. Just to help her sleep. To take the edge off. Maybe that's how it would have started.

But she knew enough about it that she scooped every last bottle into a box the day after Phoebe died. I sat in the passenger seat as she drove them to the fire station for disposal. When I asked why we had to do it right then, she shook her head. Just once.

"Don't want them in the house. Don't want that in my head for even a second."

In some way, it could have been me, too. Not hard to come by illegal substances in San Diego, but I've got an unreasonable terror of pills and a propensity for puking after anything strange enters my system. Plus, I knew right away what I had to do after Phoebe died. I had to be strong for Mom. I *still* have to be strong for Mom.

But if I didn't?

Another version of me might have ended up where Kayla is now.

I guess I got lucky.

"I'm sorry," I say softly. "I know it doesn't change anything. I know when you lose someone… I just know it doesn't matter. But I'm sorry all the same."

Kayla doesn't respond, so I turn for one of the stalls, wondering what the hell I'd even hoped to accomplish coming in here.

"Mira?"

"Yeah?"

She's still fingering her brother's bracelet. Still staring at the wall across from her with her jaw clenched and eyes watery.

"I'm sorry."

"What do you mean? What for?"

She looks up at me and her eyes are colorless. "For everything."

TWENTY

KAYLA'S WORDS SEND GOOSE BUMPS UP MY ARMS, BUT she doesn't elaborate. She slides off the sink and sways heavily, catching herself on the wall next to the sink. Then she pads outside, leaving me to stare at my ashen face in the mirror.

I'm sorry. For everything.

A chill rolls through my reflection in a shiver. I don't need to use the restroom, but I don't want to be out there yet. I need a minute. Maybe several of them.

I take a deep breath; my exhale is slow and shaky. I need to pull it together. The flat of my palms are cool against the tile on either side of the sink. Shadows circle the soft flesh beneath my eyes, and my lips are chapped and cracked.

"What is she sorry for?"

I whisper the words, but they are still jarring in the quiet of the bathroom. I shiver again. God, what if Kayla is right about me? What if I'm a mess just like the rest of them?

But someone in our group is more than a mess. Someone is dangerous.

Too many things have gone wrong to blame this all on coincidence. My dad always says if it looks like a duck and quacks like a duck—it's probably a duck.

Or in this case, sabotage.

The word feels ridiculous, but what else fits? Someone obviously doesn't want us to get to where we're going. But who? And why?

I turn on the tap out of habit. Water hisses down the drain in a sibilant rush. Should I try to talk Joyce into letting me stay here in the bar? Should I try to tell someone what's happened so far—what I'm afraid of?

The police.

I turn the water off and take a deep breath. All of this is about to solve itself. The police will come, and I'll explain all the wacky things that have gone down. Better yet, I'll tell them I'm only in high school and that will be that. They'll whisk me off to some tiny police station in a warm cruiser. Probably wearing an officer's coat. Maybe they'll even offer me some hot cocoa. No more riding with these strangers. No more wondering if all these little misfortunes and my suspicions add up to something sinister.

The door bangs open and my made-for-TV fantasy bursts like a soap bubble. Harper storms in, eyes blotchy and red. I see those spots of blood on her white shirt. She doesn't look so crisp now. She looks like something terrible has happened. Or like she knows something terrible is coming.

Harper meets my eyes and stops short.

I think of her and Brecken—all those close conversations. Josh said there's something between them, but what? Why the hell would either of them not want to get home?

I clear my throat. "Are you okay?"

"I just need a minute," Harper says, voice rough.

"If you need to talk—"

"I don't," she snaps. And then she gives me a tight, apologetic smile. "I'm sorry. I just need a minute. Okay?"

"Sure."

Josh is waiting just outside the restrooms, leaning heavily on his crutches.

"Is she all right?" he asks.

"I don't know. She didn't talk. She said she needed a minute." At the bar, Joyce is watching us with a frown. Then her eyes flick back to the guy at the end of the bar. He's finished his drink, but still seems to be staring at his lap. I wonder if he's asleep.

Between this guy and Kayla, it's like a sleeping epidemic has hit central Pennsylvania.

Brecken is back at the table, reaching for Josh's beer. His own glass sits empty beside him. Kayla watches him, but also steals quick glances at the door like she might bolt. Harper is *literally* crying in the bathroom, and Josh and I are skulking around the corner whispering. We're quite a party.

"Are you okay with Brecken drinking your beer?" I ask Josh.

"It's fine. I don't like to drink." Then he frowns. "Look, we have a problem."

I laugh with zero humor behind it. "You mean aside from the hit-and-run, the missing items, the wrecked car, the snowstorm of historic proportions…"

Josh doesn't smile or add anything to my list. "Harper called the police again, to check in since it had been so long."

"And?"

"They've picked up the kid and his father and transported them to the hospital."

"So, on a bright note, we don't have a gun-toting gas station owner after us," I say. Then I pull my lip between my teeth. "Is he going to be okay?"

"I don't know. The cops want a report, but they are still cleaning up I-80, and they have no idea how long it will be."

"We'll have to wait."

"Which could be fun," he says sarcastically. "The bar is closing soon."

"That's right." I reach for my pocket, then remember my phone is gone. I search the walls, finding an old-fashioned Budweiser wall clock above a row of whiskey bottles. The position of the hands knots my stomach in an instant. "We only have twenty minutes."

"Right," he says.

Joyce is behind the bar. She's leaned over, washing glasses in the sinks as far as I can tell. Smitty has finished his drink, and maybe he wants to go home, but he was kind to us once.

So here goes nothing.

"Wait." Josh's hand lands on my arm after my first step. "What are you doing?"

"I'm going to talk to them. If I explain the situation, maybe she'll understand. Or maybe Smitty will convince her. I don't know."

"You can try, but Harper started bawling at the bar. She wasn't moved."

I sigh. "Great. Okay, then we wait in the parking lot. If the engine is running, we'll be warm."

"Maybe we should find another open restaurant or something," he says.

I shake my head. I am *done* driving with these people. "Everything has gone wrong since we've gotten into this car. I'd really rather stay here."

Josh looks at me with an expression I can't read and my neck goes hot. I duck my head.

"I'm sorry. I'm sure I must sound completely paranoid."

"You don't," he says softly. "Everything *has* gone wrong."

I snap my head up and the intensity in Josh's eyes is clear, his focus absolute. His gaze flicks around the room—checking to make sure we're not going to be overheard. Waves of gratitude roll over me, because I'm so glad to not be alone in this moment.

"I think we need to be careful with Brecken," he says quietly. "He's stressed and volatile and he's trying to pin the blame for what happened to Corey on anyone but himself."

I tense. "He's trying to pin it on you, you mean."

He shakes his head, unconcerned. "I don't care about that.

I *know* what happened and I'm happy to talk to the police." He ducks toward me and I smell soap. "I'm more worried about Kayla. He keeps making comments about the drug thing. If he paints some picture of a deranged addict, they might buy it."

"Kayla wasn't driving," I say.

"I know, I know. I don't know how he'd do it, but…" He lets out a hard exhale. "I sound crazy. I'm making him out to be a monster. He's probably just scared."

"Maybe," I say, but I don't know if I believe that Brecken is afraid. Across the room, he's sitting at our table, his mouth a hard line and his fists thick and heavy on either side of his empty glass. He looks like he would not hesitate to throw someone else in front of a firing squad if it meant saving his own tail.

"I just can't shake the feeling that he's up to something."

Harper steps out of the bathroom and we separate instinctively, Josh's face going blank. She pauses beside us, taking in the room.

"Are you okay?" I ask her softly.

"I'm fine," she says, and she sounds it. Her eyes are puffy, and those bloodstains aren't going anywhere, but her hair and skirt are smoothed. She is put together beautifully again, but I know better now. I thought Harper was all the things I wanted to be, but there are two sides to that coin. For every moment she's held it together, there's another where she's fallen to pieces.

At the bar, Smitty stands up, donning hat and gloves and handing Joyce what looks like a fifty-dollar bill along with a kiss on the cheek. Her eyes well up she tries to give it back, but he refuses, wishing her a Merry Christmas.

He's pushing in his bar stool when he pauses, looking over at the man at the end of the bar. I look, too, a chill running up my back. That man *still* hasn't moved. Not to pull out a phone or go to the bathroom—he's somehow downed two drinks, but I haven't seen him so much as twitch.

Smitty isn't smiling at him the way he smiles at everything else. He's frowning, a deep furrow between his dark brows.

"Sir, you need to pack up," Joyce says curtly. "I'm shutting down soon."

The whole bar feels like it grinds to a halt. I'm almost convinced that this guy isn't even alive—he's *that* still. I take a couple of steps closer, ready to ask if we should check for a pulse. But then he moves, his hand dragging up to the bar in slow motion. There's something familiar about the way he moves. Something about his coat, too, when he pulls it on.

He reaches up to place a few crumpled bills on the bar and my stomach clenches. His fingers are gnarled. His coat is brown. Familiar.

I take a sharp breath that smells of hospitals and death. And then darkness engulfs me.

Total, complete darkness. My hands fly out, my throat tight with panic. I find a chair. A table. It is still pitch black.

"What's happening?" Harper asks. But it's obvious. The power has gone out.

"Just hold on," Joyce says. "Hold tight. I'm getting a flashlight."

"I've got my phone," Smitty says, and a few seconds later, a beam of light pierces the black interior of the bar. I follow the beam, spotting snatches of bar stools. Chair legs. A stranger's heavy work boots. Thin, ratty hair under a yellow hat. It's him.

I can't breathe. Can't swallow. He has to be someone else. I have to be mistaken.

"I've got mine, too," Joyce says, and another beam joins the first. They're scanning the bar, crisscrossing over the tables and chairs. "Just leave the glasses and dishes and get your coats."

"We're leaving?" Brecken asks, sounding surprised.

"No power," Joyce says. "It's ice that's done it. Won't be coming on anytime soon."

The beams cross again, and then Smitty holds his on the door, asking if we can see our things. We can. Joyce is checking the bar with hers. She clinks glasses. Rustles something behind the bar. Maybe a purse.

Then her flashlight beam swings wide, and I see a flash of cardboard-brown coat. He's moving. Coming at me. I gasp and stumble back, knocking over a chair and falling on my butt.

Light hits my eyes. I reach up to cover my face.

"I'm sorry," Smitty says, averting the beam. "Are you all right?"

"Yes, I'm fine."

"Here's your coat," Harper says, and she puts it on me like I'm a little kid.

I don't argue with her. I'm too busy listening to those heavy work boots, watching that man—the man I can't be seeing—walk out of the bar without a word or a backward glance.

It isn't possible. I have to snap out of this and hold on to what's real right now. I have to use my head.

But my head is one hundred percent sure that's the man I keep seeing.

After the rest stop, running into him at the gas station was weird. But here? It's too much. It's not possible.

But it's happening all the same.

November 15

Mira,

You're lucky I found out what happened. If I hadn't looked so carefully at all of your accounts—if I hadn't figured out all the names and places you hide—Well. Let's just say things weren't going to go well for you.

I was angry, Mira. Thinking you could deny the connection we share. Thinking you could pretend this isn't fate. That it's something you can ignore.

But I found the truth. An envelope came, thick and heavy, full of all the unopened letters I'd sent. Your friend at the art gallery must have made a mistake. You didn't live in that house. And I should have known long before now. How many nights did I watch those windows, waiting for a glimpse of your beautiful face?

But I will see your face again soon, Mira. I know you're going home for the holidays. I know exactly where to find you. Won't that be a gift? I can't wait to see your surprise.

See you soon,
Yours

TWENTY-ONE

THE MOMENT WE'RE OUTSIDE, I SEARCH THE PARKING lot. Compared to the darkness of the bar, the snow on the lot makes visibility easy. He couldn't have been more than two minutes ahead of us, but the man in the yellow hat is gone. Vanished like a phantom.

Joyce locks up and then tugs on the thickest bright blue gloves I've ever seen. She doesn't offer help, but she does say, "Hope you get home for the holiday," as she strides to her car.

Smitty waits a touch longer, asking about our fuel level and making sure we'll be warm. He recommends a truck stop that will be open, but it's ten or fifteen miles away, which feels pretty daunting. Finally, he pulls out his keys and looks toward the cars. Joyce almost has hers scraped clean.

"You all take care of yourselves," Smitty says.

"We will," I say.

We wish him well and watch as they both scrape their cars and leave the lot.

"Where did that other guy go?" Kayla asks. "The weird one."

I sag, relieved that someone else saw him. "I don't know, but we need to stay away from him."

Everyone's gaze turns on me, and a shiver runs up my back. I sigh. "I saw him earlier. At the rest stop. And then the gas station. I don't like it."

Brecken's eyes widen. "Did he see what happened with—"

"No," I correct him, but I pause because he looks worried. More worried than I think a person who *accidentally* hit someone should be. "Not that rest stop. The first one. All the way back on I-78. I bumped into him in there first."

"On I-78?" Harper wrinkles her nose. "That's like three or four hours away. What would he be doing here?"

"He *wouldn't* be here," Brecken says.

Josh frowns. "It would be an…unlikely coincidence."

"Well, call it what you want. I saw that guy. In the rest stop by the vending machines. I remember the scars on his hands and his yellow hat."

Brecken scoffs. "You—"

"Wait," Josh says, interrupting him with a raised hand. "No, I think I remember this guy. I saw him outside the stop. Yellow baseball hat, right?"

"Exactly!"

"Okay, but he's gone, so who gives a shit?" Kayla asks.

Harper crosses her arms. "I don't like some guy lurking around."

Brecken throws up his hands. "He's not here to lurk!"

"Why are you so tense?" Josh asks Brecken.

"I'm not. I'm just cold and sick of this damn storm."

"We should get in the car," I say.

Harper hesitates. "I want to check something."

Kayla and Harper cross the lot for the back of the car, where they begin rummaging. Harper, I assume, is looking for a backup battery or something. Who knows about Kayla. Maybe she's still trying to find whatever drug paraphernalia she lost.

"I'm going to scrape the car," Brecken says, but the wind has kept most of the snow from sticking, so the job is pretty easy. He's tucked inside—sulking, presumedly—in no time.

Josh steps in closer to me. "What if we leave him here?"

I look at him, snow and wind whirling around us, both of our coat hoods whipping in the cold. "What?"

"Brecken." His voice is steady. Even. "What if we leave him and go?"

I go still. "You can't be serious."

Josh closes his eyes, exhaling. "Mira, I know I sound paranoid, but I'm telling you—he hit that kid. It wasn't an accident. If he did that to a random kid in a parking lot, what else is he capable of?"

Brecken stares out the windshield in the car. Harper is still wrestling in the back, looking through the luggage. Kayla is empty-handed, wandering toward us, and then back to the car. She makes me think of a pinball in slow motion, ricocheting off every surface with no mind of her own. Finally, she circles around the opposite side of the car and gets in the back seat. She pulls her hood up and leans against the window.

"How are you so sure?" I ask.

Josh crutches a step closer to me. "Because I was trying hard to pull him away from that kid. He jerked the wheel back."

I look at him, not sure what else to say. Would anything else even matter?

He goes on, barely breathing the words. "I know Harper is determined to defend him. He has her fooled somehow, but he knew what he was doing in that parking lot. I'd bet my life on it."

"We can't know. Not for sure," I say, curling my hands into fists in my pockets.

It's cold, but the wind feels quieter. I don't know if the storm is done, but I'm grateful that it has loosened his grip for now. The silence is a gift and I close my eyes briefly to drink it in.

"Maybe we can't know," Josh says, clearly not content with my short response. "But he did steal the gasoline, right?"

"Right."

Josh is so close now, I can't see anything beyond his face. Flecks of silver glimmer in the green of his irises. "Don't you think that says something about his character?"

"No, it doesn't."

We spring apart at the sound of Harper's voice.

Heat flashes over my cheeks like a hard slap. I want to tell her it's not what I think. I want to apologize. I want to know how she got over here so fast without us hearing, but the howl of the wind makes that part clear enough.

"Harper…" I say, but I don't know what should come after. She's staring at us stony-faced, and a sickening surge of adrenaline runs up through my middle. How long has she been standing here? How much did she hear?

For his part, Josh waits her out, his expression giving her nothing. She returns the look, not breaking eye contact even when she pulls the keys from her pocket and starts the car with the remote.

The sudden noise is startling and her expression is unsettling. It makes me think there are two sides to Harper. One girl seems to be falling to pieces. And the other has the whole world held tightly in her fist. The panicky version of Harper annoys me, but when she's like this? On the plane it impressed me, but now… If I'm honest, this side of Harper is scary.

Why *is* she so determined to protect Brecken? What secret are they hiding?

"Look," Josh says. "I'm not trying to play judge and jury here, but I'm worried about you. I'm worried about all of us."

"Because of Brecken? Because he's a big, bad guy?" Her voice is a candy-coated razor.

Anger flashes over Josh's face, brief but intense, but he swallows it down, giving Harper a tight smile. "Suit yourself. I'll be in the car."

Harper whirls on me, face hard. "I suppose you want to leave him here, too?"

I hesitate. Even if Josh is right, and part of me thinks he is, leaving Brecken here feels ridiculous. There's a good chance he'd freeze to death, and I'm not super keen on letting someone die based on speculation from a handful of sleep-deprived strangers.

On the other hand, he's smack-dab in the center of all of this—the stealing, the thing with Corey—so can we risk being in the car with him again? What if Josh is right about none of this being an accident? What if Brecken doesn't want us to get home?

Realistically, what could he do? We've been through his things, so we know he's not hiding a stash of weapons or anything. How would he stop us?

Maybe hitting us like he hit Corey?

"You're awfully quiet," Harper says.

"There's a lot to consider." My last thought is still dancing up my spine with icy fingers. "A lot of terrible things have happened."

"That doesn't mean we need someone to blame. Brecken didn't cause these things."

Maybe. Maybe not. But I'm still not ready to get back in the car until I'm clear on one thing.

"Why are you defending him?" I ask.

"I'm not."

I shake my head. "Yes, you are. All of this would come down on you more than any of the rest of us. The car is in your name."

"That's why I called the cops!"

"But you're also treating Josh like he's a monster for thinking maybe Brecken is a danger to the rest of us."

"I'm not—" Harper cuts herself off and takes a deep breath, slowing down her words. "I'm not treating Josh like he's a monster. Josh is a textbook nice guy."

"So, what's the problem?" I ask. "Why not listen to him?"

"Because guys like that give guys like Brecken a bad name."

"I think Brecken is doing a fine job of giving Brecken a bad name."

She shakes her head. "Forget it. You're not going to understand."

"Then explain it."

Harper rubs her arms and sighs. "We should get in the car."

"No!"

She stops short at that, staring at me. "Mira, try to take a—"

"Okay, this is part of the problem!" I exhale hard and look briefly skyward, trying to collect the thoughts rolling around in my head. "I don't get some of this. You constantly treat me like…I don't know, like your pet project or little sister."

She looks down. "You just…"

"Remind you of someone?" I laugh. "I know."

"It's Ella's roommate," she says, and her whole face softens in pain over those two syllables. It says plenty. Still, she clarifies. "Ella was my girlfriend. Her roommate, Jane, is a freshman. She doesn't have a lot of family and I have sisters. I guess we sort of took her in. She paints, like you. Looks a little like you, too, though maybe not as short."

I nod, digesting this. It explains the way she treats me, but it sheds zero light on the Brecken situation.

"Okay, that's why you're nice to me, but what about Brecken? He stole gas in a car he's not legally supposed to drive. Then he hit a person with the same car. I know that you're smart enough to know that if the police ever do get here, you're going to get in some kind of trouble for all of this."

"I seriously doubt me letting someone drive my rental car is going to be a federal issue."

"You don't care if you get in trouble with the police?"

Her expression darkens. "Let's just say my concerns are larger than a rental car mishap."

The quiet stretches between us. I'm not sure how to reply, so I take a step to the side, my boots crunching in the snow. Everything is still. The snow holds our voices close, cushioning the sound. It feels close. Private.

Finally, she takes a breath and continues. "I got a call at the airport. I was standing in line at the car rental booth. Brecken was behind me; he actually told me which line to get in. Only a couple of the places will rent to you if you're under twenty-five."

"Wait, Brecken was renting a car?"

She shakes her head. "He was, but he decided to let me have it as long as I dropped him home. He paid for practically half of the rental. That's why he doesn't have cash."

The car door cracks open, breaking the spell of quiet between us. Brecken pokes his head out.

"What's going on?" he asks. "Are you all right?"

"Fine," Harper says without looking. "We're fine. Just give us a minute."

He hesitates for one minute, his expression changing as he watches her. I feel that invisible link between them again, a connection stretching across the parking lot. And then the door closes and the tether snaps. Harper meets my eyes.

"We were chatting," she says. "Brecken commented on the flight and complimented my bag. Small stuff. Then I got this call, you know? From home. It was my mother."

I nod.

Harper goes on, her gaze drifting downward. "I couldn't hear her very well. She was crying *so* much." She stops to take a quick, harsh breath. "The connection was bad, and there were all those stupid airport announcements."

"It was loud in there," I say.

She nods. "I had to ask her questions, because I couldn't totally understand. I had to ask pretty *pointed* questions."

"About what?"

"About my father." Something ripples over her face, a brief flash of pain before she swallows it down. Lifts her chin. "My dad's in trouble. He works for a financial firm, and it's something to do with that. The police came. They arrested him and took computers. Mom doesn't know what's happening. My sisters are home with her and they're younger. Everyone's scared and none of them understand."

Imagining it makes my chest hurt. Harper in line, asking

increasingly frantic questions. Brecken overhearing, whether or not he wanted to.

"Brecken heard you," I guess.

She nods, swiping at her eyes. She's crying. "He did. I was so scared and stuck in the middle of the stupid airport. I couldn't even get out of line, and I was so flipped out. I blurted everything to him. Every awful embarrassing thing."

"Harper," I say softly, not knowing what to say. What even to ask.

"He was nice to me, and he'd never even met me," she says. "He knows I'm desperate to get home, and I think that's why he stole the gas. I even think that's why he wanted to drive. I know, it's stupid. Total pompous man bullshit, but his intentions aren't evil."

I nod, not because I agree with her, but because I get it now. To her, Brecken is some kind of hero.

I try to play my opinion close to the vest, but whatever expression crosses my face must say I don't share her view.

"I get it," she says. "I know some bad things have happened."

"He ran over someone," I respond. There's no way to make those words sound anything other than ugly.

"That was an accident," Harper says. "*Obviously* that was an accident. Do you believe it could be anything else?"

"After everything that's happened today, I have no idea what to believe."

Her gaze is unflinching. "I believe it enough that we are not leaving him out here."

"Then we'll wait here for the police," I say. "All of us."

Brecken opens the passenger door again, and Harper rolls her eyes. Before she can complain or even take a breath to speak, he's out of the car, moving with long heavy strides in our direction.

I tense because something's wrong. Very wrong. I can't tell what he's looking at, but every hair on my body is standing on end.

"What is it?" Harper asks, and in that second, Brecken stops in his tracks, eyes fixed on something near the building. I turn to look, but there's nothing but shadows and snow and—

Movement.

Gooseflesh rises on my arms. It could have been a trick of the eyes, except Brecken is out here, and he's staring at that darkness. I scan the length of the building again, searching for something. Looking for—*there.* Another vague impression of movement in the shadows, near the corner of the building.

It's too dark to see. It could be anything. Nothing.

My eyes find their target and my heart lodges into my throat. The moving thing steps out of the shadows. It's not nothing.

It's a person.

They step into the murky light of the parking lot, snow crunching. I don't want to look, but I do. And I immediately see a familiar battered yellow hat. He lifts a recognizable withered hand and my insides freeze.

"Cold one, innit?" His voice is as gnarled as his fingers.

"It is cold," Brecken agrees. His eyes are hard, but his tone is polite. Distant and clipped, but undeniably polite. "Which is why we need to get moving."

He puts a hand behind him, waving the two of us back to the car. He's discreet, but I think the man notices. His face turns, still lost in the darkness under his hat, but tilted in a direction that tells me he's watching this. Watching our retreat.

"I'm not here to hurt nobody."

"No one says you were," Brecken replies.

Another door opens. "Everything all right?"

Josh. Somewhere behind us, near the car. I hear the chink of one crutch hitting the snow-covered pavement. I inch my way backward, but I feel the man's eyes on me. I still can't see his face under that hat and I don't want to.

"Have a good night," Brecken says to him abruptly. "Be safe on the roads."

"Just the thing I'm getting to," the man says, slurring the last bit of the sentence. "You might see I'm traveling without a car."

"I'm sorry to hear that," Brecken says.

"Looks like you've got a little space."

"No, we don't. We're all full."

"With little things like them?"

I feel the man's eyes on me. Watch them graze Harper, too. We are the *little things* he's referring too. Harper curls her fingers into the sleeve of my coat and pulls me close. Her breath shudders.

"Why don't you two get in the car?" Brecken asks. He's using the same, easygoing tone but there's an edge underneath. It matches the stress cording out the tendons in his neck.

"Let's *all* go," Harper says, her voice shaking but loud. "We're already full, so come on, Brecken."

"Now, hear me out." The man holds up his hands and I try not to inhale, not to smell that awful, chemical smell. It's mixed with liquor now. He's swaying like he's drunk, and there's something bulky in his coat pocket. I don't know what he's got in there, but it's bigger than a wallet. I think of the sign behind the gas station counter. Does he have a gun, too? Is he the danger I've been sensing?

My body knew something was wrong. Every hour, my skin has crawled. My body prickled and shivered and *warned* me that I was being watched. Maybe even hunted. And now I know why.

"I don't mean no harm at all," he says, words bleeding into each other, "and we can squeeze for a few miles. That's all I need. A few miles so I'm closer to town."

"I'm sorry," Brecken says, "We can't help you."

Harper and I start backing toward the car in wordless agreement.

"Oh, you could help," the man says clearly, no slurring in these words at all. Even the rough edges of his voice seem to be smoothing over, and it's turning me to stone. "You could help me if you wanted to. And you'll wish you had helped. One day you'll remember this, and you'll wish you'd made a different choice."

There's no question on waiting now. I trip over Harper's feet once. Twice. She pulls me up, and we scramble to the car. Brecken walks calmly to the driver's-side door, sliding behind the wheel without asking for permission. He doesn't need it.

I don't care if he drives. I don't care that he stole. In this second, I don't even care if he meant to hit Corey in that parking lot, as long as he gets us away from this place.

And away from this man.

TWENTY-TWO

I TRY NOT TO BREATHE THROUGH MY NOSE. THE MIX OF smells in this car is sending my stomach back to that topsy-turvy place from the earlier parts of the drive. Everyone's soap and shampoo and even laundry detergent mingles with the faint smell of melted snow and sweat, all layered over a residue of new-car air freshener. Not actual new car smell, mind you, because I'm guessing this vehicle has seen a parade of travelers in and out of its seats, but the artificial chemical odor that seems to fool most people.

I'm not fooled. I'm nauseated.

I shift in my seat, shoving a hand between the belt and my stomach as Brecken creeps down the snow-clogged road. Somehow in the commotion, Josh ended up in the front, and I'm back with Kayla and Harper, my shoulder bumping Kayla's every time Brecken turns. The nudges make me sicker than the smell.

I grip the seat beneath me with both hands, trying desperately to hold myself in the middle, and close my eyes, shutting out the spray of snow on the windshield and the memory of the man in the bar parking lot.

I want my mother. Not the grief-stricken, vacant-eyed version I got after Phoebe died. I want my Before Mom. I know I need to be strong for her. That's how it works now. But in this moment, I need her, too. I'm sick and scared and so tired that my eyes ache.

Before Mom would tell me *that was quite an adventure*. Then she'd push my hair back from my face while I'd choose one of the cookies that would be fanned out, *just so*, on the rectangle plate she always uses. We'd have Christmas like we did before this nightmare. Before Daniel left. Before Phoebe died.

The Christmas tree would sit left of the fireplace, my stocking would already be full, and Mom would have Bing Crosby's Christmas album playing to make it feel like home. Right now, home feels like another dimension. Something that's slipped away from this new world entirely.

My stomach cramps, and I curl my shoulders in, wondering why I can't shake this feeling of dread. Doesn't my body know that the terrible thing has already come? Plenty of terrible things. The wreck on the bridge. Kayla and her drugs. Corey on the ground. The man at the bar. It's all behind us, but my body is coiled tight, my senses sharp and searching.

My body still senses danger. And maybe that's because the danger has been with us all along. My gaze drifts over each of my fellow travelers. These people are just like me, I tell myself. We're all trying to get home.

Unless we're not.

My breath freezes in my lungs. I hold it in for one beat. Then another. It comes out in a rush. What if one of us isn't in this car to get home at all? What if one of us got in this car for all the wrong reasons?

I know someone is lying. Stealing, too. But how do I know there isn't more coming? I don't know anything about these people. I don't even know who I can rule out. Harper? I don't think so. I've seen a side to her—cold and calculating—that doesn't match the bubbly girl I sat with on the plane. And whatever's going on in her family, it's bad. How do I know she's not involved in that mess? Easy: I don't. I can't dismiss Josh or Kayla, either. Kayla has been out of it the entire trip, and I know there's a chemical explanation. Addicts are often desperate by nature, and desperate people can do unthinkable things. It would make sense for her to steal items of value, but breaking the chargers? Taking the map? That part doesn't add up.

Harper called Josh a "nice guy," but Brecken swears he was responsible for hitting Corey. Maybe he's right. I'm not sure I could see Josh mowing a kid down, but maybe he's hiding something darker beneath all the pretentiousness and patronizing comments.

Maybe.

Any of them could be behind this—behind *all* of this. But my eyes draw back to Brecken and hold. *Intense.* That's the first word I thought of to describe him. He's been champing at the bit to be in charge since we started this trip and when he's been in charge, terrible things have happened. Yet, somehow he's managed to end up behind the wheel again.

And he didn't just hitch this ride—he wanted to rent a car himself. He suggested coming to I-80 as well. The only thing Brecken resisted is stopping at the Cock 'N Bull, which is the one place we might have gotten rescued.

A thought lances through me like a frisson of heat: Where was Brecken when the power went out?

I don't know.

I stare at the back of his head, at his long thick fingers curled over the steering wheel. My heart thumps, a drumbeat of fear pulsing in the tips of my fingers. I can't imagine what he'd want from us or what he might plan. But I can't deny that when I look at him, I'm afraid.

I look around, watching the snow-covered slopes pass by. We're headed deeper into the mountains. It doesn't feel like the right way if we're looking for a gas station or a truck stop—or anything else that might be open.

I straighten in my seat, goose bumps rising on my arms. "Wait, what are we doing right now?"

"Driving," Brecken says. "Hopefully in a westward direction."

Josh and I exchange a look. He gives the merest nod, and I feel palpable relief. He sees it, too.

"I think we should look for a place where we can get a map and use the phone," I say. "The police still want to talk to us."

"They do," Harper says, "and they have no idea when they'll show up. They did give us phone numbers so we can call when we get home if nothing else." She doesn't sound too pressed. She sounds exhausted. Resigned.

Brecken's eyes flick to the rearview mirror, meeting mine. "We don't know where the station is," he says. "But we can go back if you'd like to chat with our creepy yellow hat friend to see if he knows."

His words slither up my spine.

"You said we needed to stay away from him," Harper says.

"Yes, but we're not doing what the police told us to do," I say.

"There was a power outage," Harper says. "I doubt they'd want us to sit in a dark parking lot with a scary drifter, hoping we don't succumb to carbon monoxide poisoning or whatever."

"So, we just drive off and keep heading home?" Josh asks.

"Of course not." A frown pinches Harper's face. "We'll stop the second we find something open. We *will* call."

"It's not like we're trying to get away with something," Brecken says.

I don't respond, but Josh and I share another brief look. He holds up his hand in a signal that I think means *ease up*. Or *give me time to think*. I don't care what it means. In this moment, I feel a little less alone, and that's enough.

Kayla's passed out again. Or faking it convincingly. Harper looks sleepy, too. Brecken is fiddling with the radio, of all things. And Josh seems lost in his own thoughts, a tendon in his jaw jumping. He'd better think fast, because if he's right about Brecken, we're in real trouble.

Or, wait… Am I the only one in trouble? What if this ominous feeling has mostly been mine because *I'm* the one being hunted? Brecken's eyes find mine in the mirror again and I remember—Josh's book was in *his* bag. And I either lost my phone when I was in the front seat, or when I was running through the campground. The common factor in both situations? *Brecken.* And at the gas station. I remember Harper and Brecken talking.

Josh lost a book, I lost my phone, Harper lost her wallet, and Kayla lost something she won't name. Probably drugs. Brecken said he lost something, too, but doubts are pooling in my belly, cold and slippery. Did he stage that to see our reaction?

Did he take our things?

I swallow, my throat clicking. The memory of him against that tree in the campground flares to life. His eyes were bright and his cheeks were flushed. I thought it was exhilaration from our narrow escape, but what if I was wrong? What if he was thrilled by my fear? Or by knowing he'd somehow gotten my phone from me. But why would Brecken want to hurt me?

Or am I just unlucky enough to be the one he targeted?

I force a deep breath and try to pull my mind back from the edge. I need to think. I need to find a way out of here. If Brecken is planning something—can I stop him? Can I get away?

He's big. College-football-player big with broad shoulders and biceps that tell me he could pound the tar out of someone my size. Maybe even someone Josh's size. I need to get Harper

234 | NATALIE D. RICHARDS

on our side. Kayla's too out of it to care, but Harper could make it difficult to get away from him. I need her to see that he might not be the hero she thinks.

I take a breath and look at her. "Doesn't anyone feel guilty about this?"

"Yes." To my surprise, it's Brecken. He sighs, voice gone soft. "I feel like shit about all of this. It feels like every damn thing is going wrong."

"Things *have* gone wrong," Josh says, with a pointed look at Brecken.

"This isn't fun for any of us," Harper says sharply. "This isn't part of our plan."

"I didn't think a blizzard road trip was part of anyone's plans," I say.

"Look, we all just want to go home," Harper says.

"Which is going to be difficult without phones or a map," Josh says.

Brecken snorts. "We're going twenty miles an hour. At this rate, we can probably just follow the stars west."

"Wait," Harper says suddenly, her hand raising like an urgent idea has come to mind. "Pull over."

"What?" Brecken asks.

"Pull over. Or just stop. We need to check the back."

"What do you mean?" Josh asks. "Check for what?"

"For an adapter. Some cars, especially SUVs, have power plugs in the back, right? For camping or whatever."

"She's right," Josh says, and I can hear a hint of eagerness in his voice. "Find a place to pull over."

"Laptop!" The idea is so sudden it hits my brain and my lips at the same time. I feel fizzy with the possibility. "I can charge a phone with my laptop!"

Harper's face glows with excitement, so I know she gets it. She grins. "Genius!"

"Laptops," Josh says quietly, almost in wonder. It might be nice for him to see he's not the only one with a brain in this car. He frowns. "Does your laptop still have battery? Mine's dead."

"I'm not carrying mine," Harper sighs.

"Me either," Brecken says.

"I might have a *little* bit of battery," I say. Josh twists to look over the seat at me. I hold up my hands. "Don't get too excited—I doubt I have much. I was at forty percent before I boarded in California, and I used it on the plane."

Harper touches Brecken's shoulder. "We need to pull over. Now."

Brecken finds a place half a mile up—a turn in for some long-abandoned driveway as far as I can tell. It's potentially the perfect place to pull out my laptop and charge a phone. And maybe to talk to Harper.

Harper opens her door and I start climbing over.

"I'll help you get to it," Brecken says, unbuckling.

"I'll help," Josh says, moving to unbuckle.

"No, don't." Harper grabs him. "The snow is deep, and you're on crutches. I'm sure Brecken can do it."

Panic is running like carbonation through my veins. "I don't need any help."

"It's not a problem," Brecken says, and he's already out of the car.

I don't have a good reason to argue, so I catch Josh's eyes once. I can see he's uncomfortable, but what do we do? Accuse him now in the middle of nowhere? There's no way this ends well if we do it now.

We're better off charging a phone and calling the police. We can play this game for ten more minutes. The police are our best bet.

I swallow hard and follow Brecken, stepping out into the biting wind. We close the doors, and just like that, we're alone. The occupants of the car might as well be on another planet. Wind whistles down the mountainside and the snow crunches when I shift my feet. Brecken looks at me across the top of the car and I zip my coat, feeling like his eyes are cutting right through me.

Without a word, I circle to the back and someone pops the hatch from the front. Brecken doesn't reach to open it. He watches me, unmoving, as fear runs through me like a current. I reach for the lid, and Brecken's hand shoots out to hold it shut. To stop me.

"What are you doing?" I sound afraid.

"Do you think I hit that kid, Mira?"

I shudder, resisting the urge to take a step back. Pushing against my terror to stay calm. To keep my eyes open like my mom said.

"Why would you ask something like that?"

"Because I can tell you're afraid of something," he says, stepping closer. "I just want to know if it's me."

TWENTY-THREE

I'M SIX INCHES DEEP IN SNOW AND ZERO PERCENT INTER-
ested in being here with Brecken. I reach for the trunk again and
Brecken grabs my wrist. I try to pull away, but he's got me and
he's strong.

"Let go of me." I yank hard, but he doesn't budge.

"Listen to me," he says, loosening his grip, but not releasing
me. "I didn't hit that kid. Josh pulled the wheel."

"I said *let go*."

He does. My arm drops and he exhales, his breath steaming
between us. "I'm not trying to hurt you; I'm trying to keep us safe."

"From Josh," I deadpan. "From the guy with the torn ACL."

"I don't care about his ACL," Brecken says, and then he shakes
his head, his eyes frantic. "Josh is *crazy*. He tried to *kill* that kid!"

"You think Josh tried to kill a stranger in a parking lot."

"Yes!" Brecken's eyes are wild, and his voice is a whisper
scream. "He's framing me. He's probably framing all of us!"

A fleck of spit hits my cheek and I recoil. Brecken isn't in his right mind. He is not okay, and we need help. Now is not soon enough.

I eye the trunk where my laptop rests. I fling the lid up and hear the radio playing. The wind rushing. They won't hear us unless I'm shouting, but I don't need to be loud. I *need* that laptop.

"Move so I can get my bag," I say.

"You're not listening to me. Josh grabbed the wheel. Even before that—earlier. He *wanted* me to steal the gas."

"He told you to steal the gas," I say, my voice dripping with disbelief.

Brecken grimaces before he responds. "Not exactly. But he gave me a look. In the mirror. I saw it." He steps closer to me again, voice a whisper. "I know I sound crazy, but I'm not. He is trying to make me out to be the bad guy. That's not who I am."

His manic expression sends chills up my spine. He's breathing hard and fast, and his darting eyes scare me more than anything that's happened so far on this trip. He wants me to say something and I'm grasping in the dark.

But while I'm sure that Brecken is dangerous, his words leave me with a sliver of doubt. If *I* were going to frame a person in this car, I'd pick him. He does look the part. He's got the hard face and wide shoulders of a man who could be dangerous.

What if I'm wrong about Josh?

With Brecken practically foaming at the mouth, I think I'll take my chances. I glance at the open door, at the black strap of my laptop bag, and then back to Brecken.

"Look, it's been a long day."

He licks his lips, nodding vigorously. "It has."

"We're all tired. *You're* tired."

To my shock, his eyes go shiny with tears. He nods even more vigorously. "I am. I am tired, but that doesn't change this. I know what's happening here."

I try to don a look of pure camaraderie. "Look, let's get my laptop so we can charge a phone and get the hell out of here. Let's get home, okay?"

He's not moving, and I'm done waiting. I edge closer and drag my bag out. Brecken watches on with hooded eyes. Harper opens the back door and the alarm sounds, a familiar *ding-ding-ding* in the quiet. I catch her eyes and shoot her an I-am-not-okay look.

Her brow is furrowed with worry when she stands. "What's wrong?"

"It's fine," I say, though I don't know why.

"It's not fine," Brecken says, closing the trunk and moving close to us so he can drop his voice. "I think Josh is trying to frame me for all this. I think he's behind all of this."

"Behind what?" Harper asks.

"All of it!" Brecken rails at her like I'm not here anymore. Like he's not repeating what he just told me. "Hitting that asshole. Driving away from the station. He wanted us to come up here. He suggested I-80. He's planning something!"

"You both suggested I-80, and you were driving when the boy

was hit," Harper says, her voice calm and steady. No, it's more than that. She sounds clinical, like the doctors who dealt out the details of Phoebe's prognosis. "It's normal for us to look for someone to blame for all of this, but that doesn't mean someone is guilty."

"We have to leave Josh here," he says, ignoring her. "We can't risk it."

"What are you talking about? We're not leaving him," I say. What I don't say is that Josh suggested the same damn thing about him. And I'm beginning to think it was a good idea.

"He can't be in this car!" Brecken says. "We don't know what he'll do."

"Probably read some more," I mutter.

Harper sighs. "Look, I've been thinking about this. We can't keep tearing into each other. This weather—these roads. This is an emergency. We have to work together to stay safe."

"No. Not with Josh. He's dangerous," Brecken says.

"Well, Josh thinks *you're* dangerous," Harper says. "And I think Kayla is dangerous. I'll bet Mira has her ideas. Maybe we're all just at the end of our rope and looking for somewhere to point a finger."

Brecken ignores her. "All of these things that are happening— someone is behind them. You have to see that."

"Are you so sure?" Harper says.

He doesn't answer, and her question creeps through me, cold and unwelcome. Is she right? Are we all just starting to lose it? Am I reading myself wrong about all of this?

I shiver, hitching my bag higher and pushing the thought out. "I'm getting in the car. I want to charge a phone."

I'm at the door, but Harper's half blocking the back door with her body, her arm outstretched to wave Brecken forward.

"Come on. Let's get going," she tells him.

I duck in front of her to get in. There's a scrabble of feet beside me. A sharp yelp. Something jerks my bag, pulling me backward. Harper. One strap slides off my shoulder, and my bag flips. They both fall—Harper and the bag.

I flail, desperately reaching, but it's too late. Harper's knees hit the snow as something dark and heavy slides out of my backpack. My fingers just brush the edge, but Harper reaches, too, bumping my hands with her elbow. My laptop lands with a quiet crack on the snowy pavement.

And Harper meets my eyes.

December 24

Mira,

You should have known me. I stood behind you in line at the gate. Do you realize how close we were on that bridgeway? Even closer on the plane.

I watched you message your parents and sketch in your notebook. I heard you sigh when you waited in the aisle for the man with the oversized suitcase.

You looked at me, Mira—right at me. I was sure in that moment it was fine. I would hand you these letters. Our eyes would meet and all of these long months apart wouldn't matter.

We would be together again.

But you didn't see me.

You didn't see me.

And I'm going to make you pay.

Yours

TWENTY-FOUR

IT LOOKS COMPLETELY FINE. BACK IN THE CAR, THE commotion wakes Kayla and draws us all into a tight circle around me in the back seat. I brush off every bit of snow I can see and turn the laptop over and over, trying to assess the damage. I find two cracks on one of the hinges that allows the lid to open and close. It's unremarkable, a small diagonal fracture in the case. It could be okay.

"It landed on its corner," Harper says, still brushing snow from her knees. "I'm so *so* sorry. I tried to grab it."

"Is it working?" Josh sounds worried.

"It's got a light," I say, pressing the power button. I hear a high-pitched hum winding up, and then it stops abruptly. The power button flashes yellow, yellow, yellow.

My heart sinks.

"Does it always flash like that?" Brecken asks. He's still outside to give me room, but he's leaning in.

"If so, that's annoying as hell," Kayla says.

"I don't care if it's annoying," Harper—in the front now—leans over the driver's seat to peer into the back. "I can buy you a new laptop if it's broken. But can we still charge our phones?"

"I…" I trail off, testing the power button and feeling the case near that hinge give a little.

The screen stays black and the button continues to flash. My head throbs.

Brecken pulls one of the cords from the busted charger. "Try my cord and phone. Maybe it's just the screen."

"Is it turning on?" Josh asks again.

"No, it's just…" I shake my head, pressing the power button again. The same whirring starts and then stops. The button continues to flash. I try Brecken's cord on all three ports, but there's no response.

"It's like it's stuck in suspend," I say, feeling faintly sick.

"Maybe it's just a loose connection," Harper says. "I'm sure someone can help you fix it when you get into town."

"I wouldn't bet on it," Brecken scoffs.

"Is the charger working?" Josh asks.

I shake my head and swallow hard, tasting defeat.

"Let me try," Harper says, gently prying Brecken's phone from the charger. She plugs hers in instead and then frowns. She flips the cable around. Tries it again.

I watch her, replaying that moment outside. I almost caught it. I almost stopped this from happening, but Harper bumped my hands.

Because she was trying to catch it, too.

Or was she trying to stop me?

"I'm sorry, Mira," Josh says with a sigh. "I wish I could do something."

"Me too," Harper says. I'm not sure if I believe her.

"How the hell did you manage to drop your laptop?" Brecken asks softly.

"Hey!" Josh's voice is sharp. "Don't you think you've already made this hard enough?"

Brecken throws up his hands. "Are you kidding me? You're going to blame me for the broken laptop now?"

"Oh my God," Kayla says. "Do you think we can get a break from you being a bitch-boy crybaby for five minutes?"

"No one is blaming you," I say. "Just stop making it worse."

Except it's already worse. It got twenty times worse when I dropped my laptop. Correction: when Harper knocked it out of my hands. I glance at her, a flicker of uncertainty running through me. She wouldn't have…would she?

"We need to regroup," Josh says. "We have no map. No phones. No way to charge our phones. How much gas do we have?"

"Two-thirds of a tank," Brecken says.

"Maybe we need to search the car," Harper suggests. "We still haven't searched for ports in the back. Or maybe there's another map in one of the pockets or something."

"I think we would have noticed plugs in the back," Kayla says. "Remember the Great Search Party for Mira's Phone?"

"That's right," Josh says. "We pulled everything out."

"Our bags," Harper says. "Let's go through our bags and see

if we have anything we're forgetting about. Does anybody have an iPod? Or a notebook that might have a map?"

"A notebook with a road map?" Brecken asks. "We're wasting time. You've already been through our bags."

"Let's at least check the emergency kit again," Josh says. "Maybe there's something useful back there we missed."

Agreeing, we file out again, five reluctant, weary travelers, shivering in the cold and aching from too many hours in the car. The trunk forms the center of our huddle, the focal point of our miserable half circle.

"Pop it," Brecken says.

Harper does and we start shifting bags and searching the emergency kit. There's nothing in our bags. Nothing in the kits, either. Harper pulls everything out to get to the spare tire compartment. It leaves the luggage compartment bare. We can see the seam of the back seat here, the place where the seats fold down to create a continuous storage area.

In the middle of the hinge, something glints.

"What is that?" Josh asks.

Harper leans in over the luggage and presses her finger against something silver. She recoils and inhales sharply. "It's sharp."

"It's one of those metal pulls, then," Brecken says dismissively.

"I don't think so." Harper picks at it, frowning. She pushes her fingers into the crack and her frown deepens. She wrestles and tugs carefully and I watch in shock as a long, silver-handled hunting knife emerges from the seam of the seat.

My throat tightens as she tilts it, the taillights reflected on the silvery blade.

I was sitting right there, in that seat. I was sitting *inches* away from that knife.

"What the hell is that?" Brecken asks, as if he actually doesn't know.

"It's a knife," Kayla says. "Obviously."

"What is that doing here?" Josh asks, reaching for it. It's long and mean-looking, the kind of knife you see behind glass in the camping section.

"This was in your seat," Harper says quietly, her eyes reaching mine after the words are out. "This was right behind you."

"I know." I shudder. "If I'd moved wrong it could have stabbed me."

"No," Harper says evenly. She's looking at me with an expression I can't read. "The blade was facing the trunk. Whoever put this in that crevice shoved it in from the back seat."

"The seat where you were sitting," Brecken says coolly.

Fear prickles at the back of my neck. "I'm not the only one who sat in that seat!"

Harper pales, her voice very quiet. "But you sat it in most, and you sat in it last."

"Come on, that doesn't have anything to do with anything," Josh says. "That could have been in there for months."

"Or she could have shoved it in there before we searched bags," Brecken says. "She could have hidden it there so we wouldn't find it."

"For her hunting expedition later?" Kayla asks, rolling her eyes. "Get real. Does she look like a girl who handles knives?"

"It's not hers," Josh says, shaking his head. "No way."

Harper looks uncertain and Brecken looks downright suspicious. My chest feels hot and tight like I've done something wrong, but I haven't.

"It's not!" I say, looking at Harper. She won't meet my eyes now, and I can see her face shifting. She doesn't know if she can believe me. Or maybe she wants everyone to think it's mine. And maybe what happened with my laptop wasn't an accident.

Did *she* plan this? Did she put that knife behind me in the middle of calling me sweetheart and pretending to be oh-so concerned? My stomach rolls.

"Think about it," Brecken says, shifting closer to Harper. "Who was the last person to see the map? Mira."

"Cut it out," Josh says. "This is stupid."

I want to defend myself, but there's a roar behind my ears and a lump in my throat.

"Is it?" he asks. "Because as I recall, the person alone in the car with Harper at the gas station—before her wallet went missing? That was Mira, too. The person who plugged in our phones? Mira. She was the last one to touch the map. And the person who just dropped the last device that could have charged one of our phones? Ding, ding, ding! Mira again."

"I didn't do this!" I cry. "I didn't drop my own freaking laptop, and I've never seen this knife before. I wouldn't even know how to get something like that!"

Harper steps back, face pinched. Her expression is familiar. I bet I was wearing one just like it when Brecken was standing in my spot, begging me to listen to him about Josh pulling the wheel. Professing his innocence while I looked on, clearly not believing a word.

I wonder if he felt the same way, pulse rabbiting and stomach clenched. I wonder if he felt as trapped and helpless as I feel now, with the evidence pointing at something terrible, and the truth . a slippery thing, always just out of reach. Even Josh is looking at me like he isn't so sure.

They could leave me here. They could blame this—all of these insane things—on me, and there's not a damn thing I can do to stop it.

"Who should we leave now, Mira?" Brecken asks. It's as mean as I've seen him.

"No one's leaving anyone," Harper says, voice firm.

"You aren't the CEO of this shit show," Brecken snarls. "I don't seriously want to leave her, but I'd love to know why the hell she's hiding a knife in her seat."

Josh shakes his head. "Wait. None of us could have had a knife—you can't carry a knife on a plane. The knife had to have been here before we even got the car."

"He's right," Harper says softly. "You can't fly with a blade this long." She puts the knife down in the trunk like it's suddenly burning her fingers. She stares at it, face blanched. "Think, Harper," she whispers, apparently to herself. "Just think."

Brecken doesn't miss the chance. He takes her by the shoulders and turns her to face him. "That girl has had you snowed since the beginning. She's hiding something."

I swallow hard. I feel sick and cold all over. "I'm not hiding anything."

"Oh my God, come *on*," Kayla says, sounding annoyed.

"What possible motive would she have?" Josh asks.

"What motive would *I* have?" Brecken asks. "You've been steering shit my way all this time but there's only one person in this car toting a weapon, and it's not me."

I explode. "It's not my seat or my knife, and we both know you're doing this to pass your own guilt off on someone else!"

Brecken lunges forward. "You're a little—"

Josh pushes between us. "Don't you touch—"

"It's my knife!"

The three of us freeze at the shock of Kayla's voice. There's no shame or guilt in her posture. She stands with crossed arms and her chin high as she repeats it. "It's my knife."

"You had a knife on the plane," Harper says, obviously not believing her. She's not the only one.

"No, moron," Kayla says, rolling her eyes. "I bought it at the gas station. There was a case in the back. With the fishing shit."

"When?" I ask. "You didn't have any money."

A muscle jumps in her jaw and I can tell she's thinking something over. Finally, she sighs. "Fine, I took it."

"Took it, as in, *stole* it?" Harper asks.

She lifts one slim shoulder. "The cabinet lock wasn't latched. They were practically begging for it."

I blink. "You stole a hunting knife. From a gas station."

"Please. Let's not act like you're shocked," she says.

"Why?" Josh asks, sounding bewildered.

"For protection," she says, scowling. "Newsflash: I don't know any of you."

"And you thought we were the kind of threat that requires a big, scary knife?" I ask.

She throws up her hands like this is all stupid. "It was there. I took it. I figured I'd have it if I need it. And if not, I could give it to my dad for Christmas. He loves shit like that."

"You stole a Christmas present?" Josh asks, still sounding stunned.

"So what?" Kayla crosses her arms. Not an ounce of remorse shows in her eyes.

"Holy-shit factor aside, why did you hide it in Mira's seat?" Brecken asks.

"Because you started checking bags, and I didn't want you all freaking out."

"Freaking out about someone in the car having a weapon feels reasonable," Harper says.

Kayla cocks her head. "Well, you aren't all that freaked out about driving with a guy who attempted vehicular manslaughter."

Brecken lunges forward. "I'm sick of your—"

"Enough!" Josh raises both hands, one toward Kayla and the other to Brecken. "I'm done with this. The way I see it, we have two options. We stand here and fight about who's doing what or we get in the car and try to get to a gas station or whatever else we can find."

"You're forgetting option three," Brecken says, eyes hard.

"What's that?" Kayla asks. "Leave *me* here?"

"I'm just saying, you stole a knife, and I'm not buying that you were thinking of your dad on Christmas morning when you did it," Brecken says. "What are you hiding?"

"What am *I* hiding? You want to pretend you don't have any secrets?" Kayla asks. "Funny how you haven't mentioned what *you're* hiding, Brecken."

Brecken's face shutters in an instant. "What are you talking about?"

"You shouldn't assume I'm sleeping every time my eyes are closed," Kayla says.

"What are you talking about?" he repeats, but he is quiet. And he looks like he knows exactly what she's talking about.

Kayla smirks. "I heard your little true confession phone call to your buddy."

"Shut up," he says, pink staining his cheeks.

Harper looks up. "What phone call?"

"Go on," Kayla says, sneering. "Tell them how they'll never see you the same."

"What is she talking about?" Harper asks.

"None of your business," he says.

"It feels like something we should know," Josh says..

Something groans above us and we stop, looking up. There's nothing but tree-covered mountains and snow and this terrible endless creaking that burrows under my skin. And crawls deeper. Something splinters. It's like lightning, a deafening crack that shudders in the hollows of my bones.

I can't see it. I can't see what's happening.

"Watch out!"

Josh yanks me back, but it isn't necessary. The tree falls in slow motion. The trunk of the tree lands across the road with a shuddering *whoomph*, branches catching on the slope on the opposite side of the road. Wood snaps and bark rips as the top of the tree settles.

And then there is nothing but silence.

TWENTY-FIVE

THE FALLEN TREE FORCES US BACK TO THE CAR. WE PILE in, a shivering heap of fear and weariness. The engine hums and warm air pours out of the vents, but we can't go farther with a tree in front of us. We'll have to turn around.

I feel like I'm floating above my own body, somewhere high above the car. From this distance, I can see us like the psychological experiment Josh talked about when we first set out. It's like this whole ordeal is nothing more than the worst nightmare we could collectively conjure. From here, I can almost pretend none of this is real.

Logically, I know this weird numbness won't last. This is classic disassociation—my brain's gift, letting me float away from the harsh reality to keep myself from falling to pieces. I read about this in a grief brochure after Phoebe died. Logically, I should be grateful for this feeling, because, as Phoebe's hospice nurse told us, numbness is a gift. It keeps us moving and helps us to survive the things that feel unsurvivable.

I should trust the logic in this, but logic has failed me before.

Logically, my aunt wouldn't have ever gotten sick. Not Phoebe. Not my never-drank, never-smoked, always-ate-her-greens-and-did-her-yoga aunt. She was strong and healthy. She was a woman you'd expect to live to ninety-three, the one we were sure would die peacefully in her sleep with the full moon rising and crickets singing her home.

Logically, that's what should have happened. That's the story that makes sense.

But the story that's true is different.

Phoebe breathed her last at fifty-one years old. She gurgled and groaned and rattled away minute by minute in a yellow-walled hospital room that smelled like disinfectant and death. A room that seemed as eaten and worn by cancer as her body.

Losing Phoebe taught me that when your world falls to pieces, your brain will not keep you moving. Your brain will shut down to a low static hum. Your heart will tear itself in half and ache until you're sure you'll die. Until some part of you wishes you could.

It's your instincts that will keep you alive.

Beneath the push-push-push rhythm of blood carrying oxygen to your veins, there is something else. An animal directive that will put food in your mouth when you can't imagine eating, that will stop at the coffee line in the hospital because your body remembers the need for sustenance even when the rest of you forgets.

I stood in that line one year ago, a few minutes after 3:30 p.m. After Phoebe died. I knew we'd need caffeine. We had a funeral to plan. Decisions to make. I didn't even have my wallet, and a stranger in line bought me coffee. The coffee was so hot it burned my fingers right through the cups, but instinct told me to hold them tight, to march blindly to the elevators that would take me back to the yellow room where we lost her.

Instincts matter. And my instincts are telling me I am in danger. Something bad is coming. I don't know what and I don't know how—I don't even know who. But in the marrow of my bones I'm sure that if I don't get out of this car something is going to happen. And there will be no way to stop it once it starts.

"What now?"

I jump at the voice, looking around. I can't be sure who asked, so I shrug.

"I need to think," Harper says. She's back behind the wheel, and she looks like she did at the beginning, smoothed and together. But I can still see her hands shake on the wheel. I can still see the half of herself she tries to hide.

"We have to turn around," Josh says, twisting to look out of the windows. "And it's going to be tricky. There are ditches on either side."

"Okay, we have no maps and no phones," Brecken recaps. He's back in the front, too. I'm not really sure how we wound up like this again—just like we were leaving the airport. "And since we also have no common sense about people who steal knives, I guess we're all going together."

"One big happy family," Kayla singsongs, the sweetness of her voice a honey-coated dart.

"Wait," Harper repeats. She turns sideways toward Brecken. "I want to know about the phone call."

"It's not—"

"I want to know," she says, cutting him off and holding his gaze.

The pink is back in Brecken's cheeks. He's embarrassed. Maybe angry.

"You won't get it," he says.

"Try me," Harper says.

He shrugs. "I have to change majors."

"What do you mean?" Josh asks.

"I failed biochem for the second time. Genetics, too. I can't stay in premed."

I'm confused and my voice shows it. "Wait. *That's* your dark confession? Can't you just switch to another major?"

"Obviously I *can* switch," Brecken says, "but that's not the point. I have no idea how to say this to them. There isn't another major. There's *medicine*. That's it."

Kayla sweeps a dismissive hand at Brecken, giggling. "Oh my God. I totally thought you'd knocked up a high schooler or something."

Harper turns on her. "You said you'd heard his call."

"I did! But he was all *I fucked up* and *It's bad* and *They'll never see me the same way*." Kayla's laugh is a cruel bark. "It was a whiny rich boy sob fest, but I had no idea it was all because of a widdle bad gwade!"

"What the hell do you know?" Brecken asks.

Kayla's eyes narrow until I think of the blade on the knife she stole. "I know that your biggest problem is that you'll have to find a *different* way to get even richer than you already are. Hardly the stuff of Lifetime movies."

"It's that simple, right?" Brecken asks, face contorted in a snarl. "Never mind that my parents are both doctors. My uncles, too. And my grandfathers and their brothers before that."

"So?" Kayla asks.

"So, it's expected," Harper says softly, her eyes never leaving Brecken. "His family has certain expectations."

"Expectations?" Brecken's laugh is anything but funny. "Mandate from on high is probably closer to the truth. I will be the first son in *five* generations to *not b*e a doctor. Five! And it's not because I have some alternate grand life plan. It's because I can't hack it."

Quiet descends. I think of my father holding me on his shoulders at the lake. I was seven—and listing out all the jobs I knew, and Dad was assuring me I'd be great at them all. My parents have only ever had one refrain when it came to the future: be happy—that's the real measure of success.

"I'm sorry," I say, for lack of anything better.

"Is there anything you want to do?" Harper asks. "If you could be anything at all—"

"I'd be a damn doctor!" Brecken says. He lets out a shaky breath and closes his eyes for one second. And another. When he opens them, his voice is softer. "Look, I don't know anything else.

I grew up trying on my dad's white coats. Half of my childhood pictures show me playing with old stethoscopes or otoscopes. My uncle called me Little MD for years, and it's killing me that I'll be letting all of them down."

"Can't you just join a study group?" I ask.

"Or work harder?" Josh mutters softly. It doesn't feel like he means it to be helpful.

"I've tried everything. Study groups. Tutors. Meetings with the professor. I studied four hours a night for two weeks for my final, and I still only pulled a C minus."

"But C minus is technically passing, right?" I ask.

"Passing isn't enough," he says. "My adviser strongly recommended that I consider a different major program."

"So?" I shrug. "Screw him."

"He made the same recommendation last time when I failed the courses. I retook both classes. Second time around, I failed one and only barely passed the other." Brecken shakes his head. "The worst part is I know he's right. It won't get easier. I'm not going to be able to do this."

I can't imagine my parents caring about me changing a major, but I can't imagine interrupting a five-generation family legacy, either. It's hard to piece together the different things I see in Brecken. Every time I think I get him, he slips sideways, changing my perspective.

I still don't think I trust him. For all I know, this could be an act. He looks genuinely upset, but looks can be deceiving.

"Okay," Harper says softly. She readjusts her hands on the steering wheel and nods, her voice stronger when she says it again. "Okay."

"Okay what?" Josh asks.

"I'm sorry this is happening," she says, and she sounds sincere. "I think we're all going through something right now. But we can't do anything about it, not from here. Which is why we can't stop moving. I'm going to turn around and retrace our drive back to the main road. We'll head west until we find a gas station or a police officer. Anyone that can help us get home."

"I hear you, but we've got a lot of backtracking to do," Brecken says.

"We passed a lot of roads that probably cut back up to that main drag," Josh says.

"Okay, then let's find one that heads south," Harper says. "We can take that to the county highway we were on, right?"

"Right," I say.

So, we head out. Harper does not drive like Brecken. It's been a while since she's taken a long stretch, but there's something equally unnerving about the level of care in her every move. It takes her a long time to turn around, and then she inches along in the tire tracks we made coming down this road. We roll through the valley so slowly, I can feel my shoulders tightening with every half mile we pass.

"We can go a *little* faster," Brecken says. Harper ignores him.

Josh is antsy, too, turning this way and that. Looking left

and right and even behind us. Finally, he points, inhaling sharply. "There. There's a road. Heading south on the right."

"I can't see it," Harper says.

"You have time. I could probably get out and jog faster than this," I say.

Kayla mutters, "I could build a road and get it done before she got there."

"Do you want to drive?" Harper asks.

I hold up my hands. "Sorry. You're doing great. Really."

It reminds me of Zari getting her license. She was such a wreck; she drove like an eighty-year-old woman, her hands at ten and two and her nose maybe four inches from the wheel.

For all the trouble we had, this nightmare would be ten times easier with Zari. Once upon a time, everything was easier with Zari.

I close my eyes, feeling a wave of homesickness at the thought of how things were. It wasn't wild or movie-worthy. It was just normal. And now, I don't know what that word means. God, I hope I can find it again.

Harper rolls to a stop a few feet behind a green street sign. She softly swears and I don't blame her. There are no tire tracks to follow. There is a field on the left, an endless carpet of glistening white. On the right, there is a mound of snow covering what I'm guessing is a guardrail or a concrete barrier. Beyond that, the earth slopes down sharply into a valley.

Snow is drifted across the road. Plumes of white powder swirl up into the air, turning crystalline against the inky sky. It's beautiful. Almost breathtaking. But it also looks dangerous as hell.

"How deep is that drift?" I ask, nodding toward the mound on the right side of the road. It looks taller than any guardrail I've ever seen.

"I have no idea," Brecken says.

"Let's look for another road," Harper says. "I can't even see this one."

"It's not great, but I bet it's the field," Brecken says. "It might be better around that bend."

"Or it could be worse!" Harper says. "We should keep going."

"It could take us two hours to get back at this rate. This will shave a ton of time off our trip," Brecken says.

"If we don't get stuck in that snowdrift," I say.

"No," Josh says, sounding convinced. "There might not be another one. This is where we need to turn. There's a guardrail under that giant mound. We can use that for reference."

"That's great," Brecken says. "Except we *can't see the road.*"

"Yeah, but I..." Josh pauses, shaking his head. "I think I know this road."

"Like...biblically?" Kayla asks.

"No, it just...looks familiar. Ptolemy Road. I swear I saw it earlier on my GPS. Did you see anything like this at the rest stop?"

"Maybe," Kayla says, nodding slowly. "I can't be sure, but it sounds familiar."

"You studied the map on the wall in the rest stop?" I deadpan, finding it hard to believe she realized there even was a map at the rest stop. Or hell, that we were at a rest stop at all.

"Do you remember what highway it intersects with? I know I saw an intersection," Josh says.

Kayla chews her lip thoughtfully, but eventually she shakes her head.

"You seriously want us to drive into that?" Brecken asks, gesturing out at the snow.

"It can't be that deep," I say, but looking out over the blowing slopes of white, I frown. "Can it?"

"We can always back out," Harper says. "We'll try it. And we'll go back if it doesn't work."

Harper begins to roll forward, and it's immediately clear the snow is deeper near the guardrail side. Too deep to drive through, so Harper dutifully stays to the left.

"Put it in four-wheel drive," Brecken says.

"It's been in four-wheel drive," she says, and she's still too close to the deeper snow on the right for my comfort, but I'm sure it's weird driving on the wrong side of the road. I'd probably drift right, too.

"Steer left," Josh says. "Go to the other side of the road. Near the field."

"What if a car comes around that curve?" she asks.

"Please. We are the only people desperate enough to drive through this," Brecken says.

"What if this gets worse? We could get stuck."

"It's going to be okay," Josh says.

"It's drifting because of the field," Brecken says. "See that tree line up ahead? It'll be better once we get past this. Just stay left."

He might be right about the field, and the drifting only being bad in this part. But he's wrong about going to the other side of the road. As soon as Harper eases another few feet to the left, everything goes wrong. The car lurches through a hard ridge of snow, and then there's an awful jolt, and the driver's-side tires drop. Harper yelps as the car tips, following the tires in a downward, sideways slide into the ditch beside the road.

We come to a gentle stop. My center of balance shifts, and I grip the seat hard. My stomach tilts, and my vision swirls like the whole world has gone sideways. I shake my head, but my balance doesn't settle. Because we *are* sideways, or, at the very least, listing to the left like a boat at the mercy of a big wave. I shift, trying to push myself away from Josh. I'm mashed against his body, and Kayla is mashed against me.

The whole car is tipped to the left. We drove off the road and directly into a ditch.

TWENTY-SIX

WE CAN'T GET THE DRIVER'S-SIDE DOORS OPEN AT ALL.
Harper tries, and then huffs when the door sticks. She rolls down
the windows, and the smell of snow and trees rushes in. Josh
pokes his head out to see the damage.

The window isn't mashed into the snow, but I can see from
here it's close. It's hard to process the ground at that strange
diagonal angle, but it's clear we aren't getting out of that door.

"Holy shit," Josh breathes.

He pulls his head back into the car, and I strain against
gravity, my seat belt biting into my left hip.

"Is it bad?" Harper asks in a thin, high voice.

No one answers. I don't know how she could think it's
anything *but* bad. The whole car is tilted at a forty-five-degree
angle. Basically, we're teetering off the edge of a road we never
should have tried to navigate.

"It's not good," Josh says, sounding remarkably calm.

I grab the sides of each of the front seats, trying to hold myself in place. My palms are slick on the leather despite the arctic rush of air streaming through the open windows. I'm pinned between Josh and Kayla, and everything feels too close. Too intense.

"How steep is the drop on your side, Brecken?" she asks. "Can we get out?"

"Do we have a choice?" Kayla asks. Her breath is a warm huff in my hair, but she's struggling with the door. She pulls the handle and pushes with her hands. Then her feet. I tense, squirming under the press of her weight against me. And my weight against Josh. I can feel the material from his jacket and the hard length of his arm underneath. I can feel Kayla, too, and I don't like this. Not any of it.

I unbuckle and twist my body, shove my hips out and away from the seat. My legs shake, but I crouch in the narrow space between the front seat and the back. I can't sit here between the two of them any longer. I need space. Air.

Kayla finally gets the door open, and Brecken forces his open, too.

"We need to get out," I say. I start an awkward climb to the passenger-side door. Everything about my angle is unnatural—I feel like I'll tumble backward out of the car. My stomach cramps, a warning from my body that this is not right.

Hell, nothing has been right for hours. Weeks. For the whole year, if I'm honest.

"I knew we shouldn't have done this!" Brecken says.

"You agreed to it, too!" Harper snaps. "Just get over it."

We all pile out of the car and assess the damage. We're halfway up to our calves in snow here and the other side of the car is much, much worse. It's buried above both tires, snow partly up both doors. The ditch is not deep—maybe eight feet, though it's hard to be sure. And the car doesn't look as bad as I thought, the passenger-side tires only a few inches off the ground.

Still. It's buried. This is beyond what we can do with a shovel. We need ten shovels. Or maybe a backhoe.

A certainty settles deep in my gut looking at the half-buried SUV: we aren't getting out of this snow without a tow.

I look around at the nothing that surrounds us. It's dark and cold, and there's an ache deep in my bones that feels like it'll never shake loose.

We gather quietly at the front of the car, a meeting of the minds, I guess. The wind is briefly quiet here and the silence is absolute, the snow muffling any noise the air might carry.

"What are we going to do?" Harper asks. "Should we light the flares?"

"What for?" Kayla asks. "So the abominable snowman can rescue us?"

Brecken huffs. "We shouldn't have come down here."

"Well, we did," Harper says. "We're here now."

Brecken gestures at the now useless car. "Might as well break out the campfire and the kumbayas because we're not going anywhere soon."

"We can hike out," Josh says.

"Have you seen your leg?" I ask.

He frowns down at it. "I'm not sure we have a choice. There were a few houses about a mile back, right? We could split up. Head in both directions. Whoever gets help first sends someone for the others."

"And if not, we'll just freeze to death stumbling through the blizzard," Kayla says. "Good times."

"The gas won't last forever, so if we don't get out of here, we'll freeze anyway," Harper says.

"We need to dig out," Brecken says. "We dig a trench and find something to ramp us back up to the road. It won't be easy, but we can do it."

Josh shakes his head. "No, we can't. We need help. We aren't in the Australian outback, we're in Pennsylvania. I know I saw some houses not too long ago."

"Even a mile in this will be like ten or fifteen miles," Brecken says.

"Digging out of that ditch will be like digging a grave," Kayla says.

Something about her tone chills me. I look around, surveying the landscape. The road we came from is only a hundred yards back. It curves sharply to the left and out of sight just past the field. I can't even make out our tire tracks from earlier. Not from here. But I don't remember the houses Josh is talking about. Maybe I wasn't paying attention.

I shift on my feet, trying to think. Staying here feels exposed.

Dangerous. The field on the left goes on forever, ending in a thick-looking row of trees that could be half a mile away for all I can see. What's down the valley though? Past the snow drift on the right side of the road.

I tromp back up to the road and across it. The snow is maybe twelve inches at first, but as I walk, it gets deeper. It's probably up to my chest in parts of the drift, but I find an opening, a little valley in the snow, that I can walk through.

The wind is picking up again, blasting my coat across my back. I shuffle forward carefully, not wanting to stumble off the road if I somehow miss the guardrail. But before I know it, the guardrail is in front of me. The drift to my left is enormous, but here a single swipe of my boot uncovers some of the metal rail.

I step forward, peering down the gray-white slope of the valley. It's steep here at the top, with trees dotting the hillside. It's hard to be sure, but I think the slope becomes more gradual. The evergreen branches have provided some cover and with the wind blowing the other direction, the snow on the hillside is patchier. Here and there, I can see bits of black forest floor peeking through. I crouch down, peering through the tree trunks to see what's at the bottom. Just darkness. Trees. Lights.

Lights?

My heart trips. I lost them, but I wouldn't have imagined that, would I? It had to be headlights or a house or…something. I stare until I find them again, between the spaces in the trees. They're real—I didn't dream them. It's only a few tiny yellow glimmers, but they're lined up at the bottom of the valley, which means there is a road. And those lights? They are houselights.

I squint, spotting the vague colorful twinkle of holiday lights in a window. There are people down there. Hope bursts through my chest, as warm and bright as sunshine through stained glass.

"You guys!" I shout, pointing. "There are houses down there!"

They are out of my sight, hidden entirely by the mountainous snow drift. And apparently with the wind howling they can't hear me. I shout again, but no one answers.

I stomp back across the road, fighting against the wind to get to them. My legs burn from wading through the snow, and I'm breathing fast, but I'm thrilled. It's cold, but I don't care. I could climb Everest in a bathing suit right now, because there are people! People who are not Harper and Brecken and Josh and Kayla. People who can help me get home.

When I make my way back over, everyone seems to be wandering. The trunk lid is open, and I can hear Brecken working the shovel. Harper is murmuring at him. Kayla is near them. Josh, too, but he must hear me coming, because he turns and meets me at the trunk.

"There are houses!" I say.

"What?" Josh asks.

Harper comes over and Brecken pauses. Even Kayla looks interested.

"There are houses down in the valley," I say. "It's steep, but I can get down there. I'm sure of it."

"You mean you can roll down, breaking every bone in your body," Brecken says.

Harper frowns. "I don't know. This feels like an even worse accident waiting to happen."

Brecken returns to his shovel.

"Are you nuts?" I ask. "I'm telling you there are people, like a few football fields away! We can do this. Come look!"

But they don't. And why would they? A shiver runs up my spine, and the snow isn't to blame. Because I can't imagine anyone *not* wanting to get help at this point. Unless they don't want us to get home.

"Mira, I'm going to help him get started." Harper's smile is even more patronizing than her tone. "But then I'll come look, okay? Don't worry."

"The houses are not that far," I say softly.

Josh looks down at his brace, and then his jaw tightens. He meets my eyes. "I'm going to go look."

"Your brace will get wet."

"Then it will get wet," he says. "If you think this is the way…"

"I do," I say. I touch his sleeve. "I'm going to grab my gloves and then I'm going down. If you can't do the slope, don't worry. I will get help up here. I won't leave you."

"I'm going to go check it out," he says.

I'm not sure he'll be able to get through the snow in that brace, and I'm definitely sure he won't be able to descend the mountain, but I nod, watching as he picks his way across. He's painfully slow and awkward, but I don't argue, because I feel better with the idea of having him up there. If I fall, at least someone will see.

I consider telling the other three, but decide to grab my gloves instead. I'm not letting Brecken and Harper talk me out of this. I'm going. They can stay and dig down to bedrock for all I care.

I pull the trunk of the SUV open and drag my bag closer. The latch flops open and it spills. I swear, this damn latch.

I swipe at the tangle of toiletry bags and clothes that tumbled out. Something else fell out, too. A large yellow padded mailer.

It isn't mine.

It isn't mine, but when I flip it over, I find my name scrawled across the front of the envelope in neat, sloping black letters.

I frown, pulling open the flap. There is a thick stack of smaller envelopes and a single sheet of thick, buttery soft paper on top. Perfectly organized. Dread fills my stomach, a cold, hard ball beneath my ribs. There should not be an envelope with my name on it. But there is.

My hands feel numb as I peel open the flap and tip the envelope up, dumping the contents into the trunk. The other smaller envelopes spill out in a hiss of paper, along with an assortment of miscellaneous items that must have been at the bottom of the mailer. A map of Pennsylvania, Harper's wallet, and a battery that I'm guessing is Brecken's. But my eyes lock on a familiar black rectangle with a shattered screen. My phone.

This is the stuff that was taken.

My throat tightens. I touch my phone's shattered screen

and spot one of the envelopes underneath. *Mira Hayes*. I shove everything else away and focus on the envelopes. They are all unopened and addressed to me. But the address in San Diego isn't familiar. My face goes cold as I run my finger over my name, a high-pitched whine ringing in my ears. I scan the postmark dates spelled out in red inked postage stamps. February 4. April 8. June 12. August 30. November 15.

One of the envelopes bears my first name only, neatly printed across the front. It looks fresher. Newer than the rest. A sick certainty tells me I do not want to read these. I pause, spotting the single unfolded sheet of crisp white paper. It was on the top when I looked at the envelope.

I swallow as I turn it over. I read one line and know I am right to be afraid.

I should be terrified.

Mira,

I can smell you in this car.

I can hear you sigh.

I can feel the way your breath shifts the air.

Every one of my senses is full of you, and still you don't see me.

But you will.

You aren't calling your parents again, Mira. You aren't going to Pittsburgh. You aren't going home. You'll stay here, deep in the mountains. I'll find a place, a private place where no one will find us.

Maybe then you'll see me.

Maybe then you'll understand that you're mine.

TWENTY-SEVEN

THE LETTER SLIDES FROM MY HAND, FLOATING DOWN TO the scattered envelopes below. I try to step back, and my knees go to water. I hear Harper and Brecken at the front tires. The *shink* of the shovel over and over. Kayla approaches, her steps crunching. I pitch forward, catching myself on the side of the car with my hands. I can't breathe.

Can't breathe.

But I have to.

I force air into my squeezed-shut throat and ignore the thumping of my heart. The chatter of my teeth. Think. I need to think. My gaze drifts down to the wallet. The phone. The envelopes.

They all show an address on Tribune Street. My brain searches every crevice of my memory, trying to make sense of it. What does that address mean to me? Is it familiar? I know Tribune Street... It's—

Seaspun Gallery. I had a show at Seaspun Gallery, and they

had an office where I dropped my paintings. It was my first series in gray. Not a drop of color touched my palette for those paintings, not burnt sienna or cadmium red. Just lamp black and titanium white and all the shadows between.

When was that show? A year ago? Maybe right after I got home after Phoebe died. I press my palm to my head as the thoughts spin. It had to be February. Early February. I paw through the letters, checking the dates in red ink until I find the one I'm looking for. February 4.

I rip it open and unfold the letter, scanning it quickly. They were at the show. Oh, God, this person watched me. Talked to me. I frantically search my memory, finding nothing. The show was *year* ago—it was all a blur of nameless faces and my fake smiles. All I could think about was how sad Mom was at home. But I wasn't home. I was at Seaspun Gallery. And this person saw me. And wrote about fate and destiny.

Who did this?

I blink and a flash of Brecken's dark eyes in the rearview mirror. Another of him, flushed and breathing hard against the tree. He'd talked about destiny, too. And about us, together.

We make a good team, Mira.

Destiny's on our side.

Bile rises in my throat, but I swallow it down. Take two steps back from the car.

"Hey." I nearly jump out of my skin, but it's Kayla. Just Kayla.

My hand is at my throat, the letter back in my other hand.

I don't remember grabbing it. Kayla glances at the letter. How could she not look with the way it's shaking in my fingers?

"What the hell..." she says, and I can see the shock fall over her as she scans the pile of letters. "What the hell is all of this? Is that your phone?"

Tears slide over my cheeks, hot and unexpected. My voice is a cracked, dead thing. "I don't... This was in my bag."

Kayla looks back over her shoulder and my senses catch up. I hear Harper muttering. The *shink* of Brecken's shovel. He could hurt me with that shovel. His words from the campground come back to me, sudden and terrible.

We should stick together, you and me.

I think of him cornering me behind the car. Trying to blame Josh. Trying to get me on his side. I was right to be afraid of Brecken.

I grab Kayla's arm and pull her close.

"Hey—" she protests.

"Do you know anything about these letters?" I ask. "Your stuff isn't here! Everyone else's stuff is."

She doesn't flinch. "What the hell? No!"

I don't know if I can trust her, but I can't imagine her behind this. She's barely holding on, and this isn't the work of an addict. It's meticulous. Organized. I think of Brecken's bag and shudder.

"I think Brecken wrote these letters. I think he wants to hurt me."

Kayla hesitates, then shakes her head. "What are you even talking about?"

"There are nine letters in here. Brecken wrote them." I shake the paper in my hand. "He said things today that were in this letter, and he has already run a person over. I am not staying to see what he'll do to me."

A beat passes, a thousand emotions flickering across Kayla's face. She does not speak.

"I'm going," I say, swallowing hard. "Come or stay. It's your choice."

Her eyes flick to the ditch. We can't see them well, but Harper and Brecken are chatting. My chest aches at a glimpse of Harper's dark hair through the windows. I want to warn her. I want to get her away from him.

But then I remember the way she protected him. The way everything he does softens beneath the lens of what he did for her in the airport. I won't be able to convince her, and I can't risk losing my chance to run.

I glance at Kayla, and she looks drawn. Serious. But she nods. "I'm with you."

I grab my bag, leaving most of the letters where they sit. I can't imagine touching more of them. We head out across the road, stepping through the deepening snow. I've got the large envelope still clutched in my left hand and the wind catches it, flapping it back against my sleeve. At the other side of the road, Josh looks up, surprise flickering into concern when he sees me.

Even through the wind, I can hear the now-sickening *shink* of Brecken's shovel. Over and over. Like digging a grave, Kayla said.

I shove the envelope into Josh's hands, crying. He turns it over scanning my name. He frowns. And somehow, his reaction makes the terror hit harder. I'm breathless, my words tumbling over each other on their way out. They choke over unexpected sobs. "It's Brecken. I think you were right about Brecken."

"What?" he asks. "What do you mean?"

"I can't... There were all these letters. And they were to me, but at the wrong address. He's after me. We have to get away from him."

"Slow down," he says, waving Kayla closer. "What are you talking about? What is this?"

"She found a stack of letters," Kayla says. "And all of our shit, *except mine*. Looks like she has a stalker, and she's pretty spooked."

She sounds like she's smiling, which means she's probably still high. Nothing about this is funny.

"We have to go," I say.

Josh shakes his head. "Because you found two letters? I'm confused."

I shake my head. "Tons of letters. I left them, but he wants to keep me here in the mountains. He thinks we met or maybe we did meet. I don't know. But he's acting like this is some great love story." I practically gag on the words. "It's insane. All of it is completely insane."

Josh steps back, face blanched. He covers his mouth with his hand.

"And you don't remember him?" Kayla asks, her voice lilting.

"No, but it doesn't matter," I say. "He thinks we are destined to be together. I told you. *Insane.*"

I reach for Josh, who flinches, unsettled by the letter. By everything I'm saying, I'm sure.

"Where are the other letters?" he asks me.

"Back there. I don't care. We have to go." I grab at Josh's arm and then look down at his leg. His *immobile* leg. Dread sinks through me. He can't handle this hill. He can't go.

"I don't know what to do," I whisper.

A second passes. Josh breathes. I see the pain cross his face and feel it land in my chest. How can I leave him here? What if Brecken loses it? Blames him somehow?

"Go with Kayla," he says.

I open my mouth, but words won't come. I want to say that I don't want to go with Kayla, because he's the normal one. He's the only one that picked up on Brecken, and I don't want to go down there without him.

"We should go," Kayla says.

I shake my head. "I don't—"

"I know," he says softly, gripping my arms. "I know you don't want to leave, but you have to. I'm okay. Go and get help. Go now."

"But, Josh—"

"Take her," he says to Kayla. He nods at her, firm and slow. He's made up his mind. "Stay close together, and I'll do what I can to hold him off."

"I will send help," I say. "I promise you, I'll send someone for you."

I climb over the guardrail and ease my legs into the snow. Kayla is right behind me. It's shallower here, but steep. Maybe steeper than I thought. I scrabble down, feet sliding until I find traction. My steps are awkward and high, and I'm grunting with the effort. I hear Kayla behind me, her quiet gasps punctuating my own panting.

I find a clearing on the slope where the grade eases. It's better here. Snow up to my ankles, but not as many trees. I keep my feet turned out and start moving down the hill, the sting of snow blowing into my eyes and the coldness burning with every breath.

I have to hurry. I have to get help for Josh.

But we're getting there. We're going to make it down into this valley. The houses are farther than I thought but I can see them. We are going to get help and we will be safe. I repeat this to myself over and over with every step.

We will be safe.

We will be safe.

We will be—

Something hits me square between the shoulder blades. I pitch forward, knees hitting the snow and my body slamming after. I'm falling, shoulders crumpling under as my body rolls over and down. I feel snow and sticks and pain. I spread my arms and legs, reaching for anything to slow my awkward tumble. My leg hooks over a small tree, and I stop with a jolt, my body aching at the impact, my head facing downhill.

I ease myself over to all fours with a groan, snow soaking through my jeans and gloves. I push up from the ground, trying to orient myself. I can't get off my knees. Everything is shades of gray and white—the sky, the trees, the ground. Like my paintings. Like my mind.

I replay the thump between my shoulders and tense. I know what that impact was. I didn't fall; I was pushed.

Adrenaline sings like fire through my limbs. I lumber to a crouch and scan the slope rising away from me. Trees. Trees.

Kayla.

She is tall and thin, her skirt billowing in the snow. Her face nothing more than hollows of shadow.

"I'm sorry," she says again. Just like the bathroom, her voice shaking. "I needed—I'm sorry."

All the breath is kicked out of me. Snow blows into my eyes, and by the time my vision clears, she's halfway back up to the road. I see the back of her skirt and tangled hair. I don't understand. I don't—

Kayla reaches out near a small pine tree. Like she's waiting for help. Or a gift.

I feel the blood drain from my face. Someone is on the hill with her. It's hard to see in the darkness, but I see a hand reaching. Helping her?

No. Someone is handing something to her, a small, orange cylinder. And something else—something small and square.

"You asshole," she snarls. "*You* took it."

The dark figure shrugs. Kayla closes her fingers around the bottle of pills and looks at me one last time. I don't understand. And then all the pins tumble into place and the lock opens.

She is holding a bottle of pills. Whoever that is, they just gave her pills—paying her off and returning her goods. Oh my God, he had help. Brecken paid Kayla with pills to help him. He was just looking for the opportunity. I scan the guardrail for Josh, terrified that I'll see him injured. Worse.

I open my mouth to scream for Josh, but then Brecken steps out from behind the tree and I need to run. I have to stay away from him.

Except it isn't Brecken. The shadows swallow his features, but I'd know that silhouette anywhere. My throat closes up, my mouth curdling around the shape of the name.

TWENTY-EIGHT

JOSH.

It's Josh standing on the hill. I can see the bulk of his jacket. The shaggy edges of his hair. And his crutches are nowhere in sight.

Numbness is a gift. That's what the nurse told me, and I believe her now. Because for one blissful breath I feel nothing looking at Josh. He stole our things. Wrote me letters. Pushed poison pills into Kayla's outstretched hand. He did all of this, and now he is hustling down the mountain without the vaguest hint of a limp. He is walking and I am back on my knees, watching this all unfold like I have nothing to do with it at all.

I take a breath. It smells like Christmas in this forest.

Get up.

My instinct overrides my stupor, launching me to my feet. I'm wobbly. Shivering. And it's too late. He's on me.

"Do you see me now?" he asks. "Do you finally remember?"

I open my mouth, but I have no idea what to say. I don't

remember. I don't remember anything, and I don't understand what he's asking. I'm frozen, rooted into this ground like one of the evergreens towering over me.

His laugh is a cruel joke, and it's clear I'm the punch line. "Aren't I the fool to believe you'd be smarter than this?"

"I..." No words feel right, so I trail into nothing.

"Do you really not remember me? I was wearing this same damn brace when I bought your coffee. I made everything better for you in that moment. You wept, Mira!"

His words are a hodgepodge of sounds that don't belong together and hold no meaning for me. And then something begins to coalesce, the dark impression of a truth. Someone did buy me coffee. The night that Phoebe died, in the hospital, I forgot my money and someone bought my coffee.

But it wasn't Josh! He had a beard. He didn't...

My thoughts strangle themselves to silence because I don't remember enough to be sure of anything except this: someone did buy me coffee. And I cried. Not because of coffee but because of Phoebe.

Because I was breaking to pieces.

"Oh, are we done playing games now?" he asks. "Done pretending you don't know me like you did in the gallery that day?"

Oh my God. The gallery. So many people talked to me at the gallery. By the end, I just waved and smiled and nodded no matter what they said. He steps close and I stumble back, almost tripping again. Adrenaline bursts into my legs and I turn to run, but he catches my sleeve, pulls me close enough to see the intensity in his eyes, and then the glint of metal in his hand.

"Time to go," he says, taking my arm and hauling me to my feet.

"Go where?" My voice is shrill and panicked.

"It doesn't matter. We'll be together. We'll be away, and you'll see. I know you'll see."

I try to pull myself free, and he tugs back. We struggle in the snow, and I push against him with all of my might. My foot slips and I drop back to one knee. He slides around with a grunt, grabbing my other arm. I see that metal again.

The knife. Oh, shit, he has the knife, and it's pressed right against my arm.

I arch my back and kick at his knees, but he easily avoids me, his fingers biting into my arms like teeth. The snow is so slippery. Cold. I writhe like a cat being held under water. I have to get him loose. Get him off me. I have to get away.

"Stop fighting me, Mira. Stop fighting this."

I fight twice as hard. Three times. I kick and flail and jerk and then—I fall. We both do, the thin sheet of glazed-over snow cracking under our impact. His body is on mine—heavy and hard. I want him off. Off!

"Don't fight me!" he cries.

I scream, using every bit of my energy to haul my body over to one side. Something pierces my bicep as I roll, and my scream could shatter glass. Josh loosens his grip, but the pain is an electric shock. Heat follows it, wet fire that pulses with my heart. I pull my uninjured hand up to the wound. My sleeve is wet. Snow or blood, I have no idea.

But Josh's ashen expression tells me there's at least some of the latter.

"Mira," he breathes.

I kick him between the legs. Once. Twice. He's down, keening when I kick him again, somewhere in the face. My arm is throbbing from shoulder to fingertips. My fingers are wet. Dripping dark splatters into the snow.

I reach for the knife that's skittered a few feet away from him. My hand is slick with blood, but I grab it anyway.

It's colder than ice in my grasp and the pain—oh God, the pain is nauseating. It rolls through me in Technicolor waves, sending stars across my vision with every beat of my heart. Josh snags my foot, and I'm down, knees hitting the snow and pain spiking like I've been stabbed all over again.

I feel my vision going gray but I will not pass out. I will not. I kick with both feet, catching him in the jaw with the heel of my right boot. He flops back and slides a few feet down.

Go. Go now. Go fast.

I crawl away while Josh groans on the ground. Rise to my feet even as my pulse throbs in the wound, a frantic, agonizing rhythm that blurs my vision. I walk anyway, dragging my legs up and up and up as fast as I can.

Josh is still groaning. I hear him shifting in the snow. But he's not getting up. Not yet. I use every muscle I have and every muscle I don't. I heave myself one eager step at a time until I'm at the guardrail, and haul myself over. Dark drops spatter the snow as I retrace my own tracks to the car. Whimpering. Crying.

Kayla is gone. No sign of her either direction, but Harper meets me halfway across the road. Brecken is behind her, and it's clear they've been looking for me.

It's also clear that Harper is terrified.

My breath is ragged and fast. The knife drops into the snow, a gruesome splash of red against the pristine white. Harper's eyes drag to that bloody blade and then to my face.

She raises her shovel high.

TWENTY-NINE

"STAY BACK," HARPER SAYS.

"Harper, no," I say. I can barely get out the words. The pain and my breathlessness steal half of everything I want to say. "Josh—it's Josh—no crutches… There are letters."

"Where's Kayla?" she asks. "Where is Josh?"

I point, feeling sick and dizzy. "Down. Down there."

But Kayla isn't down there. She's gone. God, why did she help Josh? How could she? And when?

No.

The gas station. I remember them talking. They were alone, and she was sick then. Feeling terrible. But she got better. He must have given her a little then. More at the bar. He dangled her along because he knew the one and only thing she cared about. He'd planned it that way.

"Did you push them?" Brecken asks. "God, Mira, what did you do?"

I shake my head vigorously. Too vigorously. My head swims

and I droop, propping my good hand on my leg. Harper tightens her grip on the shovel.

"Letters," I pant out. "Look at the letters. Trunk."

I hear Brecken's swift steps retreating to the car. I stand upright and stumble. Harper swings the shovel forward a little in warning.

"I said stay back!" Harper warns.

"The letters," I say, still breathless. "He was—watching me. For months. Kayla helped him."

I hear the rip of paper in the background. Brecken is either opening the envelopes or tearing them to pieces. My heart throbs. A *beat-beat-beat* in my wound. I sway on my feet, and Harper lets out a frightened yelp.

"Back!"

"Harper, run!"

Josh. It's Josh telling her to run. My blood runs cold as I turn, head spinning. He can't be here already, but he is. He's found one crutch and that limp is back. Blood trickles from his swollen lip. Was that me? Did I do that?

I wish I'd done more.

"Stay away from her, Harper," Josh croaks. He is utterly convincing. "She pushed us. Me and Kayla. Kayla's hurt. We have to help her."

"No," I shake my head hard. "Not true."

"She needs help." Josh drags himself forward, pain etched into his features. If I didn't know better, I'd believe him. If I hadn't seen him loping down that mountain. Coming for me.

"Where is she?" Harper asks.

"She's not down there," I say.

"Mira came at me," Josh cries. "She had that knife. She might still have it."

"Oh my God," Harper says, her eyes dragging to the crimson-stained snow.

"He's lying to you," I cry.

He's on us now, and I'm trapped between Harper with her shovel and Josh with his lies.

Fresh panic flares through my middle. Where is Brecken? Because Harper is a lost cause, and I can see thoughts falling over Josh features. He's going to use her worry. Her kindness.

He's making a new plan, right now.

"We have to help Kayla," Josh says. He's scanning the ground.

Oh God. The knife. It's right beside him.

"Stay away from me!" Harper says. Josh overplayed his hand, and now she's afraid of us both. She's holding the shovel at each of us. Josh raises one hand, his brows sad.

"I won't hurt you," Josh says. "I just want you safe. Stay away from her, Harper."

He groans like his knee hurts, leaning down awkwardly.

I see it in slow motion, and I know what this is: he's going for the knife.

I lunge, but the snow is deeper than I thought. My foot catches and I'm down, but I push myself forward, reaching. Trying to grab it before Josh.

Everything happens at once.

My palm grazes the cold blade. Harper cries. Josh's face is there. Right there. He's so close, a wolf's smile on his mouth as he takes the knife's handle, jerks it so hard the blade slices across my palm.

I scream in fresh pain, my body curling toward the new injury. Something moves in the corner of my eye. It's long and dark and coming fast.

Thunk.

Time stops. My breath turns cold and still in my lungs as my eyes lock onto Josh. I see a terrible painting in front of me. The wideness of Josh's eyes. The knife slipping from his hand.

The long dark line across his temple.

The line widens. Drips.

And Josh falls.

I scuttle back from his body, but he doesn't move. The shovel drops, and I look up.

Brecken. Brecken had the shovel. He hit Josh. Letters litter the ground around him. Opened letters. Brecken wasn't ripping them up. He was reading them. My eyes catch on a line I hadn't read.

You didn't see me.

I try not to look, but he's right there, sprawled in awkward angles and face turned toward the sky. Josh doesn't see me because Josh is gone. His eyes remain, empty vessels staring up into the night as the ivory snow continues to fall.

THIRTY

IT IS A FAMILIAR HITCHHIKER IN A YELLOW CAP WHO FINDS us first. Irony, it seems, will always find its way. We are huddled by the car, on the other side of the body.

Because it is just a body now. There's no breath, no voice, no Josh left. Not that I knew Josh. Everything I thought I knew about him was undone by the stack of bloodstained letters in my backpack.

My instincts were wrong. Brecken wasn't a monster. Harper wasn't calculating some master plan. And Josh wasn't a nice guy. He was delusional. A stalker. He invented a relationship over a cup of coffee in a hospital. And I never saw it at all.

The rugged SUV that stops at the corner of the two roads is as sturdy-looking as the driver. The man in the yellow hat jumps out, but the man driving only rolls down his window, phone pressed to his ear and his body language full of mistrust. He doesn't care for his passenger and seems to care even less for the nightmare we're presenting: blood and death smeared on fresh Christmas snow.

The man in the yellow hat seems unperturbed. He tromps heavily toward us, swearing softly at the sight of the dead boy on his back.

"God Almighty," he says, taking off his hat to reveal thinning hair. He peeks under the sweatshirt I used to cover Josh's face and shakes his head slowly.

"God Almighty," he repeats, "what happened here?"

I think he'll be suspicious, too, like the driver, who's still waiting on the other road, safely ensconced in his warm, likely blood-free, Ford. But the yellow hat man touches my shoulder with his withered fingers, and I begin to cry.

"He tried to..." My words break off in a sob and I cover my mouth.

"He was trying to take her. Or hurt her," Brecken says calmly. "We had no idea. We thought we all met at the airport, but he met Mira earlier."

"We just wanted to go home," Harper says, stone-faced.

"But he wanted her," Brecken says. He sounds angry. "He stalked her here and used us to try to take her. There are letters. It's all in there."

I shiver. I still haven't read all the letters. Looking at Brecken's stricken face now makes me wonder if I'll ever be able to stomach reading them.

"This boy followed her from the airport?" the man asks.

"No, from her home. From both of her homes," Brecken says. "It's gone on a long time."

"Where's the blond girl?" he asks. "Tall. Strung out."

"She left," I croak. "She was helping him. He gave her something to do it."

"Pills," he guesses. "He gave her a few at the bar."

"She pushed me," I say, sniffing. "She apologized in the bar because she knew she was going to help him take me. I can't believe pills would be enough for that."

"People do crazy things. For pills and less."

"I don't think we can ever understand why people do what they do," Harper says. And maybe she's thinking of her father. But her eyes linger on Brecken.

"People aren't always what we think," the man says, putting his hat back on.

I can't ignore that, because I can't convince myself that the smell lingering on his clothes and his ratty hat didn't shift my perspective. I can't deny all the ways my instinct failed me here, so I burn in shame and watch for the flashing lights of the police in silence.

This time they come right away.

My mother meets me at the hospital on Christmas morning. I expect her to be a tear-streaked wreck, but she is steady and calm, depositing her coat on the chair beside my bed and glancing at the monitor where my vitals are being recorded. She doesn't look for long. I guess I'm doing okay.

Her gaze lands on me next, and then her hands are on my face, and I am crying. Great gulping sobs that shake my shoulders and make my mostly-numb arm ache. Mom slips off her snow boots and crawls right into my hospital bed.

The hospital sheets are scratchy, and her hands are soft. She tells me over and over, "Breathe with me. Just breathe."

She said that to Phoebe, and it only makes me cry harder. I wrap my good arm around her shoulder, my hand bandaged but functional. I don't understand. I don't understand why she's strong when I pictured her rocking by the bathroom sink. Peeling potatoes for no reason at all. Staring into space and bursting into tears without warning.

Now, I am the one lost and weeping. And she is the steady presence at my side stroking my hair back from my face.

Tethering me to the here and now.

I guess my instincts were wrong about her, too.

I sleep. I don't know for how long. When I wake, the room is dark, and my mother is not in bed. She's in a chair pulled right up to my side. I can see an empty cup of coffee and an untouched tray of what looks like my hospital dinner on the table next to my bed.

Mom has notes on the back of a comment card. Surgeon names? I glance at my arm and test it out. Sore, but functional, so I don't think I need surgery. I glance at the names again.

"They're counselors," she says. Her eyes are bright, and she's looking right at me. "Are you hungry?"

I shake my head and pick at the sleeve of my hospital gown. There's a thick bandage underneath, so no hope of seeing the damage unless I want to start unwrapping all the gauze.

"Twenty-three stitches," she says. "It'll scar, but they say it's fairly clean. No tendon damage, which is good."

"Do you know what happened?" I ask, feeling teary.

"I know you've been through hell. The police are going to need an official statement later, but for now, you just sit." She squeezes my good hand and looks at me. "You're safe, Mira. This is over."

She means he's over. That Josh is dead and no threat to me. But she didn't need to tell me that. I already knew. I expect the tears that come, but the shame is a surprise.

"I sat right next to him all those hours," I say. "I thought he was a nice guy."

"I'm sure he tried very hard to convince you he was," Mom says. There's the barest shade of fury behind her expression but she is holding it in. Controlling her face.

I shake my head. "My instincts were wrong. My instinct was to stay close to him. To trust him. I can't trust myself."

"Yes, you can," she says. "You can absolutely trust yourself."

"I just wanted to get home to you. With Phoebe and Daniel...I thought you would be..." I break off with a cry. "Mom, why didn't you tell me?"

She sighs. "Maybe this is where *my* instincts were wrong."

She peels the foil lid off my cherry Jell-O and slides it over to me with a plastic spoon. I don't feel hungry but I take a bite all the same.

"Your father and I have been talking. You've been worried about his business. About me. About everyone else in the world, but not about you. And your paintings and even some of your emails." She stops and takes a breath. "We could see you were in a dark place. We thought facing Christmas without Phoebe might be enough. The news with Daniel… I wanted to delay it."

"Mom, I'm fine. Phoebe was *your* sister."

"And she was your aunt," Mom says. "You were close. And all the time that I was falling to pieces, you were so strong. I told everyone how strong you were and I was so proud. I still am proud, but I should have been worried."

"Worried why?"

Mom touches my hair, just the barest graze near my forehead. "Because sometimes it is easier to force strength for others than to allow ourselves to feel weak and hurt."

"You think I feel weak and hurt?"

"I think you need to," Mom says, cupping my cheek. "I think that's what grief does. It reminds us that we are small. That we are not in control."

"When were you going to tell me about Daniel?"

"I was going to talk to you when you came," Mom says. "Because I didn't want it to be one more opportunity for you to be strong for me."

"I didn't…" I can't finish because she's right. I came home to be strong for her. And part of me hates that she's so strong right now. It leaves me squirmy and uncomfortable and terrified.

"I hate this," I whisper. "It's too late to be sad about Phoebe. It was a year ago. And now there's all of this."

"Grief is big," Mom says. "And this is big. These things turn your world inside out. They change us. But only for a while."

"I was wrong about so much."

"Tell me what you were right about."

I turn my gaze to the window, and she rubs my arm lightly and stands up. "Find the things you were right about, Mira. Make me a list."

She gives me pen and paper and a window overlooking the highway. She tells me she's going for coffee, but she's been my mother for a long time. And she knows when I need to think.

I watch sunlight glint over the snow. I think of the bumpy landing and my frantic phone call with Daniel. I think of my texts with Zari and Kayla's bracelet and wonder if she made it out of the snow. Most of all I think of my desperate, breathless thoughts of getting home to my mother—getting through this trip.

That thought drove my every decision, because I thought my mother needed me.

Maybe that's the piece I mixed up.

I take a breath and let it out slow. Because I know what I was right about now, even if I didn't know why. My pen touches the page, and I scrawl a single line across the blank paper.

I knew I needed to come home.

ACKNOWLEDGMENTS

There are probably four thousand people I can thank here. Coworkers who are kind on a hard day. People who let me in during rush hour. Baristas who make my coffee and make me laugh. My giant fur ball, Wookiee, who always uses all 112 pounds of himself to hug me when I'm sad. Friends who lift me up. Friends who make me think. In truth, if you're in my life—if I've laughed with you or talked with you or shared a meal with you in this last year—you are part of why this is possible. Thank you all.

But there are a few people that this process is impossible without.

To Jody. Always. Your voice on the other end of the line is my anchor. You steady me in the storms, my dear friend. I can't thank you enough.

To my brilliant rock star agents, Devin Ross and Suzie Townsend, who make every bit of this process smoother and easier and more fun. I am so lucky to have you on my team.

To my unstoppable, unbeatable Sourcebooks Fire team: Eliza

Swift, whose instincts and comments turn my poopy rough draft into something I'm proud to have written, Cassie Gutman, Sarah Kasman, the art team who designed this gorgeous cover, and the marketing geniuses who do things I truly don't understand. My publishing house is the *best* because of you. Thank you.

To my wonderful OHYA sisters, but in particular Edith Patou and Margaret Peterson Haddix, who offer kindness, wisdom, and friendship. Thank you all so much.

For the wondrous librarians in my life who offer so much support, Christina and Liz and Ben with his endless Cold Car commentary. You are wonders to me. I am beyond grateful.

To so many fellow writers who help me keep my chin up when this gig is rough. Mindy McGinnis, Robin Gianna, Jasmine Warga, Jen Maschari, Carmella Van Vleet, Nancy Roe Pimm, Romily Bernard, and so many others. Thank you for getting it and for encouraging me time and again.

To David, for endless patience and understanding with the travel and the deadlines. Thank you so much for all the support. And always, always, always, to the loves and lights of my life: Ian, Adrienne, and Lydia. Every word. Every book. All of this is possible because of the joy and love and hope you bring into my world. You are the air in my lungs, guys. I love you.

ABOUT THE AUTHOR

 Lifelong Ohioan Natalie D. Richards writes books that will keep you up way past your bedtime. A champion of literacy and aspiring authors, Richards is a frequent speaker at schools, libraries, and writing groups. In addition to writing, she spends her days working at a local public library. Richards lives with her wonderful family in Columbus, Ohio. When she's not writing or reading, you can probably find her wrangling Wookiee, her enormous dust mop of a dog.

FIREreads

#getbooklit

Your hub for the hottest young adult books!

Visit us online and sign up for our
newsletter at FIREreads.com

 @sourcebooksfire

 sourcebooksfire

 firereads.tumblr.com